MW01136065

THE Rx CAROUSEL

A novel uncovering dark secrets hidden by a

prescription drug business in Silicon Valley…

The CEO of a pharmaceutical company navigates the landscape of

greed, power, politics, and medical intrigue

Anthony G. Tebbutt

ISBN: 1530189861
ISBN 13: 9781530189861

INTRODUCTION

This book is a work of fiction. The storyline and characters are all creations of my imagination to provide the reader with an entertaining and perhaps at times, a thought provoking, experience.

My fond desire is that those who have worked in the wonderful world of prescription drugs will not only enjoy the storyline but will recognize and identify some of the industry specific scenarios I have painted. Although my scenarios are all conjured in my imagination, I know from over 30 years experience that in real-life there have been incidents that do not wander too far from my writing.

For those outside of the industry, I hope to provide "insider experience" to a world that is seldom understood as well as provide answers to the many questions often posed to industry leaders. If I can bring a refreshing perspective of the inner workings of the pharmaceutical industry while continuing to maintain reader interest, it would be a worthy achievement. At times my writing may appear overly-technical. If so, I apologize but I wanted to give the reader a genuine feel for the industry along with an intriguing story.

Medical treatments and pharmaceuticals are emotional topics, drawing much attention from the media and political arena, primarily critical in nature. Some negative attention is deserved, some is not. The voice of the pharmaceutical industry is poorly represented in most public forums, and yet this is an industry that contributes significantly to the American economy. It is estimated over 810,000 people are employed in the pharmaceutical industry. It has saddened me that the industry has done such a poor job communicating the many positive aspects affiliated with the testing, manufacturing, distribution, and follow-up of prescription drugs. But, that is the task of another author; this book is strictly written for entertainment.

ACKNOWLEDGEMENTS

In my quest to become an author, I discovered writing recollections is considerably different from writing a piece of fiction. Recollections are just that, you know what happened and most of the associated hows, whys, and wherefores. Writing a novel, an author must determine where to start, where to go, and where to finish. Finally the author must pull it all together in a believable way. No easy feat.

Without the belief and encouragement of my wife Karen, this effort would have died a long time ago. My cheerleader, coach, and editor Alice Eachus kept me from going AWOL when clouds darkened. Bringing sunshine from behind those clouds are my children Heather and Jason and my amazing 95-year-old mother, Edyth.

CHAPTER ONE

"Ladies and gentlemen, we are beginning our descent into San Jose International Airport.

Please straighten your seatbacks, check your seatbelts, and turn off any electronic equipment you are using . . ."

Jonathan Grayhall was seated in his usual aisle position at the front of the business class cabin. The elderly widow sitting next to him gave a coy glance his way over her left shoulder. She had been delighted to be upgraded on the flight and murmured every fifteen minutes or so how lucky she was to be treated to business class, seated right next to Mr. Tall, Dark and Handsome!

Jonathan placed the two legal dossiers he had been reading back into a bound leather file and slid it into the deep pocket on the bulkhead wall in front of his seat. Although he was pleased with the action he had taken regarding the legal cases he had just reviewed, as always, he would mentally go over his decision several more times.

Oh well, I guess it's going to cost the company a few bucks, but I learned a lesson from my last job switch and this time I'm not going into a new position without a couple of hand selected, loyal lieutenants by my side.

Running through his mind was the action he had taken shortly after being appointed CEO of T.V. Neurologicals. Guided by the philosophy that you're only as good as the people surrounding you, Jonathan acted swiftly. He spent time with each member of the T.V. Neurologicals senior management committee, conducted due diligence over the company records, and came to the conclusion that the incumbent VP of Marketing and VP of Finance both must be replaced, and it would be best if they were gone before his arrival. Departures of this nature usually demanded an exit payment.

Job offers had already been couriered to their hand-selected replacements. Jonathan was confident only formalities closing the employment contracts remained. He experienced absolutely no guilt that by his hand, two executives with whom he had not worked one day were now out on the street, probably wondering what had caused their abrupt dismissal. Such were the breaks in the real world of big business where ultimately results were what mattered.

The jet's tires squealed as they hit the runway, and within five minutes the plane pulled to the gate. After years of business travel around the country and around the globe, Jonathan had firmly achieved Delta executive status allowing him to upgrade to business class on most every flight. With almost five million miles under his adjustable seatbelt, the executive routinely found himself in Seat 1C in the bulkhead section. This placement allowed him to be first out the door, ready to jump on the business at hand.

As he walked toward the limo lot, Jonathan grinned as he recalled the comment made by the elderly lady who had been bumped from economy to the business class seat next to him. She was quite overcome by the opportunity to be escorted to the front of the bus and travel in a style to which she certainly was not accustomed.

"Aren't you lucky that you always travel in business class!" she exclaimed to Jonathan.

He wanted to remind her of the endless hours he spent on airplanes that included weekends, holidays, and family birthday celebrations, but Jonathan, too much a gentleman, decided not to burst her bubble.

"Yes, I'm very lucky," he replied with a smile and continued to enchant her with yet another tale of his worldwide travels. As they prepared to disembark, he reached into his pocket for a few slips of paper and discreetly handed her several complimentary cocktail vouchers.

"They keep sending me free drink vouchers and I have more than I can ever use, please allow me to give these to you."

Delta kept Jonathan on the platinum frequent flyers list, which he knew entitled him to a few perks. But, free drink vouchers? That didn't make much sense since drinks were always complimentary in business class.

The sweet little lady fondled the chits as if they were fine jewelry. A sunny smile brightened her face and she gave Jonathan a wink as she slipped the perks into her purse.

"Why, thank you, kind sir!" If only she was back in her twenties, this man would be going home with her, she was sure of it!

Jonathan glanced at the black Panerai Luminor watch snugly embracing his wrist. His wife had given it to him for good luck the last time he made a career move. It was a handsome timepiece and he loved its oversized, steel case design with the unique locking mechanism. The watch had its origin in Italy, but was manufactured in Switzerland by the finest timekeepers. Panerai watches played a role in assisting frogmen of the Decima Flottiglia MAS in operations during World War II. He chuckled as he thought, what the heck was the Decima Flottiglia? He'd certainly never heard any stories glorifying Italian Navy Seals!

The Panerai read two p.m. Jonathan was pleased the flight had been on time. The date was January 2, but there hadn't been a New Year's celebration requiring recovery for the new CEO. There really wasn't much for Jonathan to celebrate. Sad memories of the home and woman he loved haunted him and were big factors in his decision to move and start a new life in Silicon Valley in the San Francisco Bay area.

The San Jose airport had changed considerably from the days when Jonathan first flew into the South Bay. He recalled the stairs on wheels that once were pushed to the airplane door by the ground crew. Passengers touched the good earth directly without a protective shelter provided by tunnels or tubes. Good luck making the run to the terminal if it was raining, but most days the hot California sun was strong enough to ripple the tarmac. This day he took the short hike up the umbilical tunnel into the bright and shiny, multi-storied terminal building dedicated to Delta. It was a far cry from the khaki shack that once housed Delta and a few other local carriers years before. Jonathan tried to remember how long it had been since business took him to San Jose. No matter, he was here now and here to stay.

The tremendous growth that had taken place in the Bay Area was the direct result of the success of silicon technology companies like Intel, Cisco, Apple, Google and today's wonder story – Facebook. With the convergence of great universities, ample investment capital, and an entrepreneurial culture willing to take risks, it almost seemed unfair that all should come together in one of the world's most beautiful settings. This was an example of "perfect perfection," far removed from the perfect storm.

Those not fortunate enough to live in the Golden State ominously warned of the imminent danger threatening California when the "big one" hit. Ask any Californian and they would scoff at the suggestion that a rumbling earthquake represented any more threat of destruction than a severe tornado or hurricane could bring when it hit other parts of the country. The main difference Jonathan surmised was that storms usually came with warning while earthquakes did not.

Several months previously, Jonathan did a pros/cons evaluation of the job for which he was being courted. He reasoned the same factors that planted seeds for growth in silicon technology should, by all accounts, foster biopharmaceutical research. To a certain extent this was already happening, reflected in Bay Area history that touted Genentech, Gilead, Syntex, and Alza to name a few highly successful companies. Not quite the world's hotspot to the extent silicon high tech was, the area's promising presence of U.S. biopharma certainly was not shabby. Other leading pharmaceutical regions included Boston, San Diego, and Los Angeles, but the greater San Francisco area was probably known as the primo location for pharmaceutical R&D.

Jonathan was here to make his mark as CEO for a relatively young drug company that he believed had a good chance of making a stock market killing for his bosses and employees. The wonderful and exciting aspect about working in the drug industry was that financial success usually brought much needed medical benefit to the general public. He caught himself before going much further with this line of thinking.

Whoa, boy! Let's not be naïve, the two do not always go hand in hand. You well know there have been several cases of executives departing a company with bags of cash, leaving the company in the red. Remember the advice that crusty professor gave you in B School, "In the Valley, things are often not what they seem."

After much deliberation, Jonathan Grayhall accepted the position of CEO at T.V. Neurologicals, a fledgling neurological company based in Mountain View, California. T.V. Neurologicals was still a relatively young company founded only ten years before by Dr. Timothy Varter.

Varter was an English physician who had grown tired of the UK's National Health medical system which he liked to describe as more aggressive and ruthless than an American HMO on steroids. And so he moved his medical practice to Los Altos, a pleasant suburb on the San Francisco Bay peninsula.

Dr. Varter was a good doctor but soon discovered he was an even better entrepreneur and an outstanding salesman. Early in his transition to the Bay Area, Varter came across a Stanford University research lab spinoff that had discovered a molecule which showed efficacy in epilepsy models. The good doctor had zero business experience, but he knew enough to see a good thing when it was dancing in front of him. Epilepsy was a condition that had unmet needs and the mechanism of action provided by this molecule could be a major breakthrough in treatment protocols.

Borrowing money from angel investors, banks, relatives, and anybody else he could convince, Varter managed to negotiate all rights to the compound and ensured the patent file was solid. Varter christened his new venture T.V. Neurologicals and joined the list of entrepreneurs seeking to make their mark in the sacred Valley.

Tim Varter was extremely effective selling his vision to the venture capital (VC) community high on Sand Hill Road in Menlo Park. The charming English accent behind the sales pitch came from a public school education at Eaton, followed by medical education at Cambridge.

The infusion of capital enabled Varter to form his company and develop the newly discovered molecule into an FDA approved pharmaceutical product that brought relief for many patients. That molecule became the breakthrough drug commonly known as Czuretrin, a medication that offered a new chance at life for thousands of epilepsy sufferers who were previously unable to gain control of relentless and frequent seizures.

Once a company evolves from start-up to a FIPCO (Fully Integrated Pharmaceutical Company), the very same venture capitalists backing the originator recognize the need to infuse a different breed of corporate leadership and often become instrumental in launching the search for a new, more appropriate CEO.

There was wisdom within this thought process as venture capitalists typically watch over their investment by accepting board positions with their corporate offspring. Often the skills required to lead a company vary, depending on where the company is positioned in its life cycle. The skills and energy required to start a company like T.V. Neurologicals were quite different than those required to advance a company with a maturing product portfolio.

T.V. Neurologicals had its IPO, Initial Public Offering, launch five years previously and quickly raised $32 million at a price of $8 a share. Sales of Czuretrin drove the stock value as high as $22 with three stock splits, but for the past year the stock had been hovering with a share price around $12 as investors pondered how and when the company was going to announce its next breakthrough. The success of T.V. Neurologicals as a company was heavily dependent on the continued performance of their anti-seizure drug Czuretrin and the development of following drug launches.

There is a blockbuster drug paradox pertaining to prescription pharmaceutical products that enjoy rapid success and basically drive the profitability of a company. The more successful the drug, the greater the potential for a substantial letdown in a company's future performance. A pharmaceutical product may build sales to one, five, or even ten billion dollars, but once the patent expires and generics flood the market, the higher the financial ascent can translate to a greater fall. The drop in sales is precipitous and is almost impossible to replace, creating a burning need in a drug company to introduce and launch new products into the research pipeline that can offset losses.

Jonathan's recruitment came through the distinguished executive search firm of Selbrick & Straggles, which was paid a substantial fee to find the right person for the T.V. Neurologicals CEO position. Jonathan guessed S&S was paid somewhere in the vicinity of $200,000. Not bad for a headhunting exercise! The firm worked hard to pry Jonathan from the company where he enjoyed the golden reputation as the youngest and brightest Chief Business Officer; he was all but promised the coveted CEO chair in the not too distant future. At thirty six years old, Jonathan had the business world by the tail and was proud of his accomplishments.

Canadian by birth, Jonathan left his home in Toronto for a warmer clime to study chemistry and the California ladies at UC Berkeley, sometimes confusing his priorities. Berkeley's offbeat campus culture suited him well and he began his love affair with Northern California. Along the way Jonathan received an excellent education at one of the nation's premier university chemistry departments.

Jonathan's first job out of college was as a sales representative for an established Indianapolis based pharmaceutical company. It was here he received excellent training and grounding from a top-tier company. A young recruit's first manager can have a dramatic influence on that individual's long term work ethic and value system. This can be a good or bad situation. Jonathan had the good fortune to work for a career district manager by the name of Murray Morgan who was an Indianapolis institution.

Of all he learned from his first boss, the most important lesson was to develop a set of values which had integrity firmly placed at the top of the list. Murray mentored Jonathan well and passed wisdom that never failed to show the young man the right path to take when faced with business and personal decisions. As he ascended the corporate ladder, Jonathan adopted Murray's practice of mentoring, generously offering guidance and career advice to ambitious young hopefuls he brought into his organization.

After three years of detailing drugs in the swinging metropolis of Chattanooga, Jonathan found himself once again "California Dreaming." Recognizing the need to hone his business acumen, he applied to Stanford's MBA program and was accepted.

Stanford offered an exceptional graduate business program with numerous distinguished professors spreading and sharing wisdom. What really impressed Jonathan was the talent he saw in his classmates, many of whom he was convinced would one day have places on the world stage. He learned that exceptional smarts, sometimes coupled with incredible family wealth, inevitably led to success in ensuing business careers; just a quick look at the list of alumni university funders proved this true. Top business schools could boast about the success of their graduates largely because they were able to choose sure bets through the admission process. Jonathan was neither a millionaire's son nor a hardship case, but the cost of a Stanford education severely depleted his assets. This gave him a greater appreciation for a hard-earned income.

Jonathan graduated from Stanford with a complement of business tools, but perhaps more importantly, the Stanford visa stamped in his career passport carried the prestige of the institution. He was heavily recruited by several leading drug companies and accepted a position in the marketing department of a leading Manhattan based pharmaceutical company known for its marketing savvy. Here he was distinguished with contributions to the success of a cholesterol-lowering drug that ultimately became the most successful prescription drug ever sold. It was in Manhattan at a school friend's party that he met Tina, a promising lawyer at a top-tier New York law firm. The two seemed made for each other and within nine months happily tied the knot.

Four years flew by before Jonathan was wooed by an executive search company to relocate to the Research Triangle in the Carolinas where he assumed the role of Chief Business Officer. Along with this title, Jonathan claimed the second-in-command position to the CEO of the U.S. affiliate of a Dutch based multinational company that was a player in the field of neurology. It was at this company that Jonathan's exceptional leadership and strategic capability skyrocketed and in five short years, he was able to take the company from a me-too player to a dominant market position in the treatment of epilepsy. Along the way he built excellent relationships with key opinion-leading neurologists and established himself as a leader of note fielding excellent sales and marketing teams to support his work.

Jonathan recognized there was a close, tight circle of top physicians known as epileptologists who were the thought-leaders in their field. By earning the trust of this elite group he was able to gain the confidence of numerous patient advocacy groups and thus positioned his company as a leader in treating epilepsy. When the top job opened at T.V. Neurologicals, it was Jonathan's track record of marketing success, deep experience in the field of epilepsy treatment, and his reputation with patients and physicians that contributed to laddering him as the top candidate.

Time and time again Jonathan was hailed as an innovative leader who made a tremendous difference in the lives of thousands of people. Victims of all ages battling this nasty, crippling disease once thought to be the result of an invasion of evil spirits now had relief from disabling seizures. The sales force in particular stood strong behind the man they perceived as one of the few who really walked the walk and talked the talk, and who had a genuine concern for their success and well being. At the same time, Jonathan's team also knew him to be demanding of excellence and knew their boss didn't tolerate fools gladly.

Earmarked for the CEO position in the Research Triangle company, it appeared a certainty Jonathan would have a long and successful career with the Dutch corporation. But fate delivered a cruel intervention to those plans.

The day he landed in Silicon Valley marked the second anniversary of the day he lost Tina, his wife and best friend, to an aggressive form of breast cancer. The chemotherapy she endured was brutal and in the end was no match for cancer's persistent advance. Within a few months of her diagnosis, Tina was gone.

Jonathan knew he had to move away from the sad reminders he faced everywhere and every day. This realization made him receptive to new opportunities on a distant coast and the chance to rebuild his shattered life. T.V. Neurologicals made the package financially attractive and offered a significant amount of restricted stock and 2.75 million in options at $11 for agreeing to lead the company into its next phase of success.

As he walked out of the Arrivals terminal, Jonathan spotted the Carey limo driver holding a sign with his name inked on it. The solitary man was wearing the obligatory black suit that looked like he had slept in it the night before. He nodded acknowledgement and the driver reached to take Jonathan's carry-on luggage to the parked black Cadillac.

Soon they were headed north on Bayshore Highway 101 to the T.V. Neurologicals facility, a short trip at this time of day.

CHAPTER TWO

Mildred

You can always spot them, Mildred thought as she settled uncomfortably into a contemporary plastic chair placed firmly against a wall in the crowded waiting room. The relatively generic beige room was splashed with an occasional abstract blotch of hunter green in an attempt to divert eyes from connecting with others. Patients and their companions were wearing annoyed and distressed scowls on pained faces and were in no mood for diversions of any kind. They had been penned in the small room far too long and all showed signs of becoming cranky.

Mildred's observation referred to the pretty, perky young blonde with shoulder length hair who sashshayed into the room balancing on three-inch platform heels. The young woman was dressed in a navy knock-off designer suit accented with a row of simulated pearls around her neck, obviously the twenty-something's idea of what a young professional should wear. The attractive young thing was carting an oversized dark leather bag bearing the name of her company embossed in gold which secreted the mysterious tools of her trade, whatever they might be.

The bag was so big that the woman was forced to use a portable grocery cart to wheel it around but more importantly, to avoid chipping her recent manicure. During numerous trips to her doctor's office, Mildred learned to recognize the ubiquitous pharmaceutical representatives who were constantly seeking "just a few minutes with the doctor."

If that polite request didn't get the desired response from the staid gate-keeping receptionist, what followed was usually an offer of giveaways (otherwise known as chachkis) magically pulled from the bag. Fancy pens loaded with black gel, 3M pads, or perhaps designer desk clocks were the usual enticements. After handing over selected baubles the question, "May I check the sample closet?" always followed. Dropping off samples was the pharmaceutical sales rep's trump card to get behind the waiting room partition and accidentally bump into the physician while he/she moved from one treatment room to another.

Occasionally the gatekeeper performed her role with the fervor of Kevin Costner in "The Bodyguard". That wasn't a pretty sight for anyone clustered in the waiting room to see, but Mildred had to say, most were friendly and maintained a professional demeanor.

The drug rep's goal was to give a detail, a two-minute presentation heralding a particular drug's benefits, while diminishing the limitations of whichever prescription drug she was selling at the time. To be effective, details had to be presented face-to-face with the prescriber. The name and indication of the drug were an intricate part of the song and dance, and ultimately made their way to the salesperson's performance evaluation.

Today's young hopeful was lucky. It probably didn't hurt that she was exceptionally pretty. Face it, pretty opens more doors than plain, which is one reason why there are so many attractive female drug reps marching into physicians' offices.

The young lady was ushered into the inner sanctum to give her pitch before the doctor saw his first patient of the day and became immersed in a busy routine. Pharmaceutical companies hit the mark when they began hiring attractive young women and loaded them with samples to gain access to doctors. Of course it didn't hurt that a highly talented segment of the work force gained access to what previously was a male-dominated occupation. Over the years Mildred had seen more and more of the exceptionally bright women ascend to the previously all male station of district manager, and a few had even floated high enough to crash the glass ceiling in the hallowed halls of the home office.

Looks of indignation from a few of the under-educated waiting room patients speared the receptionist as she allowed the young woman entrance. Just who was this filly upstart who jumped the fence? The waiting patients were not pleased, knowing this intrusion meant they would be forced to wait even longer. The woman didn't even have an appointment! The gall of it all! But Mildred surmised, business was business.

After an hour of waiting and being bombarded by endless drug commercials shown on the Med TV monitor hanging precariously over the door, Mildred was on the verge of leaving when one of the nurses peeked from behind an entrance doorway, summoning her to the winding hallway leading to the waxy white cubicles of care.

This day Mildred was led back, not to one of the six sterile patient treatment rooms, but into her specialist's spacious office. Today she had come to learn about participating in a clinical trial, a new experience for her. As Mildred and her scout snaked their way to the doctor's room of respite, she wondered how the office staff had perfected the art of admitting waiting patients just before they completely lost all tolerance and stormed out of the waiting room, cursing never to return again. Mildred *thought* she had the courage to bolt after waiting for hours, but then again, maybe she didn't. Something deep inside had always held Mildred back from standing up to be counted among the maligned masses. This was one of her life's regrets. If only she could summon the courage to be counted. Maybe there would eventually be a pill for that shortcoming.

Middle-aged Mildred, showing every one of her fifty-two hard years, plopped down in a large red leather chair in her neurologist's office, only to face another twenty minutes of waiting.

She spent the time reading ancient dog-eared magazines. Seldom did the office pay for magazine subscriptions as patients frequently recycled them out of desperation. Old medical journals were most prevalent on the waiting room tables and nobody wanted to read those magazines.

The doctor finally made his entrance, greeting his patient warmly as he ambled into the room. The prerequisite banal niceties soon aside, the professional quickly cut to the chase. This would not be a routine visit to discuss one of Mildred's many middle-age ailments; the doctor knew his patient had come today to learn about his latest clinical trial, which she hoped would accept her as a willing participant.

Mildred listened intently as her doctor described how lucky she was to be offered the chance to participate in a trial for the treatment of a condition known as restless legs syndrome.

Patients with this ailment often experienced a troubling sensation in their legs that would disrupt a deep sleep.

The eminent Dr. Rivers was seated behind his well-grained oak desk, which commanded half the room. Pewter, crystal, and teak desk accessories screamed success. On one wall hung the doctor's framed declarations of worthiness to practice medicine after satisfying the requisites at one of the leading medical schools in the country – Duke University. Mildred's doctor had arrived.

As Mildred inched to the edge of her chair to catch every word the doctor was spewing, Dr. Rivers became lost in his own thoughts even as the familiar words continued to flow from his mouth. He was remembering the long journey from his first austere waiting room filled with scarred folding chairs and faded black and white Ansell Adams Yosemite photographic prints.

His first medical practice was located in a rough and tumble neighborhood in the city of Stockton, California. In those early days his office had experienced several break-ins engineered by seedy addicts looking for narcotics. At one point the staff considered putting a sign by the door advising any would be thieves that the office did not keep samples of the hard stuff. Whenever he worked late, Rivers was careful to scan the parking lot to make sure bodies weren't lying in wait against the crumbling building walls.

It had taken time, plenty of time, but the ambitious Dr. Rivers now owned a successful private practice in the affluent suburb of Sacramento known as Granite Bay. A major part of his financial success was attributed directly to the support received over the years from pharmaceutical companies. Indeed, his relationships with drug companies went well beyond friendly visits from sales representatives, countless drug spiels, and shiny sample packs. Drug companies and their clinical trials represented an important part of Rivers' revenue stream.

Over the years the doctor had masterfully cultivated a large patient population that was quick to sign up for clinical trials, ultimately giving him VIP status in the world of drug development. Drug companies often engaged his services to conduct product trials, all aimed at receiving approval from the FDA for treating whatever illness or condition they were designed to manage. Great value was put on the speed needed to recruit and conduct such trials; in this regard Rivers had few peers among his physician colleagues.

Today Mildred Gamble was paying close attention as Dr. Rivers waded through the mandatory description of risks involved in any drug trial. He knew it was important to describe side effects carefully to minimize potential liabilities should anything untoward happen.

Companies naturally went to great lengths to ensure they were releasing a drug backed with sufficient studies so side effects were minimized, but they could never be completely eliminated as every patient presented a unique profile. The neurologist spent a few minutes describing the test medication Mildred would be taking while skillfully positioning the possible benefits she and other suffering women might eventually enjoy.

Decades before, Rivers discovered his smooth, altruistic approach was a strong motivating factor for many potential participants. Sure enough, he'd pegged Mildred as a "very caring person" and knew she would jump at the idea that her participation would help thousands of women seeking relief from what she perceived to be a horrible condition, one no woman should have to endure.

Dr. Rivers fully knew restless legs syndrome was not on the World Health Organization's list of most lethal illnesses. He knew an enterprising biopharmaceutical company grabbed a niche opportunity by positioning its compound to target women suffering from this nightly malady.

Inwardly the doctor smiled, knowing the probability of the drug working in the male population would soon follow, thus opening further lucrative trials. The initial positioning of the drug for women was a marketing ploy designed to distinguish a somewhat lackluster product. Who was he to second-guess the intentions of a pharmaceutical marketing guru with an MBA from Harvard?

Dr. Rivers readily admitted his part in the process. He would be eternally grateful for the innovative thinking that erupted from the drug industry's marketing departments. However, increased governmental monitoring of pharma promotional spending was now under the microscope, specifically designed to keep the industry from influencing the prescribing habits of doctors. Mandatory cutbacks were coming from every direction affecting sponsored educational programs, symposia, extravagant lunches, and spectacular gourmet dinners. The feds were killing the golden goose! Rivers' income would take a severe hit if he could no longer deliver patients for drug trials.

To add to the financial free-fall most physicians experienced since the advent of managed care, insurance companies were cutting into the reimbursements paid to physicians for professional services rendered, in some cases by over fifty percent. Even more troubling to many was the frequent incursion into the prescribing practice of physicians who often had to follow regimens of set protocol; only if those failed were they permitted to choose alternative treatments. The overriding consideration was the cost of drugs not available as a generic alternative. Doctors complained this hold placed them in the role of implementation robots not requiring a medical education.

It had not always been like this. When Rivers first entered private practice he was a physician fully dedicated to his patients, putting their health and well being above all other considerations. Rivers was even known to make house calls to treat his older patients. Years of battling insurance companies and the ever-present threat of lawsuits filed by ambulance chasing attorneys gradually shifted his outlook so self-preservation emerged higher on Rivers' priority roster. And thus the formation of the "Rivers' Clinical Trials Factory" grew into a thriving enterprise.

As he gave his monotone rote presentation to Mildred, Dr. Rivers' thoughts continued to drift to the good old days of pharmaceutical marketing. Long gone were the truly outrageous promotional incentives concocted by the fiercely competitive pharmaceutical reps and their home office sales departments.

Not too many years before, over 100,000 pharmaceutical sales reps pounded the pavement every single day. Today that number had been reduced to approximately 60,000 largely due to increasingly difficult physician access. There simply wasn't enough time for all reps to be seen by top-prescribing doctors. Access to a physician was incredibly important since many drugs had alternative medications that could easily be substituted, often at less cost. The name of the game was for drug companies to gain the highest share of voice to ensure a promoted drug held a position at the top of mind with those doctors who had the busiest prescribing practices.

Rivers had to confess one of his favorite pharmaceutical incentive programs, sadly now discontinued, was fondly known as "Dine and Dash." This little perk made him look like a hero on those evenings when his wife called to announce she simply could not bear cooking that night.

The perk was set in motion by the organizing sales rep informing the targeted doctor that a "Dine and Dash" had been scheduled that day for a certain time at a specific restaurant, usually a popular and exceptionally expensive dining spot. This was no Burger King giveaway.

At the end of the workday, the doctor would telephone the restaurant to place his order for a full course take-home dinner or two. He was required to pick-up the meal at the restaurant in person, and in return listened to the drug rep stationed at the establishment give a five-minute product presentation in a corner of the lobby. With this, and many other programs conducted by pharmaceutical companies, the doctor's only commitment was to listen to the sales pitch. No binding commitment required a doctor to write a prescription. It was the medical profession's version of a timeshare sales hit.

Dr. Rivers lamented the loss of such extravagant marketing freebies, but expected new opportunities would surface as pharmaceutical marketing departments schemed how to outdo the competition. Deep pockets ensured innovative perks would eventually arrive in some way, shape, or form.

"Ahem!" Mildred's attention seeking cough brought the good doctor back to the task at hand as he continued his proficient clinical spiel. Mildred long felt she seldom received the respect and attention she deserved from her doctor, but also realized she did not have the chutzpah to push back. Too bad there wasn't a trial to combat this milquetoast problem suffered by so many women. Dr. Rivers took her hint and continued.

"And so, Mildred, there will be sixty women just like you across the country participating in this exciting research. We want to find relief for all women suffering from this uncomfortable condition commonly called restless legs. The active drug discovered by the company will be compared to a placebo, or sugar pill, to determine its effectiveness. You will be on one of the pills, active or sugar, for three weeks, followed by a washout period of no medication for one week, and then followed by three weeks on the other pill. This type of trial is referred to as a double blind crossover. Blind means the patient never knows when she is taking the active drug or the sugar pill.

"Of course you'll be getting a full physical and neurological workup as part of the trial procedure. I will give you my very close personal attention. How does it sound?"

"Dr. Rivers, I can't wait to try this new miracle drug! How soon can I get started?"

Sally-Anne

The restless legs trial recruited doctors and patients from across the country. Sally-Anne Zuckerman from The Villages in Sumter County, Florida was another potential participant and not surprisingly, faced a different set of medical circumstances.

Sally-Anne was the product of a one-night stand with the star high school quarterback that left her mother a teenage single parent, struggling to raise her child with family assistance, county welfare, and whatever she could hustle on the side. Raised in a household that frequently saw different men sharing her mother's bed, Sally-Anne was a victim of abuse at the hands of several of her mother's companions. Her own mother sometimes encouraged the abuse to obtain favors from her men friends. Education was never a priority in the household so with limited skills, Sally-Anne found her way to seedy, side of the road establishments on Florida's Gulf Coast which featured topless dancing. The young woman discovered that winding her body around a pole paid well and introduced her to men of means with whom she hoped to hook-up.

Sally-Anne placed great importance on economic stability and used her knockout knockers to the fullest to fill the kitty, so to speak. Her reputation as a beach hottie grew and she earned the dubious nickname of "Sally G" for her rumored possession of an incredibly responsive G-spot. It was further rumored her trailer park neighbors would be made acutely aware if one of her male friends found the sensitive knob. Sally-Anne was sexually quirky with tastes not yet fully developed. Anything was game for Miss Sally-Anne.

The exotic dancer recognized a heaven sent opportunity when the recently widowed septuagenarian Dennis Zuckerman generously tucked tips in her satin panties while she was serving cocktails at a national convention of property developers in Miami, then later asked her to dinner at Barton G, known to be one of the most expensive establishments in the city. A glance at the final bill confirmed this May-December arrangement had possibilities.

Sally-Anne knew from experience that once she lured her prey into bed he would be putty in her hands. She didn't earn her nickname for nothing. After a whirlwind courtship, which involved sex in so many ways the old boy had never experienced or even dreamed possible, the stage was set. Sally-Anne was a fantasy come reality for the old guy. Zuckerman slipped a ring on Sally-Anne's finger while on vacation in the penthouse cabin of a first-class cruise line.

It turned out the two actually were a good fit. For the first year of their marriage Sally-Anne was sure she'd made the right decision to cement her future, despite the occasional idiosyncrasy revealed by the old boy. Thinking along the lines of a Gulf view mansion in Naples, Florida, she reluctantly relented and accepted Zuckerman's insistence on building an 8,000 square foot house in a development called The Villages located in central Florida. Several of her husband's snowbird buddies from Jersey found the Florida cattle country area to their liking and encouraged him to join them. For Zuckerman, retirement was all about playing golf seven days a week with a regular group of retired property development cronies and indulging in an endless flood of liquid refreshment at the 19th hole.

Sally-Anne could hardly believe her eyes the first time her husband drove his ridiculous, ostentatiously customized electric golf cart up and down the community boulevard leading a motorcade of his old friends. One would think they were driving actual German and Italian GT cars the way they took such pride in their collection of oversized go-karts!

Dennis' cart was customized to resemble a Rolls Royce to match the real one he kept in the garage. As long as she had her Mercedes convertible built in Bremen, Germany, a stack of credit cards, and her geezer husband could keep her happy in the sack, Sally-Anne could accept this small price to pay for her economic peace of mind.

Not having to worry about meeting the next rent payment was a blessing, and much to her surprise, Dennis was not as bad in bed as she thought he would be. This was in part due to the old guy being hung like a racehorse.

Unfortunately, life has a cruel way of playing practical jokes and Sally-Anne soon discovered that it rains, even in the Villages' heavenly haven. After a year of marital bliss, the first wave of setbacks hit the couple. Zuckerman developed prostate cancer and the resulting surgery left him with problems satisfying his young wife. Although willing and horny, he could not summon the necessary equipment to perform. Dennis tried the wave of current pills that promised great results, but found them only partially effective. His urologist prescribed self-administered injections of prostaglandin shot directly into his member, and while this seemed to work, it wasn't a procedure he looked forward to multiple times each week. Frustrated, he searched for an answer to his predicament.

This setback didn't sit well with the former Miss Sally G and the young insatiable wife found herself becoming increasingly depressed over her lack of gratification. To add to her misery, she was putting up with a ridiculous ailment she had developed. It was something her OB/Gyn diagnosed as restless legs syndrome. The OB/Gyn suggested she might be interested in signing up for a clinical trial his neurologist brother-in-law was conducting. Sally-Anne was no doctor, but she knew the cure she really needed for her "restlessness." And, it wasn't exactly in the shape of a pill! Still, she thought, why not? What have I got to lose? I may as well give the trial a try and if I don't like what's happening to my body, I'll simply quit.

Alice

Alice Peterson, a barely 25-year-old, slim, raven-haired newlywed from Alpharetta, Georgia had always been extremely shy and withdrawn. A natural beauty, she hid her striking attributes well behind minimal and often pale makeup. The lack of lipstick did nothing to accent her rich, full lips. A low-key, simple K-Mart wardrobe hung pitifully over her shapely frame.

Raised as the eldest in a family of five girls in South Georgia, Alice's home life centered on strict Baptist teachings and so Alice was the product of a structured and overly protective upbringing. Her father was a mean, abusive bastard who drove his wife from the home when Alice was only twelve. Fearing for her life, the mother just up and disappeared one day, leaving her oldest daughter and her sisters to fend for themselves.

Alice tried to divert her father's inappropriate advances away from her younger sisters, resulting in Alice enduring many nights bonding with her father in ways no daughter should ever experience. The day after Alice graduated from high school was the last time she would ever see the terrible place she called home. Her "domestic experiences" scarred Alice tremendously and created deep deficiencies, such as lack of self-esteem and worth, and an unwavering concern that no man would ever find her attractive. These worries bubbled beneath the surface throughout her young adulthood, waiting for the opportunity to explode.

A good student, Alice was able to raise sufficient financial support to attend Georgia State while she worked part-time at a local TV station. Armed with a degree in communications, Alice found a job working as a behind-the-scenes assistant in the roving reporter department of a local TV station. She eventually found a man. Her husband Tim, a gentle and loving man, fell in love with Alice at first sight, seeing her innate beauty inside and out. Alice was surprised at her marriage since owning even a sliver of happiness went against all she believed about herself.

Tim and Alice were amorously interlocked one night when, as happens with most young men, Tim encouraged Alice to experiment with different coital positions and a few other stimulating activities, bordering on kinky.

Alice was becoming increasingly apprehensive about her husband's requests, and her lack of self-confidence led her to believe she was not woman enough to satisfy Tim's needs. After several nights of refusing his requests, Alice was on the verge of panic when she suddenly felt a strange sensation tremble through her legs. The sensation caused her legs to feel detached from the rest of her body, and yet made her want to move them wildly as if shaking off demons. A sense of relief flooded over her as she could now, in good conscience, use this physical anomaly as a reason to bring an end to their lovemaking.

"Tim, I don't feel well. There's something terribly wrong with my lower body. It's like I feel a strong, uncontrollable twitching in my legs." Her husband paused mid-stroke, looking both concerned and surprised at the sudden interruption.

"What do you mean by twitching?" Tim demanded, trying to goad Alice into continuing their lovemaking.

"Well, what if it's a brain tumor or something? Like my Aunt Winnie had!" Alice exclaimed, pushing Tim off her. Tim, sensing her apprehension, knew enough not to pressure his wife further. He covered his disappointment with understanding and nurturing encouragement.

"Of course I understand, honey. But promise me you'll go to the doctor tomorrow to look into this. Just to be safe."

With that, the frustrated husband rolled over and feigned sleep for ninety minutes until he finally succumbed to slumber.

The next day Alice reached out to her best friend, Jacki Striker, a woman she met at college. Since the day they met, they were inseparable friends. Truth be told, other than Jacki, Alice didn't have another close friend she could turn to.

When they first connected, Jacki was a brilliant grad student at nearby Georgia Tech and was working part-time as a teaching assistant in a physiology class that Alice was taking at the university. Neither was partial to the Buckhead bar scene, the watering hole for the college population. Both women were movie buffs and especially loved old films, which were freely available on Turner Classics. The pair was definite eye candy and had heard just about every pick-up line from both men and women, none of them reaching success. Jacki's stiletto sharp way of dealing with flirtation was excused as being a brainy nerd with a tendency to be judgmental, seeing the world only in black and white. A tall, slender redhead, Jacki could easily have been voted the most attractive co-ed in Atlanta if her friend Alice didn't already hold that title.

The *Atlanta Journal-Constitution* did a weekend piece about Atlanta's most promising college students; there were more photos of Alice than all others combined.

After graduating from Georgia State and separated from Jacki, Alice found a love interest in Tim and they were married with her best friend standing as maid of honor. Jacki had gone on to earn a degree as Doctor of Pharmacy and found a fulfilling job working in the medical department of a small pharmaceutical company.

Cripes! Alice is late again! I wonder if she remembers which restaurant we decided on for lunch.

While waiting for her friend in a cozy booth in a quaint Irish pub in Milton, Jacki Striker recounted the complications in her own life. Her good friend had called for help to decipher her love life and Jacki eagerly responded as the Lone Rangerette, even though immersed in her own dark, massing clouds. She pondered her predicament as she swirled the straw in her third iced tea.

I can't believe that asshole in the sales division had the balls to try to recruit me to join him and his asshole cronies in their scheme to increase bonuses! Using my medical department status to encourage key physicians to prescribe off-label is a serious violation. The jerk just laughed at my objections. When I refused his offer, he had the nerve to drop a veiled threat that I should forget everything said or face severe consequences. You'd think I was being threatened by the Mafia rather than by one of my colleagues at work. Total asshole.

Jacki worked as a medical science liaison at her company and her once enviable job was not going as smoothly as she had hoped. Within the medical department, there were a dozen MSLs like Jacki spread across the country, all charged with the mandate to provide thought leaders access to the most current medical knowledge available internally and externally. What tended to distinguish this group was a reputation for deep and specialized knowledge of the therapeutic areas in which their products competed, for example, epilepsy. Being at the cutting edge of clinical and pre-clinical information for a disease like epilepsy could give the company an advantage over their competitors.

MSLs were instructed to be objective in their discourse, operating at the highest levels of integrity. Most emphatically, they were not to be involved with the sales and marketing functions of their companies. Herein lay some of the unrest that was so troubling to Jacki.

Jacki loved her job, found it fulfilling and refreshingly honest in the world of pharmaceuticals. That harmony was disrupted in recent weeks when she was approached by a few rotten eggs in sales who wanted to exploit Jacki's carte blanche, non-commercial relationship with leading physicians. The proposed action would be geared to boosting prescriptions written, and thereby their bonuses.

Feeling pressure to make sales quotas, a few slime balls on the company sales team had taken a bite from the forbidden fruit by attempting to curry favor and gain endorsements from leading physicians for medical products in expanded areas of use not approved by the FDA. In return, vague suggestions that "gifts" might be forthcoming to any and all who provided assistance to this effort were whispered.

Jacki was mortified at the mere suggestion and in a flurry of four-letter words told them to "Fuck off!" The conspirators hardly blinked their eyes, and then admonished her for being unrealistic. Finally they assured her she was passing on a good thing that another party would absolutely embrace.

As the men snaked out of her office after offering the proposition, the group of four silk suits casually mentioned it would not be in her best interest to discuss the matter with anyone. Clearly they were not going to stop in their greedy quest. Jacki knew they would find someone to play patsy for them. She recognized this might be the proverbial tip of the iceberg that could eventually sink the company.

What was most disturbing in the quagmire was the laissez-faire response Jacki received from her boss, Dr. Medrick. After thinking about the brush-off Dr. Medrick gave when she related the bizarre offer, Jacki came to the conclusion her boss was in on it. *What the hell do I do now? Who can I possibly go to for guidance?*

Jacki was facing a seemingly impossible dilemma. She loved her job and her company, but not if the canoe she was paddling was heading for the rushing rapids. She looked at her watch again; Alice was now a full twenty-five minutes late.

What a joke, me giving Alice advice on her love life! I haven't been out on a date in months. All the guys I meet are losers. That last one had possibilities, but when I found him cheating on his tax return I had to say something and brother, did he take exception!

Jacki's social life was a complete and utter bust. Men often found the combination of beauty and brains, bolstered by a stinging view of right and wrong, was not likely to fit their definition of an ideal companion.

She saw men's heads turn toward the pub's entrance and knew it was a sure sign signaling the arrival of Alice. It was comical to watch heads slowly turn as her gorgeous friend headed to her booth. The two old friends hugged and fell into catch-up conversation for a few minutes followed by moments of silence before addressing the topic that had led to the lunch meeting.

"Jacki, I feel absolutely terrible. I had to stop Tim in the middle of our lovemaking last night. I had knots in my stomach because he wanted to try new things, but when my legs started to twitch, well, I knew I couldn't continue with any kind of sex. I feel awful this happened and want to be sure it doesn't repeat. Tell me what to do, you know about these things. With your medical background, you know a lot more than most people do."

As Jacki listened to Alice's woes, her first thought was wishing she too had someone special in her life. Unlike Alice, she would most likely enjoy the world of sexual experimentation. What Alice was describing about the sudden twitching could be attributed to a condition known as restless legs syndrome. By sheer coincidence her company was conducting clinical trials for a new drug to treat that very problem. One of Jacki's work objectives was to recruit patients for the trial, but, she wondered, was it a good idea to mix friendship and business? A still small voice warned her to be careful, but a louder voice belonged to her best friend asking for her help.

"Please, Jacki, I need you to tell me what to do!" pleaded a teary eyed Alice. Jacki relented.

"Hon, you know I'm not a doctor, but coincidentally my company is administering a clinical trial that might be directed at the condition you're describing. It's commonly known as restless legs syndrome. I can certainly introduce you to the physician hosting the trials in Atlanta and perhaps he could examine and evaluate you. If you are diagnosed with the condition, he might admit you into his trial. One good thing, the drug and work-up are free." A look of relief relaxed Alice's troubled features.

"Oh, that would be wonderful! It makes me feel so much better knowing you'll be there on the sidelines should I need any advice." Jacki grimaced, but it went unnoticed.

So it was settled. The two got back to chatting about a new department store that recently opened at North Point Mall while digging into mounds of shepherd's pie, one of the tastiest items on the pub grub menu.

Jacki felt a hint of indigestion as she finished her meal. She hoped she had done the right thing suggesting Alice join the SRD 6969 clinical trial being conducted by her company.

With her friend's involvement, it would be the first time Jacki had a personal investment in the outcome of a clinical trial. For some reason that made her feel uneasy. As she mentally reviewed the many trials she had been associated with over the years, seldom had there been any problems of significance.

Jacki took another sip of her chardonnay and convinced herself all would be fine.

CHAPTER THREE

Comfortably seated in the back of the refreshingly cool limo, Jonathan drew an iPhone5S from his breast pocket. His vivid imagination conjured similarities between the modern day corporate turnaround executive and the rough and rowdy gunslinger who ruled the Wild West.

One was armed with a six-shooter while the other did battle with a Smartphone. Both frequently made split-second decisions that permanently affected people's lives. No question in Jonathan's mind which weapon was more formidable. With the right fingers, the iPhone with lightening fast technology and powerful applications won hands down. A strike from an iPhone could take down hundreds, if not thousands, human beings in a split second.

In the twenty minutes it took to get from the airport to T.V. Neurologicals headquarters, Jonathan was able to accomplish what would've taken a full week at his desk computer just five years ago. This was the electronic firepower wizardry of Silicon Valley at its finest.

In all likelihood, the OK Corral metaphor was driven by Jonathan's subconscious mind rehashing whom he would retain on his senior management team. When a new CEO is brought in as an agent of change, it would be unrealistic to assume there wouldn't be body bag casualties. There were always a few souls who didn't share the new boss's vision, management style, or simply suffered poor chemistry while wrangling with the new man at the top.

Inevitably the new sheriff in town, in past or present times, would insist on hand-chosen henchmen to cover his back as he engaged the new frontier. It was early in the game, but Jonathan had already engineered a number of terminations and replacements. Many of his first days at T.V. Neurologicals would be spent sussing out the strengths and liabilities of employees who occupied key positions within the company.

Sussing. Now, that was a funny term he picked up from his Southern friends in the Research Triangle.

Jonathan knew he didn't get to the position he held without employing good instincts; his gut told him there were two individuals remaining in the existing team he wasn't ready to embrace as members of his recently formed nucleus, but neither was he ready to pull the trigger on two long careers with the company.

The first in question was Dr. Raynard Bernstein, the Vice President of Research and Development since the company's inception. Czuretrin was well along in clinical development for the treatment of seizures by the time Dr. Bernstein was placed as head of R&D, so he really couldn't claim credit for the drug. Tim Varter had been the driving force.

Bernstein was a cardiologist by training and was strongly backing a research compound designated SRD 0011, developed under his wing for acute myocardial arrhythmias. The origin of Bernstein's discovery made interesting reading. He had long taken an interest in toxins secreted by various forms of sea life as a source for synthesizing beneficial drug compounds. Sadly for

Bernstein and T.V. Neurologicals, there was more interest in how the drug had come to be than the actual value of the compound in the treatment of cardiovascular problems.

Once before Jonathan had seen the phenomenon of a drug researcher desperate to make a name for himself, but in the process blindly push a molecule forward with astonishing disregard for red flags raised along the way. Early in his T.V. Neurologicals corporate courtship while performing due diligence, Jonathan immediately identified two ruby red flags waving madly to be noticed in Bernstein's project.

The first was that T.V. Neurologicals was perceived by physicians to be a neurology company. The T.V. Neurologicals product line was geared to treating neurological conditions exclusively. All major resources, the most significant being the sales force, were trained and geared solely to neurologists. With SRD 0011, the target would be cardiologists. Jonathan knew from his cholesterol marketing days this physician group presented a different breed of specialists, one that wasn't easy to win over.

SRD 0011 would require investment in a new business unit dedicated exclusively to cardiology and there were plenty of issues related to such a decision, cost of investment being at the top of the list. At corporate financial meetings, it was typical for management to downplay such entry barriers, trying to avoid raining on the elaborate parade required to introduce a new chemical entity into the company's product portfolio. Jonathan had been through this scenario several times in past lives and was keenly aware that much repositioning would be needed to change or add a new direction to the company.

The second issue that had nagged at Jonathan was the paucity of research conducted on the market potential for the compound. It would not be the first time one division of a company insisted on building a better mousetrap only to find nobody really wanted to buy their particular mousetrap. Amazing as it might be, companies frequently spent millions of dollars before discovering the ugly truth that "the emperor wore no clothes."

Both frantically fluttering red flags were commercial issues unrelated to the science behind the drug. Jonathan knew he would be traveling a rough road with Dr. Bernstein.

Very few R&D heads had anything good to say about commercial strategy and were often blinded by their science.

Apart from SRD 0011, there were only two other compounds in the T.V. Neurologicals R&D pipeline. The first was a drug currently undergoing testing for the treatment of restless legs syndrome in women, code name SRD 6969. Bernstein only indulged this project because it enabled him to tout that his research pipeline was not just a one-trick pony. However, SRD 6969 was not his discovery and was, in fact, a product licensed from another biotech firm in the North Bay area. Bernstein's intention was to phase out SRD 6969 or sell it to another company soon after trials were completed. This would then divert resources to his pet cardiology project.

The second product presented a challenge many health industry leaders wrestle with in their roles as corporate leaders. Ever the dealmaker, Tim Varter picked up the rights to an interesting molecule several years before. This developmental drug was intended to promote activity in what is referred to as the orphan drug market. Orphan drugs pertain to medical situations covering a miniscule patient population. Because of this limitation, the economics of such drug development is always highly unfavorable. Regrettable, but reality.

Varter's particular orphan drug was targeted at a very small population of 400-500 patients worldwide suffering from an autoimmune disease that viciously attacks brain cells, leading to a long and unpleasant death. With such a small patient population, the company could not expect a highly profitable return on its investment of people, time, and money. But, the unusual activity of the cells in the brain made this a very interesting compound for development.

Yet Jonathan made the decision to continue the investment. The old "Murray Value System" was now an integral part of his DNA and told him further development was the right thing to do. Even though the numbers were small, these suffering people were desperate for medical relief and there was not much to be found. Since fiduciary responsibility to his company was important, Jonathan could not afford to give away the product. If approved by the FDA, he would price the drug relatively high to recoup some of the costs, inevitably drawing criticism from outsiders who didn't know the full story. Such people often became irate over yet another outrageously priced drug produced by a "greedy pharmaceutical company," forgetting the alternative was to offer nothing new to treat suffering patients.

Most likely T.V. Neurologicals would initiate a program to help those who needed the drug but could not afford it. More than likely this act of good will would be overlooked by critics. It was hard to win any PR battle and as such pointed to one of the many issues faced by pharmaceutical CEOs in an industry constantly under attack, seldom afforded praise for positive contributions to society.

The other person on the executive committee who tripped Jonathan's internal alarm system was Ron Daniels, the national sales manager. Shrieks of "Danger, Danger, Will Robinson!" echoed in his ears when he thought of Daniels. Funny how a hokey kids' TV show off the air for decades could still have recall. Within minutes of meeting Daniels, Jonathan pegged him as an old-style sales manager, very much geared to the self-serving side of selling.

Jonathan reminded himself not to underestimate Daniels' easygoing Louisiana accent as one belonging to a country bumpkin pushover. This guy was a shrewd, street-smart salesman who could sell the proverbial refrigerator to an Eskimo. In the past, the pharmaceutical industry had created an art form by catering to the whims of physician customers, and Daniels was the best schmoozer in his field. Those days had long gone by the wayside.

There were countless ways the pharmaceutical industry made it enticing for a physician to listen to a sales rep's product presentation. Typically there would be an array of product samples as well as an endless supply of giveaways like buffet lunches, pens, pads, clocks, and most anything big enough to carry the company logo. Additionally, physicians were invited to seminars at fabulous resort locations, providing an opportunity to play golf or sightsee following a morning of medical lectures. Evenings frequently gave the opportunity to sip fine wines and dine on gourmet cuisine prepared by leading Michelin chefs.

One of the most lavish presentations ever witnessed by Jonathan was an event named Everything Chocolat, a promotional function rumored to be introduced by the very same Ron Daniels when he was employed by another company. The evening's spectacular was held in the ballroom of a famous hotel; one of San Francisco's finest was the scene of many chocolate fantasies.

Rounds of tables were draped in fine linens and laces with an unimaginable collection of chocolates staggered on crystal tiers, begging to be chosen by eager chocolate lovers. Large milk chocolate sculptures reflected in table mirrors commanded a glorified presence on the larger tables. Anchored in all four corners of the ballroom, mahogany bars accented with gleaming brass served only the finest California wines and rich liqueurs to accent the dark creamy confections. All expense was gladly accepted by the host company to woo doctors and their spouses, or sometimes "nieces," attending the seminar weekend.

Jonathan's college roommate worked for the host company that adopted Daniels' brainchild and once invited him to enjoy and discern what he promised would be a spectacle not soon forgotten. His curiosity piqued, Jonathan accepted the invitation. His insider status allowed the opportunity to wander the ballroom in its untouched splendor before the doors were opened to the hundreds of eager invitees.

It was astounding to see intricate chocolate carvings towering above tables festooned with billowing ivory satin and lace. Designer truffles of all descriptions were artistically balanced on ornate silver platters accented with red roses. The ballroom truly resembled a work of art. After a few minutes, Jonathan sauntered to the entrance hallway and peered down the winding walnut staircase. He could see the crowd impatiently milling below, shoulder-to-shoulder, eager to enter Willy Wonka's world. A few children tagged along, their kind parents realizing this evening would surely be a fantasy come true for little ones. Important and connected people were in the crowd too, if they were able to secure a coveted invitation. Host companies sometimes invited their competition, simply to show how a party should be done. Of course, members of the media were included, typically congregating at the corner bars.

At exactly eight o'clock the massive ballroom doors swung open with a trumpeter sounding a majestic call. This was really over the top! Jonathan watched the tsunami of humanity flood the ballroom. Within fifteen minutes almost every chocolate had been swept off the tables, leaving smears of gooey fillings slashing the fine lace and linen. Classic sculptures had been ripped apart for the chocolate treasure within. Jonathan chuckled as he thought of kids breaking ears off chocolate Easter bunnies. Greed permeated the room as guests piled plates high with chocolate as if challenged to collect as many calories as they possibly could consume in just minutes. Human locusts had swarmed the ballroom, leaving a trail of ugly destruction behind.

As he watched the mob madness, Jonathan realized the extent of his industry's entertainment excesses. Surely doctors could be reached another way! The insanity of it all deepened his resolve to follow a path less hedonistic, allowing him to bring the merits of the industry to the forefront. It deeply troubled Jonathan that the positive side of the industry equation was seldom recognized; noble acts and corporate generosity were being overshadowed by the industry's growing reputation for excessive wining and dining. He remembered wondering what patients and serious researchers would think if they were bugs on that ballroom wall.

As the black limo rode on under the California sun, Jonathan fumbled in his pocket and pulled out the *San Jose Mercury* newspaper clipping he had first read on the plane. The reporter penning the article had it right. How sad this writer's enlightened perspective was not more frequently recognized. The article carried the head "Drugs – The Good, the Bad, and the Ugly." He read the creased paper once more.

Amazing advances are being made in cancer, inflammation, gastroenterology, rheumatology, cardiology and other medical research. Extending society's lifespan and bringing a better quality of life to many are attributes the drug industry must develop to promote better awareness. There is too much focus on the cost of prescription products and not enough recognition given to the savings when the totality of medical treatment is considered.

For example, the discovery of a class of anti-ulcer drugs known as proton pump inhibitors has almost completely eradicated the need for more expensive surgical treatment of ulcers, but most likely the key takeaway is the expense of filling the prescription.

It all boils down to the fact that human nature regards healthcare as a right and people have a fundamental problem paying for the relief afforded by pharmacotherapy. To add to this negative image, the industry is extremely competitive and has basically shot itself in the foot with excessively aggressive sales programs introduced as the companies jockey for market share. There are frequently multiple pharmaceutical options for most conditions and, like any industry, drug companies feel the need to establish market dominance.

In the early 2000s, filing of False Claims litigation against several pharmaceutical companies by government prosecutors got attention in company boardrooms. Substantial fines of up to a billion dollars were levied against pharmaceutical companies and large sums paid to whistleblowers for assisting the government. A whistleblower's share in a billion dollar fine could be as high as 30 percent with no downside risk should the case not come to fruition.

By the year 2012, industry fines totaled nearly 5.5 billion dollars; almost every pharmaceutical company of significant size had experienced a lawsuit. With the specter of government litigation and the potential for exorbitant financial penalties, behavioral change was mandated in the industry and companies were forced to adopt stricter codes of conduct regarding management of operations.

The limo was approaching its freeway exit as Jonathan gazed to his right to see large buildings wearing the corporate banners of Intel, Cisco, and Yahoo. Closing his eyes, Jonathan could picture what the landscape had been before "siliconization" hit the peaceful valley. He could see himself walking across farmland, nary a concrete building in sight.

Back in the early '70s when Jonathan was a college student, a buddy by the name of John Magilla had invited him for dinner one weekend. John's family established a long history as fruit farmers in the Santa Clara Valley and owned a significant piece of land east of Highway 101 near De La Cruz Boulevard. After a hearty family-style dinner, John took Jonathan quail hunting on the far end of the property. Looking at the siliconized landscape now, it was hard to believe he once roamed that very same piece of land as a hunter.

The limo exited the freeway at Shoreline Boulevard and after making several quick turns, pulled up to a ubiquitous series of single-story structures that housed the future breakthroughs of the Valley. A simple sign announcing T.V. Neurologicals Pharmaceutical appeared bland and unassuming. The old adage "never judge a book by its cover" certainly applied to the majority of single-story buildings that housed the economic engines chugging strong under California skies.

Gliding to a stop in front of the main entrance, the CEO of T.V. Neurologicals exited the limo, took a deep breath and squared his shoulders, then quietly entered his new home.

CHAPTER FOUR

Jonathan entered the lobby of his new company without much fanfare. Not that he expected a marching band parading in feathered hats, but a few welcoming signs would have been appreciated. He finally spied a folding note board with the bland message . . . Welcome, Mr. Jonathan Grayhall – CEO T.V. Neurologicals.

Better get used to the laid back culture of startup companies where the attitude differed markedly from established *Big Pharma* who could without a second thought, afford to spend resources to maintain the aesthetics of their environment. Compare that to a budding entrepreneurial organization that struggled to meet payrolls month-to-month. No room for multinational pomp and circumstance exists in the Valley.

The receptionist seated behind a sleek chrome desk was the picture of efficiency. After welcoming Jonathan between incoming calls, she buzzed his secretary who soon appeared waddling down the hall. The woman looked ready to drop her baby right then and there in the lobby. As the soon-to-be-mommy led Jonathan to his office, he learned she would be going on maternity leave the next week, but was quick to assure him he would be well taken care of by the replacement she had personally selected and trained for the responsibility.

The way she familiarized her new boss with his office and routine left much to be desired. Her casual, laid back delivery led him to believe something was not quite right. This was not the behavior he expected of an executive assistant to the CEO.

Jonathan walked into his modest but tastefully decorated corner office and immediately noticed the inbox was overflowing with contracts to be reviewed and documents to be signed. He promptly set about organizing his new business life and waded through the pile of paperwork with the efficiency of a maestro. Just as he was about to put signatures on dozens of overdue checks, his secretary stuck her head in the doorway and announced, "Dr. Tim Varter left a message confirming he will be meeting you for dinner tonight at Chantilly and made reservations for 6:30. Other than that dinner appointment, I kept your calendar free for the rest of the day as you requested."

After making her pronouncement, the secretary started to lumber down the hall sending the message she was eager to leave for the day before heavy commuter traffic clogged the freeways.

"Thank you for making the travel arrangements to get me here. It all went very smoothly.

I'll spend the next hour or so wading through the papers you've assembled so feel free to leave for the day," Jonathan called after her, his words echoing in the hallway.

It didn't seem the secretary had to be told twice to hit the road.

Sure not what I expected from a CEO's secretary. I wonder who put the burr under her saddle. Oh well, I may as well get some work done before dinner.

The evening meal was scheduled by T.V. Neurologicals former CEO at his favorite local restaurant. Several years before, Varter had built a handsome house in the posh neighborhood of Atherton where housing started listing in the several millions. Judging from the attentive service received at Chantilly, this man was an important and frequent patron of the fine dining establishment.

The two men had met several times during the recruitment phase. Chemistry was good from the get-go and a warm relationship bordering on genuine friendship had developed. Varter held no malice toward Jonathan for assuming the helm of his company; in fact, he was delighted he could now fully pursue his latest venture, a small vineyard in Napa. Jonathan was looking forward to a pleasurable and delicious meal at the well-regarded restaurant.

Jonathan ordered a carpaccio appetizer followed by noisette of lamb while his companion chose Blue Point oysters to complement his Veal Normandy. The meal was enjoyed with a bottle of cabernet from Varter's vineyard. Jonathan learned the sommelier kept a private section for Varter wines in the establishment's cellar. Over dinner the Englishman displayed the charm and wit that had been paramount in convincing Jonathan to make his job switch, and no doubt had served the entrepreneur well in the early days of T.V. Neurologicals when searching for seed money. Just before dessert was presented, Varter took a deep breath, puffed his chest wide and made a proclamation.

"I wager you didn't know I was one of Britain's premier athletes!" From the smile that creased the good doctor's face, Jonathan suspected there was a twist to the story that was about to be told.

"Well, I must admit in all the press I've devoured about the impressive Dr. Timothy Varter, there were plenty of accolades showered, but I cannot recall reading about athletic brilliance. In which sport did you excel?"

"My dear boy," Varter began as a piece of chocolate cheesecake made its way into his mouth. "Clearly here in the Colonies, you've not had the benefit of exposure to the sport of aristocracy, known as the Eaton Wall Game."

Jonathan suspected his friend was pulling his leg, but then again, Brits did some funny things. After a few minutes describing a game that appeared to resemble nothing else on the planet, he determined the Eaton Wall Game might actually exist and domiciled at the prestigious Eaton School for Boys.

The game appeared to carry similarity to rugby, but had been played exclusively at the prestigious public school for the past hundred years. It soon became clear this game was not a product of Varter's fantasy. While seriously explaining the convoluted rules of the bizarre contest, Varter suddenly switched into self-deprecating English humor that had his young recruit howling with laughter.

"It seems that only in England a private school, for some obtuse reason known only to the English, is labeled a public school. Furthermore, said game involves an inanimate object - being a century-old wall measuring 110x5 meters that probably bears more intelligence than the collective team players. To further complicate the setting, a vocabulary only a Welshman could understand is spoken to the already confused spectators. If you Yanks cannot understand the rules of the gentlemen's game we call cricket, what hope do I have to adequately describe my athletic prowess in this magnificent wall sport? My God, there's even a hit song by the rock band Pink Floyd called 'The Wall.' What a fitting tribute!"

By this time Jonathan was laughing so hard he had trouble catching his breath. The two men strengthened their already firm connection that evening.

"Jonathan, dinner was superb and, as always, the conversation was most enjoyable and highly informative."

The men covered key corporate housekeeping issues over the meal and much to Jonathan's relief, there were no last-minute surprises. Varter sipped his espresso and for a moment reminded Jonathan of his own father about to give a bushel of fatherly advice.

"You know, Jonathan, I came to this part of the world thinking the Valley had a strange and special capability to build world-leading companies with an almost uncanny sense for inno-vation. While there is considerable truth to that statement, what I really found is there exists an equally special capability in the Bay Area which I refer to as 'the business of business.'"

Jonathan frowned to indicate he did not understand.

"By that I mean there are so many risky and innovative corporate oil wells drilled in the pharmaceutical business that you would ex-pect a greater number of company failures in the Valley. Companies should die a natural death after drilling dry wells, but the media spin-masters and venture capitalists are very skilled at morphing a good many of these companies into their next iteration, thus the whole cycle is repeated under a different guise. The name I've given this phenomenon as it applies to our business is "The Drug Research Carousel." This concept was unfamiliar to Jonathan and so he gave Varter his full attention, wondering where this story would lead.

"In this metaphor, pharmaceutical research is akin to a spin-ning carousel with beautifully painted horses teasing their riders grab the elusive brass ring.

"Picture the wooden horses representing drugs in the research pipeline, the outer ring being those thought to have the great-est potential for success. If a drug, the horse if you would, fails in clinical trials, it would probably be removed from the carousel disk with a broken part, perhaps a leg or bridle in the case of the wooden horse, and replaced with a new, beautifully and artistically painted creature. More often, this horse might be moved from one circle ring to be positioned in a lower priority circle representing a different indication or direction for the molecule.

"It would be possible for such a drug horse to regain position in the outer circle, but only with a different medical indication. The point I hope to make, if at all possible, is that it is more profit-able to reposition assets you already own, and for which you've ac-cumulated an extensive database, than explore the capital market to purchase new assets that are expensive and relatively unknown.

"Of course this isn't always possible and goes against the adage that good money shouldn't be thrown after bad, but I marvel at how often I've seen this phenomenon happen in the Valley.

"What is equally amazing is how frequently people get rich on the subsequent iterations.

I have seen millions of dollars made through effective recycling. The romantics say innovation drives the Valley; I say it's a combination of innovation and creative corporate slight-of-hand.

"And now it's time for an old man to go to bed. I'm sure you have a full day ahead at the office, let's call it a night."

Jonathan listened attentively to what his California mentor had described and tried to visualize its implications.

"Tim, thank you for a fine dinner, and especially your wise words. I suspect you have good reasons for passing on lessons you've logged during your tenure at T.V. Neurologicals. At this point I'm still digesting every bit of information I'm fed. I always appreciate learning how to expand my options in the changing business environment."

With that, the two said goodnight and headed to their respective homes. As he drove home in his rental car, Jonathan reflected on Varter's parting comments and wondered what had prompted the older man to speak so philosophically. Tim seemed to have taken a liking to the new leader of T.V. Neurologicals, perhaps he was hoping to pass on pearls of wisdom, or maybe he just had too much wine at dinner.

The concept of recycling and lack of genuine innovation seemed to be contrary to the culture of the Valley. Yet Varter certainly was no fool and his words of advice were not to be ignored or taken lightly. "The business of business" and "The Drug Research Carousel" were novel ideas Jonathan had never come across before. Undoubtedly the Valley had a history richly overflowing with innovation, but apparently Varter had seen a few blemishes in the polished presentations.

The next day Jonathan woke a half-hour later than usual, grabbed a glass of orange juice and then worked out for sixty minutes on his in-home elliptical exerciser. Finally he was ready to jog down to the local Starbucks for his grande, double-shot, low-fat latte before meeting a real estate agent who had been referred to him.

Jonathan spent several hours with the agent house hunting; at their first stop he experienced firsthand the sticker shock that hit newcomers to the Bay Area. It could only be described as being walloped with a 2x4 up the side of the head.

To keep the need for smelling salts at a minimum, it was common practice for companies relocating employees to the Bay Area to provide generous financial packages to make the transition easier. In the San Francisco area, a house could easily cost anywhere from five to tenfold the price of a home in Anyplace Else, USA.

The financial assistance offered might be a five-year decreasing stipend to help cover the considerably larger monthly mortgage financed in this region of the country. The stipend might be $1,000/month for the first year, $800/month year two, $600/month year three, and so forth.

The logic was the employee would have increasing income, usually through stock gains, to offset the diminishing stipend as the years sped by. Without special financial assistance, it would not be possible for many transfers to take place. Even with generous packages, most corporate employees still could not maintain the style of housing they typically enjoyed in Middle America. Real estate agents carried tissues in their glove boxes and pockets to mop up the flood of tears when reality hit. Many a job opportunity involving relocation was refused for the housing reason alone.

Jonathan considered himself fortunate in this aspect of his transition. As a single man he didn't have much desire to own a large house so his needs were more easily met. Without a spouse or children to consider, he was perfectly happy with a townhouse condominium his agent found off Sand Hill Road in an area known as Sharon Heights. His agent assured him he had purchased a 1600 square foot bargain for $2 million.

A frivolous reason driving Jonathan's housing decision was the proximity of a favorite haunt well known from his Stanford days. Many a night Jonathan could be found downing a greasy cheeseburger with pint of ale at a local tavern called The Dutch Goose. He suspected his hectic schedule at T.V. Neurologicals and casual bachelor lifestyle would result in many nights of not-such-fine-dining at the peanut shells on the floor establishment.

Next on his agenda was the purchase of a car. This was a task he undertook with great enthusiasm, loving high performance vehicles as he had since he was sixteen years old. Jonathan was looking forward to test driving an assortment of powerful machinery. They say the only difference between men and boys is the size and cost of their toys! Jonathan was the poster boy for this truism.

From an early age he embraced anything proclaiming a need for speed, from roller skates to bicycles, go-karts to motorcycles, and finally high performance automobiles. His strong bias for German precision cars showed on Jonathan's final list of three highly coveted automobiles. Of course there was a Porsche, he'd always admired the Carrera 4S, but it seemed there were just too many of them on California roads. And, for business purposes, a four-door would certainly be more practical.

The next car he considered was a BMW M5. Jonathan had experienced several of these fine-driving machines in the past and noted this stallion delivered performance and comfort in a more subtle manner than any Porsche could.

There was one other car that called to him. It had sleek curves reminiscent of a beautiful woman and after test driving the precision automobile down the 280 Freeway, Jonathan knew no other car would satisfy him. He settled on a metallic silver Audi RS7, a relatively new boy on the block which was honed to deliver world-class performance. The automobile also boasted drop-dead gorgeous styling, and possibly the finest interior of any car on the road. The final ribbon wrapping the package was Quattro 4-wheel drive. Fortunately the dealership had the exact car he was looking for parked front and center on the lot. Jonathan drove away a very happy man.

The final item on his California To Do list was selecting a golf club membership. Golf was one of Jonathan's favorite pastimes and he had developed a pretty solid game playing beautiful courses in the Carolinas where he posted a handicap of 11. Jonathan and his top marketing manager and good friend, Pete Ames, fought many memorable battles on the links when they were not putting it to the competition in the business arena.

Not that he was keeping score, but Ames had bragging rights for two holes-in-one while Jonathan touted just one. Undoubtedly there would be West Coast skirmishes forthcoming as there were plenty of California greens to conquer, especially around Monterey. Pete and Jonathan were a formidable business team as well as good friends and he couldn't wait to make plans for the two to reunite on the links and in the boardroom.

Keeping to a club close in the Valley, Jonathan narrowed his choices to two country clubs, Palo Alto Hills and Sharon Heights. Both had fine courses and he had lined up sponsors to nominate him for membership at each. Having played the courses several times during his Stanford days, Jonathan ultimately decided to go with Sharon Heights because it was closer to his condo. He hoped the considerable fee to join would not be wasted and he could find the occasional afternoon to tee up. He'd set a four o'clock meeting with the club secretary to finalize his membership and brought along his clubs and checkbook.

Jonathan found the man on the driving range honing his golf swing. When he saw Jonathan approach he quickly laid his golf club down and led the club's newest member to a table on the veranda.

"Mr. Grayhall, we are delighted you'll be joining our membership. I'm sure this will be a decision you will never regret." A pleasant man, thought Jonathan, well chosen for the job.

"Yes, I'm pleased I successfully passed the vetting process! Today I thought I'd give you my initiation fee and perhaps get in a quick nine holes. I noticed the club has a policy of not advertising initiation fees, but perhaps you could now tell me what I signed on for so I can give you my check."

Without batting an eye the club secretary responded, "Certainly, Mr. Grayhall, you may make the check out for the number indicated on this receipt... Jonathan gulped as the secretary passed the slip over to him

The number was far greater than the $50,000 he'd estimated, but at this late stage he was not going to back out. Expensive, but he could afford it and was convinced that as hard as he expected to work, he needed to have a recreational outlet. As he handed over the check he joked, "I thought I was joining Sharon Heights. I didn't realize I was buying the club!"

Unfortunately, the humor was lost on the secretary so Jonathan quickly added, "Just joking! Now, would you be kind enough to put me with a group setting out to play nine?"

"Not a problem, Mr. Grayhall. I see a few of the golfers from the Stanford team are here.

We have a relationship with the university, which allows playing privileges. Would you like to join them?"

Jonathan was up for playing with the kids and remembered Stanford was well represented in collegiate golf, having at one time a certain Mr. Tiger Woods as a member of the men's team. Ninety minutes later, he was sufficiently humiliated by the litany of shots the superstars of tomorrow were able to shoot. His six over par was a far cry from the twin six under pars shot by the collegians.

With a few hours of daylight remaining, Jonathan decided to drive the Audi up Highway 17 over the Santa Cruz mountain range to the seaside town of Capitola.

Pulling up to a roadside hole in the wall, he enjoyed an authentic Mexican dinner washed down with an ice cold Arnold Palmer. The sunset was spectacular as it cascaded over a picturesque view of the bay. It had been a glorious day, if only he could have shared it with Tina. He missed female companionship and wondered what his future held in that regard. Jonathan felt he was ready to find out. As darkness crept over the water, Jonathan suddenly felt very lonely. It was a long ride home.

The next morning he was back in the saddle at the office. It was already Friday and Jonathan's schedule had been hijacked by Rachel Hammer, the VP of Human Resources. He picked up his phone and dialed her extension to plead his case for skipping the session she had planned. Before he could get a word in, she breezily announced she would be arriving at his office in just a minute. Sure enough, within sixty seconds he heard a knock on the door. Always the gentleman, Jonathan got up from his desk, walked to the door, opened it and welcomed, "Come in, and please have a seat."

In walked the bubbly, smiling Vice President of Human Resources, hand outstretched as she entered the doorway. Jonathan immediately noticed that like a lot of successful executives, Rachel had a confident, firm handshake. The two had met during the recruitment process three months before and Jonathan surprised himself by recalling the details of their breakfast meeting. That morning the VP wore a navy blue skirt and fluffy white blouse with a pair of dark blue high heels that accentuated her figure. Funny, it was not like him to keep memories of how women dressed in his head.

"Good-morning, Jonathan, and welcome to T.V. Neurologicals. The employees are excited to finally have our new CEO on board and they're anxious to meet you and hear what you have to say."

With those words she had efficiently defused any possibility he could skip the planned session. Accepting he couldn't escape her orientation, he made the mental adjustment to commit to the meeting.

"Looking forward to it! Perhaps you could brief me on what you think we should accomplish." Given the invitation, Rachel launched into a tight summary of her expectations for the meet and greet session scheduled with the employees, including a heads-up about potential sensitivities within the employee population.

"Your briefing is very helpful and I see you've set up a tour in line with the culture and work environment I expect to establish within the company. Your insistence on the need for this morning's program is well founded."

Jonathan did not easily give praise, but in this case it was well deserved. Rachel was delighted to have a leader who subscribed to her methods.

Making their way around the building, Jonathan was able to make each person he met feel the genuine interest and concern the man at the top actually felt, no matter their level in the organization's hierarchy. His ability to convey sincerity won him a number of supporters in just a few minutes. He sensed any quality time spent with employees would be promisingly productive as he usually uncovered interesting information during casual communication sessions. The small investment in human capital would pay dividends down the road when he would need to cash in on goodwill for an inevitable unpopular decision not on today's current roster of issues facing the company.

Another positive outcome brought by Rachel's tour was the opportunity to witness his VP in her element. Her handling of people was not only extremely professional, but clearly demonstrated the positive chemistry this executive had with employees.

After the tour they spent half an hour debriefing in Jonathan's office. Rachel had an animated style of speaking, using her hands to good effect as she gave her account of the day's activities. Jonathan could not help but notice the absence of a ring and normally would not have given this a millisecond of thought. Why was it that with this talented person, his intuition was on high alert? They say that the eyes always tell a story and in her eyes, as attractive as they were, they told him nothing. Jonathan had a sense that behind the intelligence, immaculate dress and attractive looks, something was amiss?

"Rachel, I started the day with some degree of reluctance to participate in the meetings and tour you had planned, but I now see why you thought it was important. I must say, this has been a most productive day."

She smiled at the compliment as he continued. "On another note, I want to say I really enjoyed seeing you in action and look forward to working together in the pursuit of success and excellence at T.V. Neurologicals." Jonathan stopped to consider how he might be able to answer that question mark bouncing around in his gut.

"When I did background reading about T.V. Neurologicals executive committee members, your file was pretty thin. It seems we know surprisingly little of your background. Perhaps you could take a few minutes to tell me about yourself and what you personally would like to accomplish at this company."

Rachel paused, and then eloquently responded to his question.

"I'm originally from Indianapolis; attended Duke University where I majored in Communications and after four years with a major pharmaceutical company in the Research Triangle, I went for an MBA at Harvard. The lure of the West Coast pulled at me and for the next six years I worked for Genentech before being given the opportunity to join a promising start-up called T.V. Neurologicals. I've been here four years and my objective is to be instrumental in developing a high performance pharmaceutical culture unmatched by any other in the Bay Area."

"A worthy goal by any standard!" exclaimed Jonathan. "I look forward to working closely with you to make it all happen." The two locked eyes, a bond of trust was clearly in the making.

"Do you have family in the Bay Area?" he inquired. There was a noticeable pause and shift in her posture as if she was debating her answer.

"I used to have an identical twin sister who lived in Southern California, but she's no longer with us."

"I'm so sorry," Jonathan quickly responded, feeling uncomfortable having asked the question just to make conversation.

"Yes, it was a very sad loss for me. My sister typically kept things to herself. She didn't like to talk about what was happening in her life, but one evening after a couple glasses of merlot, she opened up more than she ever had before."

Rachel was becoming teary-eyed so Jonathan interrupted. "Rachel, you really don't have to revisit old, painful memories. I'm sorry I asked about your family at all."

After a moment of silence, Rachel quietly started speaking again.

"A few months after that evening she died giving birth to a stillborn son. Since then I've been seeing a counselor who advised me not to keep my sadness buried inside. I can't believe I'm telling you my troubles! We barely know each other and here I am dropping my life history on your shoulders."

Jonathan nodded, not quite knowing what to say as she continued. "That very evening we had made plans to have dinner together but that bastard changed both of our lives with his actions. In short, my sister had a rufie dropped in her drink at a corporate conference and was raped in her drugged state. The pregnancy just added to the tragedy of the situation."

It was almost as if she had a need to continue speaking in order to lance the poison that was stored in some distressed corner of her mind.

"I was supposed to meet her for drinks and dinner. If only I had arrived a few minutes earlier I might have saved her from that bastard dropping his vile drug into her drink. The number of times I have asked myself why I couldn't have been there for her."

By now Jonathan was really feeling uncomfortable with what he started as a casual conversation and prompted by some deep gut feeling.

"Oh my God, that's terrible! Based on what I've read about the drug, she probably didn't remember anything about that evening." He could see Rachel was struggling to hold it together, but seemed to have more she wanted to share with him.

"My sister could only remember what happened during the first minutes after she was taken to a hotel room upstairs. Because he didn't want to be identified, the scumbag wore a Halloween Scream mask until he was sure my sister was completely under the effect of the drug. The bastard!"

Jonathan recoiled in horror, thinking about a repugnant rapist assaulting a young woman while wearing a bizarre mask. What a sick puppy.

"I'm so sorry for your loss and I hope you'll find a way to get over your sadness."

"Perhaps, but not until I know the identity of the low life who raped my sister. I never intend to stop looking for him. I'm sorry, I've taken a lot of your time and I have people waiting to see me in my office. I best head over there and let you get on with your busy agenda. Jonathan, I'm so pleased you've taken the helm at T.V. Neurologicals."

Rachel offered her hand as she was leaving and Jonathan thanked her for her time and good work. He genuinely felt she was going to be an asset on his team. Rachel left him with a positive impression of her professional capabilities, but at the same time, Jonathan sensed something was very wrong. He always put tremendous faith in what his instincts told him; gut feelings had never failed him.

Something deep behind those eyes troubled him greatly. Clearly it all stemmed from the attack on her sister. It had been a long but productive day as Jonathan headed back to his condo for another solitary supper and long hours of preparation for his first executive team meeting the next Monday.

Once again his thoughts went back to the time spent with Rachel. He knew he was missing key pieces of this people puzzle but was confident that the foundation for an excellent professional relationship had been formed and answers would be forthcoming

CHAPTER FIVE

Based on what he'd learned in the three short weeks spent on-site, Jonathan knew he had much to prepare and review over the weekend. He locked himself in his home office, aka The Cave, emerging only for short hits of fresh caffeine. Monday morning came too quickly, but Jonathan felt fully prepared to coach the T.V. Neurologicals team. The game clock was ticking. It was now five minutes until his players hit the field. A dozen thoughts battered his mind.

Hmm, should I start with the watches or would it be better to end the meeting with that surprise? No! Don't second guess your plan; go with the watches to start the meeting!

Jonathan positioned himself deep in his office chair, grasped a foam basketball and primed it to fly into the small net hanging on the back of his office door. While living in the Carolinas, he'd become a rabid fan of Duke University basketball. After making a sizable donation to the school, he received an autographed Nerf ball hoop emblazoned with the Blue Devils logo. Firing hoop shots was ritualized into his morning routine along with the Starbucks double-shot latte he picked up every day on his way to the office.

Sitting behind his desk he lined up the shot. SWISH! Nothing but net. Taking shots at the toy target was a sure release for tension and made a relaxing start to any day. As Jonathan thought every morning . . . *if only I could build a dominant legacy like Coach Krzyzewski did!* Following three consecutive baskets, he set off for the executive conference room to hold his first team meeting.

It was quarter to nine on Monday morning, the fourth week of Jonathan's tenure as T.V. Neurologicals CEO. He took a place at the head of the large acrylic table and glanced over the seven empty seats soon to be occupied by his senior management team. Two of the seven still had question marks dancing over their heads. When it came to assembling the team required to achieve success, Jonathan bordered on ruthless. There was no place in his mind for compassion.

On this inaugural morning, all seven players were expected at the meeting: Raynard Bernstein, VP of R&D; Ron Daniels, VP of Sales; Pete Ames, the new VP of Marketing; Chuck Hopper, the new VP of Finance; Brian Petrowski, VP of Operations; May Li, VP of Quality Control and Rachel Hammer, VP of Human Resources and Corporate Communications. Jonathan's handpicked insiders had been in place for two weeks and were ready to cover his back against the unknown.

Poaching a player from a previous company doesn't generally result in defensive legal action, but when more than one is hired away, lawyers can be called in to plug the drain. Jonathan lured only Pete Ames from his old stomping grounds.

After he joined the North Carolina firm as Chief Business Officer, Jonathan soon took Pete, then a promising young marketing executive, under his wing. In Ames he saw a brash but brilliant marketer with limitless potential for career growth.

He had even joked with Tina that one day he wouldn't be surprised to find himself working for Ames. The two successfully built the epilepsy franchise for the Carolina company, always complementing the other's strengths while becoming the best of friends. Ames had known his mentor was contemplating a venture west and the two spent hours discussing the pros and cons of such a move. When Ames learned Jonathan had been offered the position at T.V. Neurologicals, he immediately asked what his role in the new organization would be. Jonathan knew he wasn't going anywhere without this kid in tow. That was a sure deal. In a few short weeks, Jonathan had successfully ensconced his lieutenant by his side in sunny California.

Having Ames firmly placed on his team gave Jonathan a sense of security, knowing he'd have an extra pair of eyes to uncover any underhanded politicking initiated by questionable executives that inevitably happened when a management change of this magnitude took place. On the business front, Pete brought a potent addition to Jonathan's plan for T.V. Neurologicals marketing armamentarium. The two had already consumed cases of brewskies while discussing strategies for success at their new company.

Jonathan's other ally had come by serendipity more than by direct action on his part. Several years earlier he had attended a pharmaceutical wholesaler's annual meeting and at one of the event dinners was seated next to a guy named Chuck Hopper. The two struck up a conversation and rapidly became friends, keeping the relationship going well after they left the meeting. Jonathan saw a sense of integrity in Hopper that he liked very much. With the challenges facing the industry, someone holding Hopper's value system would be a useful addition to any management team.

There was another reason for bringing Chuck's financial talent to T.V. Neurologicals. Following a series of national accounting scandals, the pharmaceutical industry was required to comply with toughened accounting standards known as Sarbanes Oxley.

For smaller companies, this upgrade in accounting requirements demanded strict control and diligence. Jonathan had the foresight to recognize he would need someone like Hopper to successfully implement changes.

Apart from his two questionable executive team members, Jonathan had to admit there was quite a pool of talent put together by Tim Varter and his VC backers. He would give the two question marks the opportunity to prove their value, but vowed to act quickly if they did not step up to the plate.

On each leather chair around the impressive contemporary table, Jonathan had placed a box wrapped in dark green leather-pocked paper that screamed, "Open me!" As the minute hand approached nine, the executive team drifted in and took their seats.

Management psychologists have drafted numerous pages on what could be learned from where an individual chooses to sit at a management meeting. Jonathan had collaborated with a consulting psychologist to develop his own method of uncovering what he needed to know about behavioral psychology. The gift he had placed on the chairs was part of his personal evaluative process.

All were curious about the contents of the package which was apparently a gift, but no one dared pick up the box without a nod from the new man at the head of the table. Finally, with flair and flourish, Ames picked up his box, held it high above his head, and shook it like a baby's rattle. Jonathan correctly predicted the inquisitive marketing VP would be the first in the group to make a move.

Jonathan glanced around the room and looked into each pair of eyes long enough to make a connection before moving to the next. After this little exercise clearly announced who was the alpha dog, Jonathan was ready to get started.

"Good morning, and welcome to our kick-off executive committee meeting. The seven of you represent the key functional areas at T.V. Neurologicals. It will be essential we all perform our roles in an exemplary manner to achieve the vision I've set for this company. Most importantly, we must achieve our goals in a timely manner, and so I have a gift for you. Please go ahead and open the packages you're all so interested in."

As if a start gun had exploded, the seven unwrapped their packages with varying amounts of enthusiasm, Bernstein being the least enthusiastic and Ames attacking his box like a ten-year-old on Christmas morning. When the contents were revealed, exclamations filled the room as everybody examined a shiny Seiko watch.

Jonathan was a watch aficionado; his personal collection boasted several luxury timepieces including a Breitling Chronomat, Cartier Santos, IWC Portuguese, Rolex Daytona and his favorite, the Panerai Luminor. A Seiko watch placed in a far lower price bracket, but was still considered to be a quality timepiece. Jonathan paid for the gifts himself, knowing that would have more impact on the giving. On his left wrist was the same Seiko Chronograph model he had gifted to his team.

"Please accept this small gift as a reminder of our first team meeting, but more importantly, keep in mind the clock is ticking on the patent expiration for Czuretrin. It's critical for T.V. Neurologicals to have a successor product ready to launch next January." Jonathan knew this was a genuine challenge, but was absolutely essential if the company was to survive.

"Don't feel obliged to wear your gift every day, but please put it in a prominent place to serve as a constant reminder of the urgency needed to make our deadline."

Jonathan had taken great interest watching each team member unwrap the small box, feeling this simple act could be quite telling. Critical observation was a skill he picked up when playing poker. Being able to decipher facial expressions and body language could make the difference between winning the pot and losing a pile of chips. Not a perfect tool, but often useful.

Psychological profiling is a well-known technique generally used for personnel development and is pursued voluntarily. On this particular Monday morning, there would probably be a collection of disconcerted and nervous executives sitting around the table had they realized they were unknowing participants in a customized profiling model developed by Jonathan and his consultant.

Jonathan felt a hint of guilt about not sharing this exercise with Ames and Hopper ahead of time, but had no problem leaving the others on his management team in the dark; such was his absolute focus on success.

Ames's expression contained youthful enthusiasm and he appeared to enjoy a break from the usual corporate "bored-room" meeting. Hopper served in financial capacities where giveaways were rare and was delighted to be on the receiving end instead of paying the invoice.

True to his background in operations, Petrowski took pleasure in playing with the complex dials on the chronograph to see how they functioned.

Li came from a wealthy family and displayed no telling signs about what she thought or was feeling, remaining highly inscrutable.

Hammer admired the shine on her wrist and looked genuinely pleased with the watch. She caught the attention of Daniels who couldn't take his eyes off her. Not wanting to give him any indication that could be interpreted as the least bit positive, she exited the conference room before he could approach her.

Bernstein looked at the watch with bored impatience; he was perfectly happy with his fifteen-buck Timex and certainly didn't want to feel indebted to this new thorn in his side.

And then there was Daniels, clinging to the other end of the spectrum. The accumulation of expensive material goods was important to this man. The watch he walked in wearing was a gold Rolex President, retailing at over $20,000. Daniels had obtained his bauble for a discounted five grand hawked by a boyhood pal, now a fence in his old New Orleans neighborhood. Daniels enjoyed broadcasting material success and wasn't pleased with what he saw as political pressure to wear a common team watch. The embarrassment and chagrin he felt was poorly camouflaged.

As he surveyed the room, Jonathan caught Daniels glancing at Rachel in more than a casual way, but he couldn't be certain. Lord, he hoped those two weren't hooking up!

Jonathan and Daniels first met on an earlier recruiting trip. A dinner had been set up at Evia, an authentic Greek restaurant in Palo Alto. Daniels' Brioni suit and Cartier cufflinks did not go unnoticed, but even more telling was the third Beefeater martini before dinner. After cocktails Daniels ordered a Silver Oak cabernet, involving the sommelier in a lengthy discussion regarding which year would be most appropriate for their meal and why Napa grapes were superior to those harvested in Alexander Valley. Daniels appeared confident he was on solid ground at T.V. Neurologicals given the sales numbers he had delivered over the years. Unfortunately, the man wasn't reading his prospective new boss well. Had he done so, he might have passed on the after dinner cognac.

Jonathan kept his thoughts to himself. In his corporate experience it was never a good sign when sales managers showed tendencies to excess of any kind. Despite his flamboyant actions, Daniels hadn't attained success by being unaware of the external forces surrounding him. As the evening progressed, he realized he had overplayed the sales bravado card and now would have to give serious thought to redeeming himself. The evening ended politely, but without bonding.

The icebreaking gift-giving gesture completed, Jonathan launched into his vision for the company while planning to discuss and analyze the collected profiling data later with his consultant.

Jonathan turned his focus on the absolute need for the next big product. He detailed how business was to be conducted and presented his expectation of results orientation. As part of his weekend preparation for the Monday meeting, Jonathan had asked Chuck Hopper for a review of the previous year's financials as well as the business plan for the current year. He wanted to send a strong, no-nonsense message about the importance he placed on hitting the numbers. Jonathan's demeanor became gravely serious as he made his final point.

"In the end, it always comes down to numbers to determine success or failure," he stressed. "You can get a dozen 'Atta boys' but they're soon forgotten and offset by a shortage in net income. Sometimes a team that achieves good numbers several years in succession is accused of sandbagging. My response to that is they've never hung anyone for coming in above budget expectations. But under budget? Well, that's another story and not a pretty one."

The change in the new CEO's demeanor was evident to all. It was almost as if Jonathan was cloaked in a new persona when it came to his absolute dedication to results. This was a man who was unaccustomed to any business shortfall. Even Pete Ames shifted uncomfortably in his seat and hoped his boss and friend would follow-up with comments about the importance of results, but not at all costs.

When the young CEO thought his key financial points had hit home, he steered the conversation to the next topic - the R&D pipeline, the lifeblood of any pharmaceutical company.

"Raynard, would you please provide the team with a review of the status of SRD 0011, SRD 6969, and the orphan drug?" Delighted with the opportunity to talk about his baby, Bernstein spoke with high praise for the two recently completed phase III clinical studies.

"With regard to SRD 0011, I am delighted to report the two Phase III studies were completed on time and on budget." Hopper shifted uncomfortably in his seat knowing that to-date, over $350 million had been spent on the two trials.

Late Friday evening Hopper received an unexpected additional $50,000 invoice from the Clinical Research Organization managing the studies. Yet another of many frequent oversights he had discovered in Bernstein's department. Hopper had yet to discuss this new wrinkle with Jonathan.

Bernstein continued. "The code has been broken and we're in the process of analyzing our data in preparation for the forthcoming meeting with the FDA."

The financial VP looked at Jonathan and suppressed a chuckle because the nod Jonathan subtly gave signified he knew the BS was getting waist deep. The nod signaled for Hopper to keep on top of budget expenditures, which Jonathan already recognized were hemorrhaging out of control.

"So, by next Tuesday we expect to have initial results and I remain confident of success." With that Raynard started to sit, but Jonathan quickly addressed him.

"Raynard, I would like to hear about the remaining pipeline products, please." Bernstein looked like a deer caught in headlights owned by a Mack truck.

"I really don't want to take up the team's time discussing those projects. I have serious doubts about their ability to meet end points and besides, we'll need every dollar of our clinical budget to finish the toxicology studies still outstanding on our lead product."

"Okay, you've made your thoughts on the matter crystal clear," Jonathan responded in a firm, unyielding tone. "But, I would still like to hear more, particularly about SRD 6969. The grapevine seems to be loaded with chatter regarding that project."

"As you wish," replied Bernstein with a condescending air. "But I must warn you, it is my firm opinion we shouldn't be throwing funds down that drain."

Clearly agitated, the researcher began speaking about the restless legs drug product. "SRD 6969 was not identified using targeted, receptor-based research techniques, as was done with 0011. This is an old molecule with rights held by a struggling East Bay company that has been around for some time. Tim Varter was able to pry it away as their balance sheet looked weak and the molecule sale to T.V. Neurologicals enabled that company to survive for another six months."

Bernstein went on to describe the history of SRD 6969 and how it had been a marketing driven study. He was careful to show as much disdain for the word "marketing" as he could. He explained the science and receptors involved in restless legs and why the drug had very low probability of success.

But Jonathan hadn't been catnapping the brief time he'd been at T.V. Neurologicals. He enjoyed employing MBWA (Management By Walking Around) since that technique often presented interesting tidbits of information. On one of his early walkabouts he shared lunch at a table of clinical monitors for the SRD 6969 trial and they provided fascinating feedback that never would have reached his ears if he had depended on Raynard.

"Tell us about the anecdotal reports from the trial sites and the problems regarding the return of excess clinical trial drug material."

Raynard glared at Jonathan, his face reddening as minutes passed. *What was this man doing talking with my staff and why were they sharing information not approved for distribution? Somebody is going to get an ass kicking for this!*

"Yes, well, I believe you are referring to unsubstantiated reports from trial physicians who expressed some surprise at unexpected results described by their patients. Let me stress there is no controlled data, only anecdotal reports suggesting the product has a distinct and pronounced effect on the female sex drive, enhancing pleasure from the act.

"The matter first came to light when we were unable to recoup excess clinical product after the trial was completed. The participants refused to give it up and it wasn't until physicians pushed the conversation that the full story behind the unusual patient behavior was revealed."

The buzz around the table grew to monumental levels. This was the first Ames had heard of these results and almost jumped across the table. Since joining the company, the new marketing director had scoured information in the product pipeline and no mention of these unusual findings was in any report made available to him. Initially Ames was furious with the head of research for withholding this incredible finding, but his anger soon gave way to waves of excitement. If SRD 6969 proved to be a female Viagra®, the drug would be a blockbuster of untold proportions! Not surprisingly, Bernstein was exceedingly unhappy with this reaction as it pulled attention away from his own special project. Jonathan interrupted the buzz, now reaching crescendo levels in the room.

"Just a reminder, we also need to continue the investigation of the orphan drug in the pipeline, I want to make sure this small but important program is not lost given the overriding focus on SRD 0011. Before we break I have a few final remarks."

It had been quite a meeting and around the table reactions were running rampant.

"I believe I was brought in as CEO to take speedy action where I deemed it to be necessary. In doing so I apologize I haven't had the time to debate some of my decisions with the management team.

"My first action was hiring a compliance officer who will report directly to me. She has a seat at this table and would be with us today if not for an appendicitis attack. She is recovering well and will join the team shortly; please stop by and get to know her. I strongly believe the environment in which we operate today demands strict adherence to the guidelines the Office of the Inspector General set forth. Severe financial penalties are in store for companies that run afoul of the restrictions. I'm well aware T.V. Neurologicals has had no issues to date, but that's no guarantee potential action will not be brought against us in the future. You've probably heard of a substantial case recently settled for a billion dollar fine, with violations dating back more than five years. Companies taking proactive steps to bolster corporate internal compliance systems have had a stronger defense in such cases."

Deep lines furrowed the brows of Ames, Daniels, and Bernstein. Their departments would clearly be affected by this action. Although he espoused a style of participation, Jonathan would unilaterally make important decisions when he thought they were necessary.

"My second decision is directed to you, Pete. I would like an urgent commercial assessment conducted on SRD 0011 to be on my desk within two weeks. An external expert opinion should be part of the assessment so that T.V. Neurologicals retains objectivity. We need to determine if this drug fills a need in the marketplace."

"This is preposterous!" blurted Bernstein as he jumped to his feet. "I will not tolerate such a frivolous use of corporate funds that could be spent on research!"

"That call is not yours to make," answered Jonathan in a calm voice that successfully covered the irritation he felt. "It is an exercise that should have been completed long ago and we most certainly will need answers when we confront the pricing authorities. We also need adequate answers to give the medical press who have been hounding me since my arrival." Jonathan paused for effect before adding, "Raynard, please sit down."

Raynard took his seat angrily as Jonathan continued. "Are we clear, Pete?"

"Crystal," exclaimed Pete who looked like he just found the golden goose. He'd been given the green light allowing him the freedom to explore what potentially could be a blockbuster drug that previously had no blocks in the playpen.

"This brings me to the last agenda item of the day. Once again it centers on the pipeline.

We're playing a hand with three cards," he began, using a poker analogy to get his point across.

"Three cards we will turn over at the appropriate time.

"SRD 0011 will be turned over next week when trial results are submitted with the commercial evaluation to follow shortly thereafter. Our wild card is SRD 6969. Apparently very few researchers believe it will be successful treating restless legs, but coincidentally the molecule presents the potential of being a blockbuster treating female sexual response. It's my belief we can't put all our hopes on one research project," Jonathan stated confidently.

"We need a fallback. As such, I am directing our research team to provide a plan to gain proof of concept for SRD 6969 in female sexual stimulation, or however we choose to define the indication. I want this plan to be on my desk, along with the commercial assessment, in two weeks."

The CEO paused allowing his words to sink in. "The orphan drug project is not expected to be a factor contributing to the wealth of the company in a commercial sense. From what we know, I think it fair to surmise the product, if successful, would contribute to the moral fiber of T.V. Neurologicals."

Pete Ames thought Bernstein was going to stroke out on the spot. He saw his face shade to bright purple and swore he could hear the man's heart pounding across the table.

Bernstein had to remind himself to breathe and took deep swigs of air to keep from passing out. He had to find a way to stop this meddling fool from disrupting his plans. Any disturbance in his timeline would seriously waylay recognition by the research community which Bernstein believed would be heaped upon him in mere weeks.

"One final point before we close." Jonathan paused and looked around the room slowly to make sure he had everyone's full attention. "By now you are all well aware of my emphasis on achieving results. I want to make it clear that I place equal importance on the manner in which these results are achieved, which is reflected by my decision to appoint a compliance officer."

The inaugural management committee meeting came to a natural conclusion when there was nothing more to be said. Ames and Hopper left animated and smiling, looking forward to a rollicking ride with the new sheriff in town. Ames was pleased Jonathan had acknowledged the importance of taking the right path in his closing remarks. Hammer and Li seemed to take things in stride and their body language did little to reveal what they thought of the morning's events.

As Hammer walked out of the meeting room she again caught Daniels looking in her direction. Petrowski was still intrigued by the moving parts on his Seiko, continuing to push various knobs in sequence on the chronometer.

Daniels sided up to Bernstein on the way out and whispered, "I know we haven't seen things eye to eye in the past, but it may be in our best interest to pool resources and tackle issues of mutual concern."

Raynard had no love for the likes of Daniels whom he viewed as a sleazy salesman, but found himself nodding in agreement as the two conspirators walked down the hall.

Still seated, Jonathan thought how much he disliked the unilateral action approach he had just taken. He preferred to build consensus, but during his career when he'd been thrust into a new business environment, there was always partial regret when he looked at his actions in hindsight. Was he acting fast enough to satisfy his instincts? This time around Jonathan was determined to take a strong lead.

As he left the room Jonathan was surprised his thoughts were not directed at the strategic challenge ahead. Instead his thoughts whirled around Tim Varter and the sage advice he had offered at dinner a few weeks earlier. What was his new mentor trying to tell him?

CHAPTER SIX

"Time is money" is an expression that certainly holds true for drug companies when patent expirations are in countdown mode. Patent expiration is trial by fire for every pharmaceutical company that has produced a blockbuster product. It is essential to find ways to increase the speed in which clinical trials are administered and run in order to replace lost sales to generics. The race to get new drug approvals by the FDA becomes the core competence all companies strive to win.

SRD 6969, the T.V. Neurologicals compound undergoing testing for restless legs syndrome, seemed to be progressing at a reasonable clip, but the results experienced by Mildred, Sally-Anne, and Alice were not what had been anticipated by the company sponsoring the trial.

Mildred

Three months had passed since Mildred's first meeting with Dr. Rivers to begin her participation in the drug trial. She was desperately hoping to find relief for the aggravation she experienced every night from this hideous and unexplained condition.

Tonight as she lay in bed listening to her husband's contented snoring, she giggled like a schoolgirl. She was still keeping Harry up at night, but it sure wasn't her legs that were restless! Harry was delighted with the transformation in his wife's bedroom habits and with their relationship in general.

Just one week into the trial, Mildred sensed something was happening to her body, physically and mentally, and it had nothing to do with restless legs. She was feeling sexual sensations never experienced before and it seemed her thought patterns were different, although she couldn't describe exactly what was she was experiencing.

Slightly concerned at first, she thought maybe the problem was the result of some weird hormonal imbalance, but her worry was soon dismissed when she concluded the sensations weren't uncomfortable and her mood was happy and upbeat. By week two of the trial she felt an overwhelming urge to have sex with her husband whenever possible and the intensity of the urge reminded her of the desire she felt on her honeymoon in Carmel thirty years before. She fondly recalled that special first time he entered her and how her body had shuddered under his touch.

One night two weeks into the trial, Mildred and Harry started their normal nighttime routine, only Mildred didn't have sleep on her mind. For the past few years the eleven o'clock ritual never varied. Unmake the bed, change into cotton pajamas, perform bathroom duties, and wish each other a chaste "Good Night" before meeting the sandman. Except on special occasions, Harry rolled on his side with his back to Mildred. This night he suddenly felt his wife's hand fondling his manhood using strokes that genuinely surprised him.

"Sweetheart, what are you doing?" Mildred had never initiated lovemaking in the thirty years they'd been married, no wonder the man was confused and almost alarmed by her forward action. Mildred snuggled close to her husband and whispered suggestively, "It's been awhile since we made love and tonight I want you inside me." Harry was shocked and rolled over to see what unknown wanton woman had uttered those words.

To his surprise Mildred was totally naked. With one quick move she straddled him and took him inside her wet and welcoming channel. Harry gasped with pleasure and again wondered who this wild woman was who'd crept into his bed impersonating his wife. Mildred rocked back and forth searching for deeper penetration while moaning like a Saturday night heathen. Another first. Harry had never heard his wife utter *any* sound when they made love; she was generally stone silent and never hinted at pleasure. What happened over the next twenty minutes was simply indescribable for this long married couple.

Mildred took control of their lovemaking, deliciously exposing places her husband had never seen before. She was intent on experiencing her own pleasure as orgasm after orgasm waved through her body. Harry was astonished by this woman who was now demanding the best he could offer. Growls of pleasure filled the bedroom that seemed to come alive as raw, unbridled sex drew the walls in tight. Mildred's passionate initiation rocked a sexual reservoir in Harry that neither knew existed. As she lay on the bed that once was used only for sleeping, Mildred experienced aftershocks of sexual pleasure like she had never known before. She was a happy, satisfied woman, but knew she would soon want more. But for now, Mildred and Harry lay side by side, totally spent.

"My God, that was fantastic, but where the hell did it come from?" A completely depleted Harry barely had the strength to get the words out.

"I think somehow, someway it must be related to the drug I'm taking in that restless legs trial. Ever since I began taking the pill

I've been feeling different and really good about myself." Harry leaned over and kissed his wife gently on the lips.

"Be sure you keep a good supply of those pills on hand when the trial is over," encouraged Harry. "Once the company finds out what gold they hold, they'll sure charge a fortune for a prescription. But you know what? I would happily pay a fortune for a night like this!"

Sally-Anne

Things were certainly heating up in The Villages. Sally-Anne Zuckerman was experiencing sexual stimulation like she'd never felt before. How much was due to her natural body chemistry and how much could be attributed to the experimental drug was difficult to determine. The only thing she knew for certain was she had developed a voracious sexual appetite and her husband was having an increasingly difficult time meeting her demands.

One major reason Dennis Zuckerman felt his wife was incapable of being satisfied was that his own ability to perform had suddenly gone the wrong direction after surgery for prostate cancer.

After a few high PSA scores in the teens and a positive biopsy, Dennis elected to undergo a radical prostatectomy that would extract the cancerous tissue but would also involve possible nerve damage. Initially he found the little blue pill called Viagra® and its cousins helped him achieve the necessary response with his equipment, but it didn't last for long. He now was forced to undergo a most unpleasant method to stiff his dick. A direct injection of prostaglandin into his organ was the only method that seemed to work. The prepping involved and uncomfortable injection brought a real cold shower to any passion the old man hoped to feel. Dennis found himself seeking new avenues to meet Sally-Anne's increasing demands. He could accommodate her maybe once a day, some days twice, but needles assaulting his Johnson two times a day was all he could handle.

After a round of golf at the club and a few drinks with his buddies, the foursome's typical conversation about women and sex became heated.

Zuckerman instigated the conversation with a shot across the bow.

"Kowalski, I bet I saw more up and downs in that round than you ever saw in your bedroom!"

His golfing companion shot back, "Watching you putt today, I would say you're having trouble finding the hole!" This drew a big laugh from the four men.

"You gotta be kidding!" Zuckerman exclaimed. I gotta beat my wife with my putter to keep her away so I can recharge my driver. Again guffaws circled the table.

"Tell you what," Kowalski offered, "if you need any help keeping the lovely Miss Sally-Anne satisfied, just call on your old buddy and I'll be happy to rattle her tin cup."

Dennis' first reaction was to punch the ass right in his alcohol induced, bulbous nose, but then he recognized the possibility of a win-win situation opening before his very eyes.

Kowalski's jab had given him an idea. Dennis had always wanted to watch his wife get it on with another man or woman, but never had the nerve to suggest it. Harboring secret voyeur and cuckold tendencies for much of his married life, Dennis started to figure ways to introduce the explosive topic to his wife.

Should he casually mention he couldn't help but notice her heightened sexual state that seemed to result from that stupid drug trial she was on? Then later work up the nerve to ask how she would feel about inviting a friend into their bed? A three-way could be most satisfying for all parties and it sure would be an enjoyable way to take the pressure off his performance. What the hell, Sally-Anne just might agree!

Flushed with excitement at the thought of watching his wife grinding on another man or a well endowed woman, Dennis left the club early to test his persuasive powers on his hot little sweetie.

Driving his ostentatious golf cart at the top speed of 18 mph, he made it to his front door in ten minutes. He was getting so excited about this sexual proposition he might not need an injection for the occasion!

In his haste to find Sally-Anne, Dennis didn't notice the blue BMW convertible parked across the road, nor the empty wine glasses on the kitchen table. As he climbed the stairs, Dennis paused when he heard heavy panting and moaning coming from his bedroom. He deftly stepped to the door and peeked around the frame. There was Sally-Anne, spread eagle, writhing with pleasure as the club's two Argentinean tennis pros had their way with her.

Well, isn't this an interesting development! Now, how do I take advantage of what serendipity has delivered?

Always the opportunist, Dennis found his camera in the hallway closet and quietly snapped shots of the threesome as a little bit of kinky enhanced the show. After capturing shots that might be too much even for *Hustler,* he headed downstairs and poured himself a glass of cabernet. Dennis couldn't wait for the trio to traipse down the staircase. He wondered how they would explain what was going on. Oh well, what they didn't know wouldn't hurt them. The erotic photos would give him the leverage he needed to bend Sally-Anne's promiscuity to his will. He chuckled wickedly at the thought of his wife bent deep over the back of the boudoir chaise lounge.

Alice

It had been another steamy night in the Peterson's Alpharetta bedroom. Tim was admiring his beautiful wife while she stretched like a satiated lioness on the bed beside him.

"Why are you looking at me like that?" she teased. The transformation in Alice since she joined the crazy drug trial had been nothing short of miraculous.

"I thought you were asleep, but now that you're awake I want to make love to my beautiful wife one more time."

Tim roughly parted his wife's legs and once again the couple was locked in a passionate embrace, taking great delight in each other's body. Their lovemaking was beautiful and enjoyable in so many ways. The shy, mousey girl, always in the background had surprisingly blossomed into a vivacious, beautiful young woman who carried herself with self-confidence, so unimaginably different than just weeks before.

Tim had always seen Alice's underlying beauty and was thrilled it was now out there for all to see. What wasn't on display was the intensity and urgency Alice made love and the crashing multiple climaxes she experienced. She had also developed an adventurous appetite for sex toys to enhance the intensity of their arduous lovemaking. These pleasures were his alone and Tim considered himself the luckiest man on earth. Totally exhausted, the two were on the verge of falling asleep, peacefully replaying scenes from minutes before.

Alice recognized she was undergoing both a physical and sexual evolution. The ingestion of SRD 6969 had increased her sexual quotient and had also stretched her personal ambitions. She was actually starting a new career as a television reporter!

Shortly after she started the trial, Alice surprised Tim when she interviewed against hundreds of other women for a position with the local TV news team as a roving reporter. Her husband could hardly believe his wife had developed the chutzpah to try out for the job. He was only too happy when she dragged him to shop for a trendy wardrobe aimed at accenting her voluptuous body, and was really over the moon when she beat all contenders for the job. Within months Alice's star had soared to the heavens and fans were demanding more exposure for this bright new television broadcaster.

Alice's Twitter account surpassed a million followers and her sweet but sultry face smiled from the cover of every local entertainment magazine. The station was bombarded with calls for special appearances by their new star. Ribbon cuttings, community panels, supermarket openings – everybody wanted a piece of Alice. The top brass recognized they had a diamond in the rough and assigned their leading network anchor the task of coaching Alice to network stardom.

Yes, Alice Peterson was a very happy woman, but there was a vague nagging nugget in the back of her mind that disturbed her. The clinical drug had all but solved her issue with restless legs and certainly boosted her sex drive, but more importantly, Alice felt her self-confidence explode. Was it really only the effect of the drug?

On the sexual front there was absolutely no question the drug had made a tremendous difference, and what a wonderful difference it was! She giggled as she remembered the sensations that had pulsed through her body just in the past hour. She had climaxed countless times and had brought her husband to new heights by responding aggressively and creatively to his lovemaking. *God Bless SRD 6969!*

But that one nugget continued to niggle when quiet surrounded her as she tried to fall asleep. Taking off her makeup before climbing into bed, Alice noticed a line in her forehead that she hadn't seen before. This minor imperfection concerned her greatly, far more than it should. She made a mental note to schedule an appointment with her newly found cosmetic surgeon to rectify the problem. With that decision firmly made, she dropped into a peaceful sleep.

Alice's phenomenal ascent to stardom had not gone unnoticed by her good friend Jacki Striker. She'd heard water cooler talk about behavioral changes observed in patients administered 6969, but what she saw in her good friend Alice was so dramatic that it scared her.

Fortunately the changes in Alice all seemed positive, at least from what Jacki could observe.

Briefly reviewing the overall trial results, she couldn't find any report detailing negative changes in personalities.

On the personal front, things were not going well for Jacki. With Alice's personal escalation, blossoming confidence, and independence, Jacki was seeing a lot less of her old friend. Perhaps in a misguided manner, she put blame for this on the T.V. Neurologicals drug.

What was far more troubling was the situation brewing in her workplace. Always one to follow the straight and narrow, Jacki was greatly disturbed by recent attempts to involve her in a scheme to drive sales of Czuretrin. What exacerbated the situation was the suspected involvement in these nefarious activities by her immediate supervisor. Jacki's strict code of ethics could no longer ignore what was happening all around her office.

She felt trapped.

Jacki knew she was facing the possibility of a difficult confrontation with her employer, a situation she didn't want to develop because she genuinely enjoyed working for the company.

Café Pharma, a pharmaceutical web trash site that served as watering hole for rumor mongers, was buzzing with activity. Posts were always anonymous leading to some pretty outrageous and disgusting comments.

On rare occasions there might be a kernel of truth in the postings, and for that reason the site was occasionally frequented to pick up useful tidbits. While surfing Café Pharma, Jacki found a thread describing a case recently won by a local legal firm that had taken aggressive action on *qui tam* whistleblower cases. The case involved a single whistleblower reporting excessive drug pricing.

In Jacki's situation, the legal question would concern off-label promotion.

From what she read there was no clear downside to whistle blowing, and it could be a compelling course of action for the millions of dollars such cases generated for whistleblowers' bank accounts.

Jacki rationalized there couldn't be *that* many negative repercussions if she just set an exploratory meeting with the named law firm. The website indicated initial consultations were free, what did she have to lose?

CHAPTER SEVEN

On this particular morning Jonathan breezed into his office a little later than usual, accompanied as always by a Starbuck's grande latte. He settled behind his desk, picked up the little Nerf ball and squeezed it vigorously between his hands before taking multiple shots at the basket fastened behind the door.

After two minutes swooshing imaginary free throws that would make Larry Bird jealous, Jonathan decided it was time for a little MBWA through the office complex. Not that he was looking for trouble, but this casual walkabout exercise often proved to be illuminating, sometimes in odd ways.

He casually dropped by several departments where his visibility as CEO wasn't particularly strong and chatted with staff members about their families and interests, finally asking for input and ideas about how T.V. Neurologicals could be made better. Good ideas often came from the least expected sources.

One office on his list of important places to visit was that of Dr. Raynard Bernstein. As he reached the researcher's office door he recognized it was not by chance that this visit was not the most anticipated. If he had his druthers, he would have gladly skipped this stop. Nonetheless, he knocked twice.

"Come in," came an unenthusiastic voice. This was the first time Jonathan had visited Bernstein's office and was immediately struck by the size of the research vice president's suite. It expanded more than two hundred square feet over what Jonathan's CEO domain offered and was fully decorated with expensive contemporary furniture.

Most dramatic was a prominent aquarium featuring colored lights that seemed to change hue every twenty seconds. Inside a half dozen box jellyfish floated gracefully. The jellyfish were the source of toxin from which SRD 0011 had been extracted and subsequently formulated. The effect of the colored lights radiating on the translucent floating bodies was hypnotizing in its savage beauty.

"Good morning, Raynard, I thought I'd drop by to see if you have any last minute thoughts before we fly to Washington for our meeting with the FDA." Jonathan found a small, uncomfortable chair in front of Bernstein's desk and took it. It seemed the egotistical researcher had deliberately chosen this particularly styled chair so he could be placed at psychological advantage over visitors. Did Bernstein really go out of his way to be a prick?

"No, nothing to add to what I previously stated," he replied with exceptional disinterest. Jonathan was ready to leave this awkward setting but decided to try a different tack to see if he could form any connection with this man.

"That's quite an aquarium you have! There's definitely amazing and exotic beauty to such venomous creatures. I have to admit, I know very little about them." Raynard's mood changed instantly as he was called to speak on one of his favorite topics.

"Well, let's educate you then," Raynard pompously directed.

"The box jellyfish is in a class that includes fifty identified species, each having tentacles covered in the ocean's biological booby traps known as cnidocysts. You see, each cyst contains a tiny dart needle and a pocket of poison that in combination has been referred to as the most explosive envenomation process presently known to humans. Once the dart penetrates the skin, the cyst shoots toxin through the needle causing it to enter the victim's bloodstream, ultimately affecting the cardiovascular system by increasing blood pressure to the point of potentially stopping the heart. One Box jellyfish carries enough poison to kill 60 persons. Knowing the toxin had an impact on heart function is what led to our investigation and synthesis of SRD 0011."

"Sounds delightful," Jonathan commented drily. "From what little I know, the tentacles and accompanying cysts can cause pretty hellacious pain and scarring when they come into contact with skin."

Raynard continued on a roll, clearly enjoying discussing his favorite topic.

"Well, yes. There have been occasional deaths reported from the sting of box jellyfish, but there are steroid treatments that offset the venom, provided they are given soon after the exposure. One thing for sure, victims will undoubtedly experience severe pain not only at the cyst injection site but throughout their entire body. You can count on those unlucky buggers being out of commission for quite awhile."

Jonathan walked over to the aquarium for a closer look at the ghostly bodies suspended in the water.

"I can certainly understand your enthusiasm for this creature and the compound you have synthesized." His gaze studied the construction of the large, customized saltwater aquarium. To the untrained eye, the jellyfish inhabitants looked very much like the familiar Portuguese Man of War. He noticed the nasty barbs jutting from trailing tentacles. An ugly beak-like structure was imbedded in the clear body and gave the impression of a nose sitting in the center of a face.

"I know there are many drugs that originate from Mother Nature's endless store of molecules. In my early days as a sales rep, we were told of the discovery of a fungus that evolved into the development of the antibiotic class known as cephalosporins. It is widely noted a scientist observed the ability of a certain fungus to keep the sewage flow from the island of Sardinia relatively clean from certain bacteria and…"

Jonathan stopped talking, seeing Raynard was not listening to a word he was saying. He was too immersed watching the graceful vertical movements of his office pets.

"Anyway, I just wanted to drop in and remind you that we must remain objective from both clinical and commercial perspectives when we meet with the FDA. See you in the morning."

Raynard glared at his office portal as Jonathan exited.

Oh, how I would love to see my children's cnidocysts embedded in your smug ass, Mr. Jonathan Grayhall! You come waltzing in spouting market-ing nonsense bent on turning my world upside down, disrupting my im-portant research. Well, we'll see about that! Raynard Bernstein is not one to be trifled with!

Bernstein was a serial underachiever wearing overachiever's clothing. A graduate of Germany's Heidelberg University, he had an undistinguished university career followed by a stint as a practicing physician. It didn't help that his father was a professor emeritus at the university. He saw several classmates go on to win accolades in the medical field, including a Nobel Prize. In fact, the noted prize had gone to his younger sister and he could still hear his father's words pierce him to the core.

"Raynard, you are a great disappointment to me. I fear you are not going to live up to the Bernstein tradition of excellence in science."

Feeling the need to find success, Raynard's solution was to move to the United States where he hoped to find better fortune and finally gain the respect of his father. Despite his best effort, his

CV remained uneventful having served in subordinate positions before landing his place at T.V. Neurologicals. He knew he was extremely fortunate to hold this coveted research role; it would likely be his last opportunity to make a name for himself. Bernstein was not a vile person, but he was certainly tormented by demons of his own creation.

He gazed at his children, intoxicated by their continual flow across, up, and down the belly of the tank.

If only...

CHAPTER EIGHT

When Jonathan left Raynard's office he felt like he'd exited from the Palace of a Thousand Dung Heaps. His disdain for Raynard's egotistical self-serving manner was difficult to mask as he wrestled with how to lance this human boil and rid himself of the pus.

As much as he wanted the poison gone, he knew he had to have all his T's crossed and I's dotted to avoid ruinous settlement costs for wrongful dismissal. Evil men do evil deeds, and Jonathan was convinced one of Raynard's deeds would eventually catch up with the jackass. Until that time, Jonathan would have to attend to the myriad of other challenges facing his company.

Deciding to continue his walkabout, Jonathan dropped in on his new hire, compliance officer Jennifer Wright. During his career, Jonathan found he had an uncanny ability to read corporate tea leaves, if that's what they could be called. He had long recognized the carelessness displayed by many in the drug industry in the pursuit of increased market share, often by utilizing questionable practices and then justifying these actions by insisting,

"Every company does it." Jonathan recognized the fragility of this defense, hence his wholehearted support of a thorough compliance program initiated at T.V. Neurologicals.

Jennifer Wright came to Jonathan's attention through a T.V. Neurologicals board member who claimed she had saved one of his firm's portfolio companies a great deal of money through her handling of an investigation initiated by the Department of Justice. Such investigations frequently involved high-powered bureaucrats who seldom completed an audit without finding enough infractions to justify their existence.

It was clear from her resume that Jennifer had demonstrated the talent for early identification of high-risk issues and had solid experience establishing programs and procedures to keep employers from straying off the straight and narrow. She possessed the communication skills and temperament necessary to deal with high-powered government bureaucrats who seldom, if ever, completed an audit without finding fault. It was often not a question of "whether;" more likely, "how much is it going to cost?"

"Good morning, Jennifer. Good to see you're settling into your office, but only if your physician has given you the green light to start working again."

Pleased Jonathan showed interest in her personal well being before launching right into business, she grasped his outstretched hand.

"Thank you, I'm feeling just fine and have been given clearance to earn my paycheck. I've even had the opportunity to familiarize myself with a few issues we touched on earlier." Jonathan motioned to the more comfortable chairs around a coffee table squeezed into one corner of the small office. This might be a longer conversation than he expected.

"Good to hear. When we last met I described places where I thought T.V. Neurologicals might be vulnerable. But, first things first. As discussed, the announcement of you being assigned a seat on the executive committee and reporting directly to me underlines the importance I place on your role."

They both knew the committee placement wouldn't lead to establishing warm, fuzzy relationships with some members of the existing management team. In a company that had previously operated without a strong corporate conscience, the new standard operating procedures might take some getting used to before becoming part of the corporate culture. Because Jennifer had Jonathan's ear, jealousies were bound to crop up.

"I'm anxious to hear your preliminary report after scratching the surface of what's going on around here."

When Jennifer leaned forward with confidence and authority before responding, Jonathan was pleased. Handling compliance issues was not a job for someone who wasn't comfortable taking control.

"You promised I would be busy and there would be real opportunities for me to make a difference. My cursory review tells me that you certainly didn't exaggerate. How much time do we have?"

Jonathan immediately recognized his new hire was testing him by asking how much time he would allocate to her briefing. His answer would reveal the true level of importance he placed on her input.

"We have as much time as needed," he replied.

Settling back in her butter leather easy chair, Jennifer made ready to launch into her initial report. Watching Jennifer cushion herself, Jonathan almost chuckled when he remembered the phrase, "Looking for a soft place to fall."

Jennifer downloaded her early findings and Jonathan's brow furrowed as he intently listened to her words. He recognized that in her hands this woman wielded a scalpel. The fine blade was slicing into serious issues that could dramatically affect the ability of T.V. Neurologicals to compete, but more importantly, to survive.

In recent years actions had been brought against companies resulting in mind-shattering fines that could absolutely cripple a small growing company like T.V. Neurologicals. Many cases resulted in "consent decrees" which were most often settlements between a company and a branch of government without admission of guilt or liability and which required the company to take specific actions. These actions often had a devastating impact on the freedom with which a company could operate. One comment often heard was, "Competing with a consent decree is like going into a boxing match with both arms tied behind your back!" Yet if the prescribed behavior outlined was not satisfied, climbing between the ropes of the imaginary boxing ring wasn't going to happen, instead a prison cell could be waiting.

Pharmaceuticals used to be such a fun place to work. The good old days are gone forever; it's a new world out there!

Jennifer alerted her boss of three principle areas of possible exposure: drug pricing irregularities, inadequate promotional materials, and off-label promotion. She couldn't guarantee there weren't more snakes hiding in the weeds since the grass had grown thick and high during the previous T.V. Neurologicals administration, but these three were serpents coiled to spring.

"The media and politicians love to describe the pharmaceutical industry as immoral and without conscience while pursuing sales growth. My observation is, apart from the occasional bad egg typical in any business setting, most misconduct I've uncovered was not deliberate in nature. More often than not, the offense was the result of a changing legal environment. What may have been acceptable practice just yesterday was deemed unacceptable in today's environment. Unfortunately new regulations are often retroactively applied, leaving many companies vulnerable and exposed."

What a grim outlook this portrays, Jonathan thought. This was not breaking news to Jonathan, but confirmed what he had concluded through his own analysis.

"Is there any light at the end of the dark tunnel?" Jennifer was a savvy manager and was not about to leave her new boss stuck in a quagmire. She described a path offering a good chance to avoid much of the mess.

"Jonathan, you can't change the history of this company. Whatever happened has happened and can't be altered. I'm sure you've heard the expression, 'The best defense is a good offense.'

"Well, that has never been truer than in this situation. If we end up in a legal battle with the State Attorney General, the very best we can do is show we've taken every step possible to get our house in order. To that end I recommend we bring in outside experts to conduct an audit of T.V. Neurologicals practices and to develop standard operating procedures to minimize the likelihood of future infractions.

"We then put a full-court press to implement such procedures throughout the company. The reality is there will continue to be infractions because we are imperfect human beings. At our best we will reduce occurrences, but you and I both know we'll never be able to eliminate every potential issue."

Her powerful impromptu report was given with such conviction and compassion that Jonathan had to smile. He jumped out of his chair and exclaimed, "This is now one of my highest priorities. Get the best darn audit team you can find and I'll let the organization know you have my full and unmitigated support to dig through any and all potential matters of concern."

For the first time since arriving at T.V. Neurologicals, Jennifer realized she'd made the right decision about joining the company and was pleased and grateful she would have the essential backing from the top to make a difference.

"Jonathan, our industry is unique because it is so highly regulated and subject to huge financial penalties for infractions. On April 18, 2003 the Office of the Inspector General in the Department of Health and Human Services published a twelve page, small type bulletin providing guidance and expectations for pharmaceutical manufacturers. The scope of the guidelines covers a broad landscape and my judgment is that our focus at T.V. Neurologicals should address pricing and off-label promotion."

There was a pregnant pause while Jonathan processed all that had been said. "I'm not surprised; these areas tend to come up frequently when a case becomes public. Please go on."

"T.V. Neurologicals pricing irregularities pertain to the issue of ensuring certain government accounts receive the best price available. The multitude of contracts negotiated with hospitals, HMOs, PPOs and numerous government accounts lead to complex methodologies that can exist to calculate a drug's bottom-line pricing. This is far from being an easy fix; different experts frequently come up with different numbers. We must bring in valid auditors with pricing expertise; perhaps use former government employees who have joined the lucrative world of compliance consulting.

"Secondly, homemade detail aids are a flagrant violation in our industry and as the name suggests, involve a misguided attempt by a company sales team to cut and paste their own promotional piece in the belief they can do a better job of presenting the sales proposition. Frequently these efforts approach the arena of off-label promotion. Companies are required to take promotional selling materials through an exhaustive review process that includes marketing, medical, regulatory, legal, training and operations departments. Off-label promotion probably represents the greatest financial exposure for most pharmaceutical companies, and is therefore of highest interest to prosecutors. Prosecutors build cases for huge levied fines based on the inappropriate use of drugs and the resultant cost of misused drugs used for unauthorized illnesses."

Jonathan's body language showed the frustration he was beginning to feel. "I am very familiar with off-label use as I marketed epilepsy drugs prior to coming to T.V. Neurologicals. There was use of anti-epileptic drugs for indications other than seizures. What drives me up the wall is the public doesn't know it is legally permissible for physicians to prescribe off-label. In many cases a drug may be effective for an unapproved illness, but that information cannot be conveyed by pharmaceutical salespersons. The salesperson is, of course, tempted by the potential of increasing sales which will result in a substantial sales bonus."

Jennifer raised her hand to indicate a question; the disarming move made Jonathan smile. He had to give her credit for defusing a potentially explosive moment.

"One of the points I often hear at compliance conferences is drug companies should establish and complete trials, resulting in gaining FDA approval. Is this a reasonable solution to the problem?"

This very question was frequently posed when the topic of off-label promotion was raised. On the surface it seemed to be a logical solution.

"In many cases that is indeed what happens, however, more often than not there isn't enough time left in the drug's patent life to make the huge investment profitable. Each new indication is similar to getting a new drug approved.

"Jennifer, this has been extremely useful, but I have to move on. Is there more we need to discuss today?"

"I know this is a lot to dump on you, but you needed to hear the naked truth about what the company is facing. I'm very comfortable with all we've covered today so don't feel guilty about moving on to your next crisis."

Jonathan managed a weak smile.

"Thanks, Jennifer. The next step for you will be a briefing session to include the entire senior management team. Please schedule the meeting for two weeks from today."

The young CEO knew these were issues that had to be addressed on multiple fronts and would need the support and cooperation of his entire front-line management organization. He thanked Jennifer once more and left her office. That little voice in his head recognized this was not a T.V. Neurologicals situation that would accept a quick-fix solution; they were in for the duration.

For the first time since arriving at T.V. Neurologicals, Jonathan felt an uncomfortable spasm clutch the pit of his stomach. If the company were to lose a case brought by a whistleblower in conjunction with government regulators, there could be a significant monetary fine along with heavy restrictions placed on the company's ability to operate freely.

T.V. Neurologicals did not have the deep pockets larger pharmaceutical companies enjoyed. Such a horrific scenario would severely hamper the launch resources of any new drug such as SRD 6969 and could force T.V. Neurologicals into entering other strategic arrangements involving unknown alliances. The forced sale of the company might even be required. Jonathan's brain felt like it was being stabbed by a hundred needle pricks. Each represented a direction he hadn't contemplated when he assumed his CEO role, but clearly needed to be considered given the unexpected dynamic environment.

After hearing the strong threat of possible compliance battles, Jonathan needed to lift his spirits and he knew where to go to make that happen.

He meandered through the marketing department, making sure he took a moment or two to acknowledge the folks working hard to increase the company's sales. He came to Pete Ames's open door and walked in. Behind a massive pile of papers decorating the world's messiest desk sat his VP of Marketing and good friend, Peter. Sudden thoughts of bygone days he and Pete shared in their previous positions made him smile.

"So, are we building a base for a bonfire here? But, before you set the blaze, I think you need to throw a few green papers bearing the image of Andrew Jackson in my direction." Jonathan was referencing the last golf game the two played when he narrowly won their bet by sinking a birdie on the 18th hole.

"Christ, I don't believe how lucky you were that day! Your damn ball hit the flagstick! By all rights that sucker should have gone right off the green and into the water."

"Hey, it's what you write on the card that counts, not how pretty you look." Jonathan took a seat at the small coffee table in a corner and motioned his friend to join him.

"Tell me how my strategic marketing guru has interpreted our company's situation, and it better be only good news." Pete knew full well his boss meant he wanted the full picture, warts and all. The marketing maverick leaned back in his chair as his fingers created a tent six inches in front of his nose. This was a ritual Ames went through whenever he was about to make a profound statement.

"In golf terms, we probably have a double-bogey, a par, and an eagle."

"Go on," encouraged his curious boss.

"It's fine to spend time on the research portfolio, but a key message should be directed to the sales and marketing teams. We must continue to be successful with Czuretrin because that's the drug that keeps the lights on." Jonathan nodded in agreement.

"The double-bogey is Raynard's folly. All the preliminary research I'm getting indicates this is a drug looking for a reason to be prescribed, and I'm sure you agree, that's always a losing proposition."

"Well, you'll get no argument from me on that count. I've been concerned about that very thing since I performed initial diligence on the company. Tell me more about the other two, what do you make of them?"

Ames's face lit up.

"Let's do some flying with the eagles, Jonathan. If SRD 6969 delivers on the promise to enhance sexual pleasure for women, we are definitely big time in the money. Early research suggests the drug could actually mimic the growth curve of Viagra®."

"Are there downsides you've been able to identify?"

"The major concern I have is it's not unusual for drugs in this category to show positive early results which are not sustainable in the long run. Sometimes this is due to side-effects, but other times the drug works differently on a human body after the system becomes adjusted to it."

Jonathan stood and paced around the office caught in deep thought.

"Well, we really have no choice but to roll the dice because our only other hope is a par."

Pete shook his head.

"I have this feeling deep in my burned-out, alcoholic liver that the orphan drug could be a sleeper. Don't give up on the molecule until the last putt is sunk." Ames always weaved magic when he used golf metaphors. Jonathan was already feeling much better; he had great confidence in Peter's intuition. His friend's gut feelings had proved accurate time and again in North Carolina.

Peter knew his boss and friend well and could tell angst was roiling inside him. He caught the look covering his boss's face and knew he was going through a tough time – Tina!

"Hey, the honeys in California are hot, I'm off to investigate the playing field at a bar in Mountain View tonight, want to join Rachel and me?"

"Rachel? Good grief, Pete, you certainly didn't waste any time making that move! I have to admit she's a very attractive woman and I find her damn good at her job…" Jonathan hesitated.

"Okay, out with it, why the pregnant pause?" Jonathan was embarrassed that Peter could read him so well.

"Don't know what it is that I picked up on. Hey, you're a master at business golf and I'm experienced in the art of women. Best

I can describe would be to use an expression I heard a long time ago – 'Things are not always what they seem in the Valley.'"

Pete threw both arms high above his head in a mock expression of frustration.

"All these years and you still don't know me. She's taking me to a bar to introduce me to California surfer girls, she is not my date. Hell you were the one who always warned me never to shit in my own backyard."

Jonathan rolled his eyes as if to say there was no hope for his friend. The two laughed and Jonathan was off to his next walkabout. His lightened mood darkened as he headed to see Ron Daniels.

CHAPTER NINE

R on Daniels paced back and forth in his executive office. He cursed the name Jonathan Grayhall over and over with each measured step. Life as VP of Sales had been grandly profitable for so many years, thanks to hefty bonuses received from the high performing Czuretrin drug. The aphrodisiac effect his position of power had on impressionable ambitious female sales representatives was an added perk.

Five years before Daniels had been caught in a corporate downsizing frenzy at a major pharmaceutical company where he held the position of top performing regional sales manager. Through his contacts he'd heard about a small West Coast neurology company that was launching a novel, breakthrough product for the treatment of epilepsy. The start-up company planned to launch their premier product in the U.S. using seventy-five of the best salespeople money could buy. That company was looking for a results-oriented leader to pull it all together. Daniels was not Ivy League material; however, he came equipped with a formidable reputation of owning considerable street smarts and a will to win that enabled him to beat out the 100 or so competing for the top dog position as T.V. Neurologicals national sales manager.

He chuckled as he recalled his literal beating of a rival that took place in a San Jose topless bar, ensuring the man's quick withdrawal from the race. After his appointment, Daniels whipped his high-performing sales team into shape and soon began to reap the rewards. Sometimes a prescription product did not live up to the promise demonstrated during clinical trials pre-FDA approval, but Czuretrin delivered on every level and developed a loyal physician/patient following.

T.V. Neurologicals was still a relatively small company compared to the big boys on the block, but with a current sales force of 275 bonus-driven individuals dedicated to calling on top epilepsy prescribers, the company was a presence to be reckoned with in the target market. Additionally, commercially oriented field-based resources included a managed care team whose whole purpose was to deal with reimbursement and politically savvy state government managers for Medicaid/Medicare.

Medical resources included highly specialized Medical Science Liaisons (MSLs) to support top-tier medical specialists. As vice president of sales, Daniels enjoyed the bounty brought by the breakthrough drug for treating epilepsy, a high, unmet need marketplace desperately searching for a product that combined efficacy with a good safety profile. Rarely a week went by when there wasn't a letter from a patient thanking T.V. Neurologicals for Czuretrin, praising the difference the drug had made in their quality of life.

The perks enjoyed by Daniels were many - handsome sales bonuses, lavish incentive travel awards, an unlimited entertainment budget, executive luxury car, and adequate means to purchase the occasional bauble like the gold Rolex Daytona he wore on his wrist every day.

The year when the sales curve experienced the inevitable slowdown, Ron Daniels had no trouble looking the other way when a few of his more aggressive sales managers pushed their teams to promote FDA-unapproved indications for certain types of pain. Entering into virgin markets, albeit illegal, allowed sales to soar once more.

His stomach tightened when he thought of the witch bitch compliance officer Grayhall had hired. She had already poked her nose into his business and was asking questions that gave him heartburn. She was now in the process of setting up an external audit that would review sales practices and procedures. The T.V. Neurologicals sales chief started to feel the noose tightening around his neck.

Of the many illegal ways to give sales figures the old boost in the arm, Daniels personal favorites were off-label promotion and homemade sales materials. The former method often provided good financial return while the latter placed most penalty risks, if caught, squarely in the lap of the offending salesperson. Daniels was meticulous in his efforts to cover trails that might lead back to him as an instigator or supporter of such illegal tactics. In turning a blind eye to the activities of certain sales managers, he took great pains to ensure there weren't lurking emails or smoking guns leading back to him. He made sure everything risky was handled verbally, nothing to put the screws to him. Words created the perfect "he said, she said" scenario and could never be the basis for a strong case against anybody.

When it came to homemade in-house detail pieces, Daniels expected red flags to be pushing up like poppies. He knew occasional misguided sales representatives would become impatient with the verbiage of the sanitized brochures produced by the highly regulated marketing department. Said rep would resort to creating a personalized "Dear Doctor" letter or would manufacture a cut and paste binder to meet his/her sales needs. The concocted messages frequently presented a biased point of view and unsupported claims. It was possible such evidence could find its way into the hands of the meddling compliance woman Grayhall hired and if that happened, there would be hell to pay.

There was another potential area of exposure that concerned Daniels even more. It involved unapproved activities surrounding a small number of district managers collaborating with MSLs. When the concept of developing an MSL team was first proposed three years earlier, Daniels was the most supportive executive team member at the table, but probably for the wrong reasons.

The legitimate concept was to establish a team of highly educated, medically trained individuals who could provide high-level information resources upon request to physician specialists. Daniels found an out-of-bounds way to capitalize on this potential resource, discreetly of course. A few aggressive district managers put out feelers and recruited several materially oriented MSLs to assist in nefarious off-label practices. Simply put, medical personnel would leverage their strong relationships with a prescribing physician to expand the use of the pharmaceutical company's products not yet unapproved for associated indications.

The results stemming from these shenanigans were frequently dramatic. There were several areas in which a drug was highly effective, but trials to gain approval had not been completed and filed with the FDA. There were always creative ways a sales manager could reward such "outside assistance."

Daniels got wind that one of his sales managers had approached a particular MSL based in Atlanta. Apparently the target MSL was a straight arrow and word came back she had reacted badly to attempts to recruit her to support the dubious activities going on in the back office. She vehemently threatened to report the incident to internal compliance.

Such a report would have serious consequences for the T.V. Neurologicals sales team. Should the woman decide to take her accusations to the next level and actually become a whistleblower, well, that could have horrific implications. Huge fines, consent decrees, loss of jobs, and even criminal charges would be plastered on the company's billboard. From what Daniels had read in industry journals, MSLs were front and center in whistle blowing cases. Hell, if he had it to do all over again he could easily picture himself filing a *qui tam* lawsuit and collecting a cool $20 million for his effort. He cursed himself for not taking advantage of that opportunity years earlier. He would be set for life.

Back to the problem at hand, Daniels made a note to begin to formulate ways to discredit the offending MSL in the event she pursued her complaints.

Daniels grabbed a paperweight and hurled it across the room to vent his building anger. Still, as vice president of a highly successful pharmaceutical company, he really had it all - money, women, power! Just yesterday he'd read an article in *Sales and Marketing Management* that described the pharmaceutical sales culture quite accurately. He found the magazine in his inbox and flipped to the article for review.

Many leading pharmaceutical companies embrace a corporate culture where the sales force is the *primary internal customer. The root of this thinking likely goes back to the historical fact that the drug industry has been driven by the importance of direct sales contact, the one-on-one relationship between doctor and salesperson. Not to say other elements of the marketing mix are not important, of course they play a vital role. However, there are not many industries that traditionally require the army of sales representatives as evidenced in Rx drug marketing.*

On average, a U.S. pharmaceutical company's sales force requires 550 persons to cover key GPs and 100-175 to work with medical specialists. The typical sales call lasts no more than a few minutes. This limited time frame led to the need for multiple sales force reps if a company was to increase the frequency of sales presentations to a targeted doctor. This meant some companies doubled-up and had two sales reps selling to the same doctor, sometimes promoting the same product. The purpose of duplication of effort was to increase the frequency of physician presentations, assuming this would increase prescribing. Physicians rejected product doubling and today it is a less common practice. One powerful driving force facilitating entry into physicians' offices has been the delivery of drug samples. Samples allow the doctor to gain personal prescribing experience with a product. Patients know samples are available and often ask for them to reduce medical expenses. Sampling of drugs is typically an American phenomenon and certainly is not seen to the same extent in other major markets.

In spite of many challenges, most industries would sell their corporate souls to boast income statements as attractive as those seen in the pharmaceutical industry. Even the least sophisticated investor would quickly surmise that gross margins and income before taxes tends to be attractive, thereby permitting relatively high sales and marketing expenditures.

Oral drug products frequently enjoy large gross margins because costs to manufacture can be relatively low. There have been cases when a tablet may cost five cents on the dollar to manufacture. Patents prevent cheap copies from coming onto the market during the early years of a product's lifetime. While patents are granted for 21 years, the meaningful patent life of a pharmaceutical is generally less than 10 years due to the time required to conduct clinical trials and assemble a dossier to submit to the FDA. Time is then needed for FDA review and approval.

Pharmaceutical sales forces are highly motivated by bonus programs. It would not be unusual for a top sales person to achieve a bonus of up to 50 percent of their base salary for outstanding performance. Poor performers receive little to nothing in additional compensation. On average, bonus payouts to a sales force could amount to 25 percent of base compensation.

With so much money at stake, there has always been the risk that stray cats will seek unapproved ways to expand sales numbers, and consequently their bonuses, by stepping outside the rules. One glaring example of how this might be done is by promoting unapproved indications, i.e. off-label. An interesting observation is doctors are allowed to prescribe off-label, even as a drug salesperson must steer clear of promoting this loophole. Management up the entire sales ladder is culpable for actions taken on the field level, no matter what was provided in the way of sales direction. This breakdown often results in the initiation of compliance departments so a company pro-actively monitors behavior to ensure guidelines are met.

Pharmaceutical sales had been very, very good to Ron Daniels but now that asshole Grayhall was threatening to derail the glory train. He had to act quickly. At that moment his thoughts were interrupted. Daniels heard whispers coming from outside his door.

"Sonovabitch, it's the boss man making the rounds!"

━━┼┼━━

In the final round of his day's MBWA, Jonathan prepped himself for the mental jousting that lay ahead. He debated which of the two men he least looked forward to seeing.

Jonathan approached Daniels' office door and poked his head inside.

"Good morning, Ron. I thought I'd check in with you to see how sales are doing."

What I really want to know is if you realize this is the last day of the month and our flagship product is only 90 percent to budget.

"In fact, why don't we take some time so you can walk me through your area of responsibility in more detail than the last time we met?"

"Good to see you, Jonathan, and you'll be pleased to know the backorder we filled today will take us to 98 percent. When the production lot is released by QC, we will be at a whopping 104 percent!"

The rapid and canned response given by Daniels did not surprise Jonathan. He did not underestimate this man who wouldn't be in a senior leadership position if he was lacking ability. Pity the man chose to use his talent to travel down a dark path.

As the conversation ping-ponged around the table, both played their cards close to the vest. Daniels appeared comfortable with his perceived solid standing, showing not a care in the world. Jonathan was being careful, but not unduly negative in his choice of words. Their discussion continued for almost an hour; there was much Jonathan wanted to probe about the sales snapshot and projection for Czuretrin.

"Tell me, Ron, last year when you saw the writing on the wall showing sales of Czuretrin were peaking at one helluva level, what was the direction you set for your sales management team? What did you tell them to do to keep the sales curve from flattening?"

This was the key question Jonathan had wanted to ask in the first five minutes of the executive committee meeting.

"Well, boss, that presented my boys and girls with a real challenge and many offered suggestions I flatly rejected because they violated OIG guidelines."

Daniels clearly demonstrated how he had managed to fight his way up the mountain; it wasn't by blabbing on topics that required discretion. For the remainder of their discussion, verbal parrying was front and center, Daniels capably offsetting every attempt by Jonathan to uncover unacceptable promotional practices.

Jonathan knew he had a lot of work ahead at T.V. Neurologicals. He had to grow the sales and market share of a product approaching maturity while simultaneously transforming the culture of the company to recognize the growing importance of heeding compliance guidelines set by the Office of the Inspector General.

The biggest challenge likely lay with the T.V. Neurologicals sales force because the team had been extremely successful selling Czuretrin, and so doing had earned substantial cash bonuses for increasing sales and market share. Under these circumstances it was unreasonable to assume stricter promotional guidelines would be received with high fives. Rather, they would be perceived as an obstacle making it harder to maintain desired compensation levels.

Jonathan's thought about the legacy Daniels was creating at T.V. Neurologicals. On the positive side, the company had fostered a culture that clearly rewarded growth and market share increase, exactly what any business would want to see. On the negative side was scant consideration given to behaviors involved in attaining those golden sales. How could he, as the CEO of T.V. Neurologicals, maintain a required competitive spirit and at the same time strip his sales team of what many would perceive as their most effective weapons?

One thing for sure, the leader of the company's sales force was going to require tremendous character and skill to keep the team motivated. It was Jonathan's assessment that Ron Daniels was not up to the challenge in that regard.

"Wrapping up then," Jonathan summarized, "I am depending on you to deliver results concerning our market-leading product Czuretrin. I hope I have conveyed the importance of achieving such goals within the guidelines prescribed by the OIG."

"Crystal clear," assured Daniels. He jokingly stood at attention and saluted Jonathan, a move he immediately recognized as a poor choice. Jonathan turned and walked out of the office without a further word.

CHAPTER TEN

Over the past weeks Jacki had not been idle during her off time. She had intensely researched the topic of whistle blowing in the pharmaceutical industry, covering the good, the bad, and the ugly. Much of what she learned led her to today's introductory visit to a leading Atlanta law firm with a track record for successfully filing cases in this arena.

She copied one of the most striking things she learned from her Web search.

The False Claims act is a law designed to reward a person who is aware of a company or individual who has defrauded the government resulting in a financial loss. The whistleblower is allowed to file a qui tam *lawsuit to recover damages on the government's behalf with the intent to have the government join the case if it decides after investigation that there is merit in proceeding. The law states that only the first to file alleging fraud can continue, the filing must be within six years of the misbehavior and then is placed under seal. This means it is not disclosed to the public or the defendants and therefore is not to be discussed with anyone other than the attorney for the case and the government. The rewards can be lucrative for the whistleblower, typically between 15-25 percent of the total recovery. These cases do tend to be very expensive and lengthy and may remain under seal for two to three years.*

The Atlanta lawyer Jacki met was a senior partner in the national firm Queen and Wilson; Jacki had to call in plenty favors to arrange the meeting. The lawyer's name was David St. James and the man didn't waste much time with small talk once Jacki settled into the leather chair to the right of his large mahogany desk. The two got down to business stat.

The discussion had a strong business focus, but at the same time St. James was patient as he listened carefully when Jacki described what she regarded as suspect activities happening at her company. The attorney knew from past experience there certainly was potential for extremely large financial settlements in such cases, with a healthy portion going to the firm representing the whistleblower if the case was won.

Jacki carefully went over the proposal made by the unethical salesmen. The suggestion that she use her close relationship to inappropriately influence her key physicians to expand off-label use of Czuretrin, how she refused and the ensuing veiled threat were all detailed. She described her reasons for concern that her supervisor may be tied into the scheme. After Jacki finished presenting her prepared argument, she sat back to take in what the senior partner had to say.

"Jacki, I've listened to your allegations of inappropriate promotion for off-label indications and your description of the attempt by certain in your sales staff to involve you in a scheme that certainly has the makings of illicit activity."

He seemed to hesitate so Jacki jumped in and asked him flat out, "And, what do you think, is there a case to be made?"

David St. James, attorney-at-law, was not only a talented lawyer, he was a professional who wasn't out to make a quick buck like a cheap ambulance chaser. It was for good reason Jacki's friends had suggested his name, knowing he would advise her wisely.

"I have seen dozens of cases involving *qui tam* and the outcomes have been generally as you would expect, in favor of the government. After all, they tend to take cases already stacked in their favor.

"For the most part I've seen societal good come when egregious behavior on the part of offending companies is justly punished. As you might expect, not all ends well. Occasionally I've seen unfortunate outcomes. Plaintiffs, perhaps like you, are convinced the whistle blowing route might be the best way to fix a company's problems. I can guarantee you, that won't happen and often the eager proponent is regarded as a pariah within the company and eventually in the entire industry. I'm telling you this because I sense by listening to your story that your heart isn't in this."

Jacki was speechless. She digested his words and knew he was right. St. James continued

"Ironically, from the client's point of view, the more successful outcomes have been with those who were in it for the money. In your case Ms. Striker I can tell that you are motivated by more altruistic goals."

"Mr. St. James, its no wonder you're a highly successful attorney. You really read people well. I hope I didn't waste your time. Thank you for your excellent advice which I promise to follow."

David St. James stood up and walked Jacki to his office door and took her hand to shake goodbye. Before letting go he offered, "Jacki, I want to thank you for spending the afternoon with us to discuss the basis for a *qui tam* lawsuit. From what you've described, I'm fairly certain there have been infractions of the false claims act by personnel at your company, including senior management.

"I think it took courage to speak with my law firm about filing a suit. Just because our decision today is not to pursue, it by no means obviates the course of action another party may take. What I heard today is sufficient to convince me that you are probably on to something and in all likelihood you aren't the only one with thoughts of filing. However, having the government join us in the litigation process generally requires the hurdle to be set higher, and in my opinion more would be needed in the way of hard evidence. So, we shall see."

Jacki was taken back; this was not what she expected to hear.

"So, can I take it this situation can go no further? Your firm has no interest in filing?"

"On the contrary. I want to emphasize how much we would like to participate in what looks like a case with merit. The problem is the perpetrators involved have been careful not to leave damning evidence of their activity, so it becomes a 'he said, she said' situation. Should another pretty young lady walk into my office with strong evidence to back up her observations, or should you change your mind about going ahead, my door is open. Just remember, once the word is out you're going against your company, you'll become a demon to the industry."

The two said goodbye and Jacki found herself giving David St. James a hug. She replayed what she had heard. There appeared to be a good case developing, but it required the collection of substantial reams of hard evidence. She hadn't realized whistleblower cases could take up to three years under seal. That was a long time. Jacki was also having trouble dealing with the pariah stigma that came from ratting out her company. She knew deep down she didn't want to leave her position, but neither could she work in a culture that violated her values.

Words of advice uttered long ago from her father came to mind. "If you are not part of the solution, you are likely part of the problem."

A lot to think about, but how on earth could she be part of the solution? For now she looked forward to returning to Alpharetta where she was meeting Alice for dinner at Marlow's, one of their favorite eating spots.

CHAPTER ELEVEN

Atlanta's rush hour traffic was the usual mess so it took Jacki a full seventy minutes to make the straight shot up Highway 400 North to Exit 8. After the ramp turnoff, it took another fifteen minutes to get to the strip mall where Marlow's Pub snuggled between a high-end boutique and an Apple computer store.

Arriving at the same time, Tim dropped off his wife and Jacki could see from the expression on his face that he was not a happy camper. The two friends hugged and quickly ordered glasses of the house chardonnay. Jacki had not seen Alice for almost six weeks and was flabbergasted by her friend's stunning appearance. It wasn't that she did not look great before but every person, male and female, in the restaurant was stealing a look at the beautiful brunette, trying to guess which movie she had starred in. What an incredible makeover! Alice's make-up, hairstyle, and overall sleek appearance were way over the top. Adding to the total package was the aura of self-confidence enveloping her old friend.

"Girl, I'm going to be perfectly honest here. I'm blown away by your stunning new look and how together you seem to be!"

Receiving such a compliment from her oldest friend teased a broad smile over Alice's pretty face.

"Well, I tried hard to look my best for you, but there's still *so* much work to be done!" Somewhat taken back by Alice's comment, a puzzled Jacki asked, "What do you mean? Are you talking about your new job at the TV station?"

"Don't be absurd. I'm talking about the ghastly imperfections all over my face and body! I must get them fixed as soon as possible." Jacki started to argue but Alice quickly cut her off.

"I need to have my nose bobbed, cheekbones accentuated, chin smoothed, and I really think a nice way to round off everything would be with a Brazilian butt tuck." Jacki was truly shaken but then realized her friend was probably putting her on.

"You *are* kidding, please tell me this is a joke you're playing. You have the looks every woman in this restaurant, no, make that all Atlanta, would die for. Now stop playing with me."

The beautiful girl who had every man in Marlow's captivated by her striking good looks wanted to have extensive cosmetic surgery to fix what she somehow perceived as imperfections? Something was definitely wrong with this picture.

Alice just smiled, took a sip of chardonnay and said nothing.

As the evening rolled on, discomfort and unease settled between the two friends. Jacki noticed an edge to Alice's conversation she had never seen before. It was a change in mood and behavior that wasn't necessarily for the better. Particularly disturbing, Alice, who always spoke of her husband as her anchor and credited him with her growth and development, was openly flirting with strangers in the restaurant. Jacki wondered the unthinkable, was Alice having an affair? Crazy thoughts swirled in her head with each bizarre comment that came out of Alice's mouth. Jacki was happy to end the evening.

"And I owe everything to you and your wonderful company. I can't thank you enough for helping me get into that clinical trial. I feel so fortunate to be one of the patients who responded well. You know, the trial was blind so participants never knew if they were taking a placebo or an active dose, but in my case it was evident something was happening to me, inside and out. When they broke the trial code, I was sure the drug truly had remarkable properties. I'm now enlisted in a longer-term follow-up." Alice squealed with excitement while grabbing her friend's hand and squeezing it tightly.

Jacki felt a swish of acid batter her stomach. Was she seeing the behavioral side effects she had heard about regarding the experimental drug? Worse yet, was she partially responsible for turning her best friend into a cosmetic surgery junkie like the vain bevy of Hollywood celebs? Jacki felt terrible and knew she had to do *something*, but didn't quite know what.

Her head was already spinning after her meeting with Mr. St. James earlier in the afternoon. How much more could her head handle before exploding like a kid's balloon? Alice's behavior genuinely baffled her, and Jacki hoped any resulting actions from taking the drug wouldn't spiral out of control.

The evening couldn't end soon enough for Jacki. She pulled their waiter aside and asked he call a cab for her friend, giving a lame excuse to avoid driving Alice home. The changes she saw in her friend were extremely disconcerting and Jacki felt she might say something she would regret later. She no longer knew the person who'd been sitting across the table at dinner. Gone was the humble, gentle girl she'd known and loved in college, and in her place was a self-centered narcissist interested solely in appearances. Their friendship couldn't continue while Alice was acting like a selfish brat and Jacki felt sad at the thought she may have set the wheels in motion by suggesting her friend participate in the trial.

Alice's cab finally arrived and was announced by the hostess. The two women got up to leave and attracted attention from several men ogling them in the mirrored bar backdrop as they slipped on their coats. Jacki reached to hug Alice good-bye but instead Alice grabbed her friend's head between her hands and planted a deep, wet kiss on her mouth. Jacki pulled back in shocked surprise.

"Alice, what are you doing?" she demanded in a low whisper, trying to avoid drawing any more attention to what had just happened.

"Just giving those horny guys something to think about when they go to bed alone tonight!"

Jacki shook her head hard to chase the demons away and briskly walked out the door to her car.

All the way home, Jacki could feel an ache rumbling in her gut as piercing streams of light signaling a migraine flashed behind her eyelids. As she battled a plague of negativity, Jacki struggled for answers to the many dilemmas she was facing, but the more she thought, the more confused and upset she became.

On the verge of a meltdown, a welcome impression suddenly blew the fog away. The next month Jacki had scheduled a trip to her company's home office in California for a week of medical seminars. Through Linkedin she'd seen a message that her friend Jennifer from Georgia Tech had coincidentally taken a position at the company. Jennifer was a graduate of Emory Law and had chosen a career in Corporate Compliance. Jacki felt she was close enough to Jennifer to confide her situation. Almost immediately a sense of calm centered in Jacki's core and she felt things would work out all the way around. She remembered a sign she'd seen at a lunch counter a few days earlier, "Not to spoil the ending or anything, but everything will be okay." With determination, Jacki knew she would eventually conquer her concerns.

While in California she planned to visit her brother Ravi who owned a flourishing tugboat business. He'd invited her to visit during the West Coast's annual Fleet Week and promised a great time. Oh boy, Jacki badly needed a good dose of R&R!

CHAPTER TWELVE

The pretty young woman began to stir, slowly stretching her arms. With some difficulty she opened her eyes and surveyed the room zigzagged with bright patterns of sunlight. Panic overwhelmed her when she didn't recognize her surroundings. Feeling dizzy, she tried to recount the evening before. To her dismay she just could not remember anything that had happened. A sense of dread filled her senses as she realized something was terribly wrong. Her throat was dry, her head fuzzy, her movements slow. The woman became aware she was naked, spread across a bed in a strange room. Brutal reality crept into her consciousness. She began to cry. The woman realized her vagina was wet and sticky – she had been violated. A pitiful wail escaped her parched lips as she buried her head and sobbed deeply into the crumpled bed pillow.

Ron Daniels whistled as he walked out of the Union Square Hotel lobby and hailed a cab to take him directly to T.V. Neurologicals where he'd left his car the night before. Daniels made it a point to frequent management workshops dealing with "Diversity in the Workplace" such as the session held in San Francisco the day before.

His interest was not governed by the subject matter; it had more to do with the typical profile of many of the attendees. A large number of subscribers to the diversity sessions were attractive, female Human Resource professionals with tendencies to dominance when it came to their relationships with men. Daniels loved it when women who were known in the '60s as female libbers were reduced to submission before his depraved wants and desires. All it ever took was a few minutes in the hotel bar, a tricky sleight of hand, and soon he would be closeted in an upstairs hotel room with his woman of choice. He was the one doing the dominating once the door was closed.

Daniels had been playing this perilous game for years without incident and felt the risk was well worth the reward. The game excited him like nothing else could. Admittedly he thought the gig was up and he was in deep shit a few years before when he walked into Rachel Hammer's office.

He was in the process of exiting his potentially career-limiting situation at a Louisiana based company by applying for the VP of Sales position at T.V. Neurologicals. In the corporate offices for his initial interview, Daniels was startled when he encountered the interviewer, thinking she was one of the unsuspecting playthings he had conquered at a seminar in New Orleans five years previously. He remembered the distinctive eyes he had distracted so easily with a funny story, allowing him to drop a magic med into his target's pink Cosmopolitan. That evening's choice mumbled something about meeting her sister for a drink before the two planned to enjoy dinner together. For a split second Daniels considered making it a threesome that night, but decided it was too risky. Still, that was some wild night he had in the Big Easy.

Thinking Rachel Hammer was his target on that sex-filled steamy night in Louisiana, it took incredible self-control to appear nonchalant during his first-round T.V. Neurologicals interview. He tried to pretend he was meeting the woman for the first time, but his eyes searched for messages the prim and proper interviewer might be sending. As the conversation moved forward, Daniels became more comfortable, thinking it was fortunate the slipped rufie had done its job well. Ms. Hammer clearly did not send any sign of recognition.

The T.V. Neurologicals hopeful was able to get through the interview without missing a beat and felt strangely aroused that his conquest had displayed absolutely no recollection of ever meeting him before that morning interview. Was he mistaken? Could it be she wasn't the woman he had abused so thoroughly and delightfully? He replayed the events of that evening in his mind.

The woman in New Orleans had been one of his first tests back when Daniels was a sales rep pushing a drug for sleep issues. He'd managed to illegally obtain a sample of the product during a routine visit to the company warehouse. He marveled at how quickly the clear, odorless, tasteless capsule he dropped in the target's martini glass left the woman acting completely inebriated in just minutes. He easily led her back to her hotel room where he savagely ravaged and abused her for several hours in ways she surely would not have enjoyed or tolerated if sober. He left early the next morning while the drug still carried its effect. Daniels' experience with the drug was true to the label. It had incredible amnesiac properties so his victims remembered nothing of the violations that took place after ingesting the phantom drug.

Suddenly it hit him, of course! This was the sister his conquest had been waiting for that night. The similarity in looks, particularly around the eyes, was astounding.

The cab pulled into the T.V. Neurologicals parking lot and Daniels directed the driver to one of the side entrances since it was now almost noon. He rushed up the back stairs, hung his jacket on an antique brass coat rack, and finally settled behind his desk.

With a flurry of activity, the rapist started to sift through his in-basket with not an iota of remorse. Just another day at the office.

⟫⊹⊹⟪

A few hours later, Daniels was looking out his window. He had insisted on an office that overlooked the asphalt parking lot even though the lush green view was far better on the opposite side of the building. He waited until he saw Grayhall get into his car and leave for an appointment he'd set with a board member, information Daniels had gathered from his inside connection.

Once he was sure Grayhall's car was well on its way, he made a beeline to the CEO's office. There he found Susie Quattro, now permanently ensconced as the president's secretary after the very pregnant woman who held the position previously announced she was staying home with her new baby. At least that was the official story. In truth, Daniels seeded nasty rumors about the father of her child, which created an intolerable work environment for the young woman. The secretary's sudden resignation enabled Daniels' confidante Susie to be placed in a position to relay privileged information as he needed it. This was how he kept tabs on his boss's schedule. Daniels approached the secretary, did a quick 360 to make sure nobody was watching, and slipped his hand high under her skirt.

"What perversion do you have in store for me tonight?" he whispered.

From behind, he put both hands under her skirt and roughly rubbed her pubic area. "I sure liked the last time when you dressed in a nurse's uniform! But, let me guess, a priestess will hear my confession tonight?" Susie pushed his hands away and straightened her skirt.

"Hey, Mister Ron Jeremy," her pet name for her lover referring to the porn star. "No playing with the merchandise in the office. I can't afford to lose my job. As for tonight, you'll just have to wait, but I hope you're prepared for domination."

Daniels grinned. He liked the sound of what she had in mind.

"I booked a site visit at the downtown Grand Carnarvon for six this evening, followed by complimentary in-room champagne and dinner in the Presidential Suite," came the sultry reply. "By the way, a package you ordered from some sports store arrived in the mail room and will be delivered to your office in the morning. Is it something for me?" she coyly asked.

"Not this time, sweetheart, but I promise there will be plenty of other occasions for presents." A married man, Daniels was having his affair with Susie for two reasons. She certainly had a fine body and was a great lay, but she was also a fearless conduit allowing him to find chinks in Sir Grayhall's armor.

T.V. Neurologicals was not the first place Daniels had used administrative staff in this manipulative manner and it usually worked well. If questioned or caught, Daniels always managed to escape with little more than a verbal warning. But, sifting out information this time would require all the ammunition he could muster to keep his position on the T.V. Neurologicals executive committee. Besides, he was having fun with the young, but exquisitely experienced trollop.

Daniels gave consideration to taking Susie right then and there on the desk in plain view of anybody sauntering by, but sanity prevailed and he turned and headed out the door.

"I've got a few errands to run, but I'll see you later. I'm looking forward to ravishing that sexy bod of yours tonight, young lady!" Susie pouted to express displeasure at his rushed departure.

"You just arrived and you're leaving already! I'm beginning to wonder how much you really care about my feelings."

Susie was getting clingy, a definite signal it was time to move on. Daniels left her with the promise he would make it up and would really get into her later that evening. She giggled at his lame innuendo. A little warm-up session would have been nice right then and there, but there were more important things in play.

Daniels' next stop was Bernstein's office. Even though the two had been working together for almost five years, this was the first time he'd entered the R&D corner office housing the much-heralded aquatic display. He knocked to announce his arrival.

"Come in," called Bernstein. "C'mon over here for a closer look and I'll introduce you to my little pets. If you stand right close to the Plexiglas, the little darlings will float toward you."

Daniels did as suggested and slowly four ghostly bodies moved toward their perceived prey. Even with Plexiglas guarding him, Daniels felt threatened by the floating creatures and backed away. Suddenly overcome by an eerie sensation, Daniels broke into a cold sweat and he could swear that the creatures developed eyes that were staring at him as they moved closer. He bumped into a table where several Petri dishes marched in a row, all containing slimy material and Bernstein's voice brought him out of his trance.

"Be careful! You don't want to get any of that gelatinous ooze on your body – it might be a tad painful." Bernstein grinned. He obviously was enjoying the discomfort Daniels was experiencing.

"What the hell are you doing? This isn't a lab, it's a frigging office, for God's sake!" Daniels abruptly plopped in a chair on the opposite side of the room. Bernstein launched into his canned lecture as if speaking to a total idiot.

"As you know, SRD 0011 was harvested from toxin secreted by the cnidocysts of the box jellyfish. From time to time I milk the wonderful product of their biology so my important research in cardiovascular medicine can continue. Of course I extract the material under safe conditions downstairs in my lab, but I need to keep the small sample you see on the table for demonstration purposes."

Bernstein gestured to five containers filled with milky fluid. "I've harvested enough toxins tonight to initiate another clinical trial, all from the little fellow I temporarily relocated in this portable cooler box which functions as an aquarium."

Creepy was the word that crossed Daniel's mind.

"Are you confident you can gain access to Grayhall's office and to the file?" Bernstein asked. "I need to be absolutely sure so I can implement my plan."

"Well, I'll have to undergo great suffering in the buxom arms of Miss Quattro tonight, but will take a bullet for the cause to get the certain key in her purse that will allow me entry. What's in that file that's so damn important to you anyway? "

Bernstein paced the room a few times before settling behind his large desk.

"Next week Grayhall will be presenting at the San Francisco biopharma conference, an extremely important investor event as you know. No doubt he will use the opportunity to describe his plans for the T.V. Neurologicals research pipeline and I'm sure he will announce the demise of SRD 0011.

"I believe I can catch him off-guard by introducing my concept for an improved back-up product to SRD 0011. SRD 0011 is a mixture of two isomers, commonly described as mirror image molecules, and I've succeeded in isolating and separating the active isomer. I believe this approach will enhance the efficacy and safety profile of the product. Grayhall will have no alternative but to put the new molecule back into the research queue and ultimately the focus of research at T.V. Neurologicals will be reinstated."

Bernstein sat back with a proud, satisfied smirk covering his face as if he had discovered the cure for cancer. Daniels was not impressed.

"So, I ask again, why did you insist I gain access to the executive office?" He wasn't sure he really wanted to hear Bernstein's answer. "What is it you have in mind for our good friend?"

Clearly displaying irritation with the question, the researcher began his explanation. "Tim Varter commissioned a study on the single-isomer compound conducted by a fly-by-night company. They erroneously suggested the product had serious toxicology issues and should be buried. To my knowledge, there is only a single copy of the report in existence and it's buried in the executive files in the CEO's office. We must retrieve it before Grayhall has a chance to discover its existence and thus put the kibosh on my research."

Externally one would think from his facial expression that Daniels was impressed with Bernstein's proposal. Years of sales psychology had given him the ability to control his demeanor effectively. Internally, Daniels' guts were twisting into knots and secreting a flood of acid.

This idiot Bernstein was once again completely absorbed in his own research world fuelled totally by his desire to build a reputation as a leading researcher! In Daniels' opinion, the R&D head had no clue what was happening in the real world around him. Bernstein had not come to grips with the market research conducted by Ames indicating there was an uneconomically small unmet need for a product of this nature.

Even if this single isomer was safe and effective, it would likely find little acceptance in the marketplace. Besides, this was a strategy that would have zero benefit for the immediate threat faced by Daniels. Bernstein had conceived his stupid plan with only his salvation in mind. More importantly, it was a strategy that had zero chance of success; the man was an asshole academic who had no concept of how business worked.

A thousand thoughts rushed through Daniels' troubled mind. He had to figure out a way to take advantage of Bernstein's single-minded focus. If it meant throwing him under the bus, so be it. Better him than me, he thought.

At that moment Bernstein's cell phone rang and he stepped out of his office to take the call; his iPhone indicated the call originated in Switzerland. A minute later he returned and noticed

Daniels had stepped over to the workbench and was examining the extracted toxin. The sudden interest shown by the sales manager intrigued Bernstein.

"Well, doc, keep working on your idea and I'll do my best to get you that report you so desperately want in your hands. In the meantime, keep your creative brain working on ways we can remove our common problem from the picture."

With that comment Daniels headed out of the office leaving the unsuspecting Bernstein clueless that the biggest threat to his future was not with Jonathan Grayhall, it was with the man who had just left him wondering.

CHAPTER THIRTEEN

Jonathan had a lot to think about as he, Raynard, and a cadre of the finest R&D brains at T.V. Neurologicals boarded the United jet to Washington for discussions concerning the direction and flow of the T.V. Neurologicals pharmaceutical pipeline.

The FDA perspective was simple. Review analysts wanted to see a drug demonstrate efficacy in the targeted medical condition and determine if any potential side effects outweighed the drug's benefit to the patient. Frequently, the terms "primary and secondary endpoints" would come up. A simplistic lay interpretation would be that a primary endpoint was the targeted objective and the secondary endpoint was an objective of lesser importance or even an unexpected outcome uncovered.

FDA meetings could mean life or death for a company. Navigating the bureaucratic maze demanded a unique understanding of the psyche and motivation not only of the huge governmental agency's regulatory guidelines, but also of the lead reviewer. A difficult reviewer could cost a company billions in lost revenue if he or she did not find a drug's efficacy and safety evidence compelling. Certain reviewers had become legends and graced the unofficial "Hall of Blame" for the termination of several company research careers.

Jonathan had participated in several of T.V. Neurologicals rehearsals and was not pleased with Bernstein's performance. It was evident the researcher continued to display a bias for his pet project SRD 0011, in spite of the fact it had become clear the future of the company lay with SRD 6969. Jonathan had not been shy in communicating his vision to the management team and yet Bernstein did not seem to get it.

If they were fortunate, the orphan drug protocol would prove to be clinically effective and would provide additional revenue, but the general consensus was the drug would not be a financial pot of gold.

As the flight attendant announced their departure for Ronald Reagan airport, Jonathan gathered his thoughts and directed his thinking to the more pressing task at hand. He had to make potentially game changing decisions about the company's strategic direction. For the remainder of the flight he closed his eyes and played conflicting scenarios through his mind.

The flight was uneventful except for an inebriated congressman who was trying to grope his young intern. When Jonathan threatened to tie up the overweight asshole and have him locked in the toilet, he came to his senses and aided by a couple more shots of vodka, fell asleep. The airport police came on board and led the disgraced member of Congress away while the jerk pleaded innocence and name-dropped dozens of government bigwigs.

After a short trip form Reagan International, the men gathered in a nondescript meeting room where Raynard and the T.V. Neurologicals team spent over an hour actively discussing the recent clinical results of SRD 0011 with respect to its primary end points. They were trying to determine if the FDA would accept secondary endpoints as sufficient evidence to proceed with the drug's development without having to repeat the first trial. Decoding the jargon, SRD 0011 basically failed to prove what it set out to do. Much to Jonathan's chagrin, Bernstein was attempting to negotiate acceptance of the program without repeating the first trial. The SRD 0011 discussion went pretty much as Jonathan had anticipated; it was not well received.

The second item on the FDA agenda was monumentally important and required presenting the government watchdogs with results of the initial proof of concept study for SRD 6969 in sexual dysfunction. In all his years, Jonathan had never witnessed such a positive reception by FDA reviewers; it left him speechless. He decided the FDA bought the story outright and overselling would not add benefit so he skillfully closed the meeting before the allotted time.

The icing on the cake came when a reviewer caught Jonathan in the hallway and asked when he was coming back with data on the orphan drug. Interest had recently been expressed within the division. This was an unexpected and well-received bonus. A line from a song echoed in his mind, "Now don't feel sad, coz two out of three ain't bad."

The much anticipated FDA meetings over, Raynard Bernstein and Jonathan exited the federal building and slid into the black Carey limo waiting to return them to the airport. The expressions on their faces and obvious body language sent clear signals the mood of the two men was polar opposite.

"So, Raynard, what's your conclusion about the direction of the R&D department following our meeting today?"

Jonathan was afraid he knew how Raynard would answer, but had to give his VP the opportunity to express his views anyway.

Bernstein took a deep breath, put his index finger on his chin as if to signify deep thought and offered, "I thought it went rather well for SRD 0011. We should definitely move forward with the second trial to provide the FDA with the additional data they require."

When the words came out of Raynard's mouth, it was all Jonathan could do to refrain from throwing the man out of the limo onto the busy beltway.

"Raynard, for heaven's sake, the reviewer made it clear the data was not compelling and his words indicated a second trial could *possibly* shed new light, but he was not optimistic." Jonathan had to sit on his hands to keep from slapping the researcher silly.

"You know how expensive such a proposition would be, it would virtually swallow our total research capacity at T.V. Neurologicals. Have you forgotten that just last week at our executive committee meeting Pete Ames did a bang-up job presenting market research that clearly demonstrated a lack of market need for such a compound?

"Conversely, the research commissioned on SRD 6969 was the most exciting I have seen in years. The potential for the product knows no bounds. Where is your head, man?"

Raynard stuttered as he tried to answer before Jonathan could rip into him again.

"You witnessed the reaction of the FDA reviewer to the proof-of-concept presentation on our new product, which I would describe as the most enthusiastic I have seen in all my years in the pharmaceutical industry. Did you not hear his reference of a possible expedited review for SRD 6969 and do you not understand what that would do to our stock price?

"I'm already getting calls from brokerage houses asking about our 'female Viagra®.' It seems word is getting out via both research doctors and advocacy groups hearing from patients in trials experiencing the positive side effects from taking SRD 6969."

Jonathan had to catch himself before he went totally berserk and struck the idiot sitting next to him. That would surely result in an HR lawsuit of enormous proportions. Bernstein looked like he was close to having a stroke. Probably nobody had ever spoken to him in such a way during his decades in the business.

"By the way, I don't ever want to be surprised in front of the agency like you pulled off today. That stunt of introducing the single isomer as a better path for your pet drug's development was totally inappropriate. I will have your ass as grass if you so much as think about taking such action again without informing me.

"And one more thing. Know I am fully aware of your lack of control over the trial budget. Hopper informed me of an additional spend of $50 million with a contract research agency which you neglected to mention to me. I need you to take the necessary steps to shut down all activity surrounding SRD 0011. I will prepare statements for the financial community, but you also need to understand this change of course is significant insider information and we are prevented by law from prematurely discussing such information or engaging in any market trades of the stock."

Jonathan stopped before his fists would fly. He turned his head and looked out the window for the remainder of the drive to the airport. Dr. Raynard Bernstein was apoplectic.

How dare this commercial upstart speak to me in this manner! He wants to take away my opportunity to go down in history with the discovery of a breakthrough compound. This jackass wants my Nobel Prize!

Bernstein had never seen his boss so worked up and sensed unbearable tension creep through the limo's interior. A twitch of tightening in his chest quickly caught his attention. There, he felt it again! That sudden squeezing sensation he first experienced several days before after Daniels left his office so abruptly.

That day he could only account for four toxin-filled containers, but was absolutely positive he had harvested five. For the life of him he couldn't figure it out, but even more alarming was he couldn't locate his portable aquarium which housed one of his babies. Daniels was surely not so reckless to have absconded with his specimen. Or was he? The unrelenting twitch in his chest was scaring the shit out of him. It was probably nothing to be concerned about, but he made a mental note to pay a visit to his internist for a complete check-up.

As he searched out the limo window, Jonathan's thoughts moved to another pressing matter that had to be faced. At the beginning of each year, T.V. Neurologicals investors met in San Francisco. If he could inform his eager audience that the company was on the fast track to the approval of SRD 6969, it would have a positive impact on the stock price and Jonathan's degrees of freedom to operate the company as he saw fit.

CHAPTER FOURTEEN

Come the first of every year, the San Francisco Bay Area Biopharmaceutical Kick-off took place at the Fairmont Hotel. Financial wheeling and dealing was in full force during four days of condensed presentations, meetings, and no-calories-spared dinners. Four full days of energy and fuel started the New Year right.

Typically a leading investment bank sponsored the blue ribbon event with much at stake for up and coming companies seeking capital or strategic relationships. Many fed their voracious cash flow needs by hatching deals during the annual conference. Attendance was by invitation only, and was a highly desired and coveted summons for those involved in the industry. The kick-off was the ultimate place to be seen and press the flesh.

It was Monday morning of "Bank Week" as Jonathan liked to call the business extravaganza. Stoked and wound tighter than an eight-day clock, he'd freed his morning to prepare for the afternoon presentation he'd been asked to give. The importance awarded to the T.V. Neurologicals song and dance routine was evident as at the last minute Jonathan's presentation was moved to a larger meeting room one floor up due to heavy interest in the company's product pipeline.

A creature of habit, Jonathan stopped at Starbucks to pick up a latte on his way to the office. One of the first to enter the employee parking lot, he was early enough to find a parking spot close to the building's entrance. Jonathan was dead set against special executive parking privileges, believing all employees should have equal opportunity to park in a convenient location, the best spots available to those arriving early.

He swiped his ID card and entered the far side door and bounded up to his office. As he breezed past Susie Quattro he ordered, "No visitors this morning, Susie! I need to concentrate on polishing my presentation and preparing for the meeting in the city this afternoon."

Ritually, Jonathan removed his jacket, tossed it at the chrome coat rack, settled comfortably in his leather desk chair, and finally stretched his hands around his knees in mock Final Four fashion readying to sink a round of Nerf free throws.

His typical routine did not allow him to quit until he sank ten in a row. On this lucky morning, his first ten shots were nothing but net. That exercise behind him and hoping it was a sign of good things to come, Jonathan got down to business and began to review for what could possibly be the most important presentation of his career.

Most presentations by his fellow CEOs were downright dull and boring. Fortunately, Ames and Hopper lent their creativity and expertise to put together an amazingly zippy slideshow, incorporating a few of Tim Varter's words of wisdom.

After a few hours of review, Jonathan was confident and ready to go even though it was still early. He always enjoyed trolling the hotel lobby before a conference to see whom he might recognize and to mine veins of scuttlebutt.

Two major roads led from the Valley to San Francisco. This day Jonathan chose to maneuver his Audi along the more scenic Highway 280 and took a chance testing the car's magnificent acceleration on one of the straights. When the turbochargers kicked in, his body pressed heavily into the contoured seat and he felt a strong adrenalin rush. At 110 mph he thought it might be time to slow down to avoid pressing his luck with the California Highway Patrol. It was a relatively easy ride into the city this time of day; there was not a cloud in the sky, very untypical for San Francisco. After parking his car beneath Union Square, it took just a few steps to reach the wide welcoming entrance of the old hotel.

Invitations were required to be presented to one of several security guards working the event, but Jonathan had forgotten about this roadblock. After fumbling through his pockets he eventually found the coveted ivory card at the bottom of his briefcase. A quick flash and he was in like Flint. Lunchtime was fast approaching, but the turmoil tumbling inside his gut sapped any appetite Jonathan could muster. The CEO found a seat at a small table in the crowded hotel lobby where he could transfuse more coffee. The coffee was hearty and strong and seemed to accentuate the key points in his presentation. He was distracted when he noticed a shadow creep over the table.

"Excuse me, the lobby is pretty crowded and you have an extra chair. May I join you? My feet are killing me!" There stood a stunningly attractive woman with beautiful expressive eyes. Jumping to his feet, Jonathan pulled out the chair for her and beckoned the waiter for more coffee.

"By all means, this chair has your name on it and I was holding it until you arrived. You realize I had to fight off several Liberian bankers, but now I see I put my life on the line for good reason."

The lady laughed and Jonathan was relieved his attempt at humor wasn't too corny.

"How fortunate I should meet such a chivalrous gentleman in the midst of this dangerous setting. I thank you, kind sir."

The fact that the woman was gorgeous and held the attention of every man in the lobby did not go unnoticed by Jonathan. She was wearing an emerald business suit with a lacey white blouse peeking under the jacket. Navy pumps highlighted a long pair of legs. Her hair was worn in a style he had seen on top models, short and combed artfully to one side. As if she didn't have enough stopping power, her hair was a halo of shiny, fiery red. Very attractive, but somehow she didn't strike him as the banker type.

"Having you join me has certainly brightened my day. To what event or person do I owe my thanks for bringing you here?"

Jonathan had not felt such a strong first connection with any woman since his wife died, even though there had been no shortage of beautiful women trying to land the eligible widower. She studied her tablemate flirtatiously; chemistry was definitely bubbling.

"Thank you for the compliment. I'm here to listen to a CEO speak. He happens to be the head of the company I work for and I'm interested in what he has to say."

The two locked eyes for what seemed a long time; it was almost comical to watch the fireworks ignite. Eventually the woman broke the silent eye contact with a warm smile.

Lord, she was actually blushing!

"A friend of mine in the home office got me a pass to get into the session. It might sound silly, but I want to see and hear first-hand the caliber of the man who's leading my company."

"And which company will the lucky man represent to this most distinguished audience in San Francisco?" Jonathan teased. He was actually quite impressed by the young woman's determination to hear what her leader had to say.

"His name is Jonathan Grayhall and the company is T.V. Neurologicals, a small company located in Mountain View."

Jonathan coughed and almost choked on his coffee, but managed to contain himself. He quickly decided to remain anonymous, at least for the time being.

"So tell me, you seem to be a bright, successful participant in the drug industry, what do you want to see in the leadership direction set by your CEO?"

As they sipped their coffees, the young beauty rattled on about the importance she placed on industry values in a business charged with the wellbeing of the sick and suffering. She confided she felt integrity was paramount when dealing with people's lives and stressed the importance of pharmaceutical research, which was what had attracted her to her career choice.

Curious how she might handle current criticisms of the industry, Jonathan asked her opinion of the alleged wrongdoings reported by the media. Careful to avoid specifics, the woman spoke of concerns she had about temptations surrounding off-label promotion and the foolishness of creating homemade presentations. For ten minutes Jonathan listened to her eloquently offered opinions and when he was sure she'd finished, he took his turn to address the issues.

One issue at a time, Jonathan described where he stood on values in the industry and what steps he would take to correct apparent misbehavior or misappropriations. He went into great detail about the role of compliance and the need for CEO support. He placed high importance on separating a company's drug research and sales interactions with prescribing physicians.

Clearly this man was a corporate leader, Jacki thought. She listened carefully, eagerly taking in all this good-looking stranger was saying and couldn't believe how much he mirrored her own views. She was absolutely convinced his man was intelligent, had vision and leadership, and damn if he wasn't handsome as sin! She wondered which company was lucky to have him on board and wished she could attend that presentation. She would gladly skip the T.V. Neurologicals session to listen to this man speak and was about to ask his name when the conversation was interrupted. A VIP host from the sponsor bank whose image was plastered on every poster in the hotel tapped Jonathan on the shoulder and announced, "Fifteen minutes to show time, Mr. Grayhall."

A blank look fell over Jacki's face as she processed what she had just heard. Realization hit when she recognized the name and now understood whom she'd been chatting with for the last hour. Her face flushed with anger at the seeming deception, but mostly she felt excited and pleased she'd shared coffee with the company boss. Mr. Grayhall was everything she expected in a corporate leader, and geez, he was charming as all get out!

Before she could say a word, Jonathan smiled and admitted, "Yes, I'm the guy holding responsibility for your company and I must say, I really enjoyed our time together. Hearing your passion is refreshing. I promise you won't be sorry to be an employee of T.V. Neurologicals. As much as I would love to continue our conversation, I have another engagement I can't miss.

"I assure you I am never this forward, but I am going to break the mold by asking you to spend time with me this Saturday. Would that work for you?"

There was no way Jacki was going to pass on such an opportunity, but she had promised her brother she would join him on his boat over the weekend.

"I'm so sorry, but I promised my brother I would spend Saturday with him."

The disappointment on Jonathan's face was evident and so sincere that Jacki felt terrible refusing him.

"But, my brother asked me to bring a friend along so maybe you'd like to join us on the Bay to watch the planes perform for Fleet Week." Jonathan's face lit up like middle school kid when favored with a smile from the cutest girl in the class.

"That's the best offer I've had in years! Yes, I would love to join you. In fact, you made my day." The two exchanged cards and phone numbers. Jacki left him with her "special look" and added, "Break a leg this afternoon. I'll be cheering for you."

A boyish grin swept across Jonathan's face. As he dashed into the crowd he shouted over his shoulder, "With you on my side, I'm already a winner!"

The presentation room was up several floors and Jonathan took the stairs two at a time with a bounce in his step. He was definitely feeling energized by the conversation he'd just had with the stunning woman who worked for him. "Jacki," he murmured. Saturday could not come fast enough.

A packed, standing room only ballroom greeted Jonathan as he entered through the side door. People were actually standing six deep in the doorways. He guessed he would have a very receptive audience to hear his pitch. He took a chair on the far side of the stage and as he shuffled his notes, saw Jacki walk to a seat in the middle of the second row where she had placed her coat earlier.

"Time to focus," he told himself as he pictured his presentation like a shotgun loaded with double shells, each containing heavy gauge ammunition.

CHAPTER FIFTEEN

The eager young host investment banker walked to the podium and reviewed Jonathan's CV for the audience. He then invited the CEO of T.V. Neurologicals to take the stand.

Jonathan stood and calmly took the several steps to reach the microphone. He looked over the audience appreciatively and smiled. Over the years he'd learned it never hurts to smile, even when faced with a hostile crowd.

Sitting smack in the front row were Ames and Hopper ready to lend moral support. Behind his two old friends was his knockout new friend. He smiled at her causing Ames and Hopper to turn in their seats to find the target of Jonathan's unexpected glance. When they saw Jacki they gave Jonathan a poorly hidden thumbs-up, which caused him to blush in front of God and everybody. His two lieutenants were brilliant, but behaved like high school nerds sometimes. That was one of the reasons Jonathan was so fond of them.

The T.V. Neurologicals CEO took a deep breath and clicked the first slide.

It never ceased to amaze him how many bankers were young enough to be his progeny. The influence they carried with so few years under their collective belts was surprising if not shocking. Nearly all had MBAs or MDs and it could be unnerving to have baby-faced analysts pose a slew of penetrating questions.

Deep in the audience were faces he recognized. There was a mass of CEOs from leading companies shopping for acquisitions. Dealmakers from investment banking and venture capital firms hailing from Sand Hill Road wore their usual predatory faces. The ever present cadre of financial analysts, many fresh from B Schools, presented the front flank along with the more seasoned veterans. Completing the mix were a few hundred representatives from all walks of the biopharma industry.

Like the majority of conference presentations, the first matter Jonathan covered was the current financial performance of the company. When the numbers spoke, the audience listened since the impressive figures shouted good news. He was off to a great start by declaring Czuretrin showed strong gains in market share while providing the current consensus that the company would exceed analyst expectations for the year. *Bang!* Jonathan pulled the trigger on the first of his shotgun shells.

The scene was set to fire the second shell, a review of the research pipeline with special focus on the developments relating to the potential blockbuster SRD 6969.

Jonathan was a master at captivating his audience and soon had the most cynical, critical crowd of analysts hanging on his every word. He described positive market research findings, the acceleration of clinical activities, positive proof of concept, and ended with his coup de gras - the FDA had spoken in terms of moving on the fast track. Those two words, fast track, had a captivating effect on the entire room. There was barely any thought given to the news that the SRD 0011 trials had been shut down.

Analysts had come to the same conclusion that Jonathan had, the market need for SRD 0011 was not sufficient to justify further investment. As for the orphan drug, it stimulated some interest but clearly the blockbuster potential of a drug that enhanced female sexuality was enormous and overshadowed everything else.

The T.V. Neurologicals presentation went on for twenty minutes followed by ten minutes of Q&A, most of which focused on SRD 6969. Jonathan was pleased with the way things had gone, but one troubling question asked by a young Asian who looked like he had just graduated from high school bothered him.

"Mr. Grayhall, there appears to be considerable juggling of existing assets and no new products have really been added to your pipeline stream. I am reminded of the pea hidden under a shell in the old sleight of hand game." The young man was trying to get a rise from Jonathan but the seasoned CEO wasn't going to take the bait. He shot back quickly.

"The strategic repositioning of the T.V. Neurologicals product pipeline is constantly under review as new information is learned about our assets. We absolutely need to be sure of what we have on hand before jumping into unexplored and uncharted waters swimming with products which might possibly be added to our existing portfolio."

At this point Jonathan clicked his remote to play a ten second video. A carousel of colorful horses pranced to honky tonk melodies. He hoped the colorful metaphor would gain traction with the analytical crowd.

"I often describe the pharmaceutical research done at T.V. Neurologicals as a spinning carousel with horses for the courses. Sometimes the equine figurines are taken off the round platform with a broken part, perhaps a leg or bridle, and replaced with a new beautifully painted creature ready to run for the brass ring.

"Other times a horse might be moved from the less visible inner circle to be placed in a position of greater prominence in the faster spinning outside ring." Jonathan recounted the remaining metaphor much as it had been shared with him at dinner so long ago.

The buzz in the room escalated. The audience was clearly captivated by news of a female Viagra®. This audience saw big dollars coming their way, whether buying, selling, financing, or investing. Nodding heads and wide-eyed looks were telling indicators that Jonathan had scored the winning goal. He was especially aware of several prominent pharmaceutical entourages gathered around their CEOs immersed in heated sideline meetings.

Jonathan continued. "My point is, it is much more profitable to reposition assets a company already owns and has accumulated a deep database assuring validation than it is to go into the market and purchase new assets that are expensive and relatively unknown.

"Of course, this is not always possible and generally goes against the adage that good money shouldn't be thrown after bad, but I marvel at how often I've seen this phenomenon occur in the Valley. Just last year Biomandics in Oakland and Agrathapore in Santa Clara had great success using this strategy. Plenty of money was returned to their investors."

As he searched the faces in the audience, Jonathan could tell they bought the rationale for his research pipeline strategy. His allotted time was over, but a significant gathering was waiting with more questions. All were ushered to an adjacent room so the next presenter could prepare for his trial by fire.

Pandemonium reigned in the smaller anteroom. Everybody wanted a piece of Jonathan - bankers, media, and job seekers. What really grabbed his attention were the half-dozen CEOs from the most prestigious pharma companies taking the time to congratulate him on the job he was doing at T.V. Neurologicals. Many asked for meetings to discuss alliance possibilities.

"Alliance possibilities" was the polite way of saying, "We're interested in buying your company!"

Selling T.V. Neurologicals had not been a consideration when Jonathan first signed on as CEO. "Go it alone and build a bigger, stronger company" had always been his vision. But, the situation had changed and it might be time to give this alternate approach its due. The young Asian analyst who looked like a high school student once again asked an insightful question.

"How does T.V. Neurologicals intend to fund the launch of this blockbuster potential in a therapeutic area not served by the company's sales force?"

Without blinking an eye Jonathan gave his response.

"Mr. Kirpalani raises a valid point and I suspect he knows we are blessed with multiple options involving financing a product launch of this stature. There is always the self-financing option which strong sales of Czuretrin makes attractive. But, what Mr. Kirpalani really wants to know is, would I consider discussions with other companies? It was almost as if a lightning bolt had sent a shock through very chair in the room as the audience strained to hear Jonathan's next words.

"My answer is that I will take whichever strategic option gives SRD 6969 the support to achieve its full potential. Mr. Kirpalani, just so that I am clear, I believe that potential is on the far side of huge." A muffled roar swept the room and even the young analyst had to smile.

With this comment, Jonathan opened Pandora's box. He was willing to consider all options and this news sent the room into a flurried frenzy.

It was a successful afternoon presentation by any standard. Most would have called it a day at that point and basked in the glory of the moment. But not Jonathan. There were several workshop sessions he wanted to attend. The omnipresence of *qui tam* lawsuits at all levels of the industry was the theme in many of the sessions. By the end of the long afternoon, Jonathan came to the conclusion it was not a question of *will* there be a T.V. Neurologicals suit filed, but rather the question would beg *when* will the bomb hit and what can we do to minimize the threat such charges would bring.

Conference evenings offered opportunities for banks and larger venture capital firms to entertain and network handsomely. Every banker jockeyed to get the next hot prospect to attend his dinner or cocktail party and number one on the dance card was the T.V. Neurologicals CEO. Jonathan's exciting and innovative presentation was the topic at every social gathering. Big money generally came with mergers and acquisitions and T.V. Neurologicals was now well positioned in the game.

Jonathan could have been surrounded by eager investors until the wee hours of the morning but instead he elected to make a few appearances at carefully selected functions and then call it an early evening. Better to keep the T.V. Neurologicals suitors eager for more than hang around too long.

Besides, it had been a long time since he'd felt warm feelings for a woman and he wanted to think about that. His chat with Jacki had kindled something he'd been missing for a long while. He wanted to be in good form on Saturday for the boat cruise around San Francisco Bay. Surprisingly, the accomplished CEO actually felt a little nervous like a high school kid going on his first date.

CHAPTER SIXTEEN

It had been twelve months since Jonathan first arrived in San Jose. Twelve months! Plenty had come to term for the company over the short period of time. Surprisingly, Jonathan found his social life was moving along just fine and he was finally emerging from the dark catacombs that held him captive after Tina's death.

Looking back, Jonathan wondered how he ever brought himself to leave this paradise called Northern California so many years before. Yes, the cost of living was exorbitant and housing prices ungodly, but to offset these complaints was the promise of California weather which was often called boringly beautiful. There was an endless string of things to do, places to visit, and exquisite food to enjoy. Because of his grueling work schedule, Jonathan had to pick and choose which delights he would sample. At the top of his list were compulsory visits to Carmel and Monterey and jaunts to the wine country of Napa and Sonoma.

In the more immediate locale, his favorites included weekend ferry rides to Tiburon and lunch at Guayma's, one of the many fine restaurants along the wharf. Equally enjoyable was time spent on sunny weekends in Sausalito highlighted by a fantastic breakfast at the Lighthouse followed hours later by a waterside lunch at The Trident which boasted some of the finest abalone eaten by man.

But today was special. Today he was looking forward to the boat ride on the bay. When he arrived at the appointed slip along Fisherman's Wharf, his eyes searched for one of the ubiquitous motorized launches. Instead, moored before him was a handsome tugboat that was beautifully maintained. A Matt Damon look-alike wearing a captain's cap jumped onto the wooden dock and shook Jonathan's hand warmly.

"Hey, you must be Jonathan. My big sister told me all about you. My name is Louis, but most people call me Ravi. Welcome aboard the Cadillac of tugboats, I call her Jacqueline."

It was one of those rare times when two people immediately recognize a solid new friendship had been established as Ravi began to describe the history of tugboats in the San Francisco Bay.

Jonathan climbed aboard and promptly almost fell overboard when Jacki appeared from below deck looking absolutely stunning in a flowing white jumpsuit. The fact she had literally almost knocked him overboard was not lost on all who witnessed the incident and was the source of jovial conversation for the next hour.

Jonathan was surprised to learn Jacki's brother owned a tugboat, a vessel he'd never boarded before. He knew this was going to be an exceptionally great day on the water, especially because the lady with fiery auburn hair was with him. Sipping wine while gentle swells lapped against the tug's hull was mesmerizing, topped by watching dozens of aircraft fly overhead with the Blue Angels as the sky's star attraction.

Ravi hired a special caterer for the occasion as he was hosting friends and business associates along with Jonathan. Guests were presented to an outstanding display of Dungeness crab and shellfish scooped from local waters, served with never ending bottles of chilled French champagne and Napa's finest wines.

Without warning, several blue and gold Navy jets teased the waves just a few hundred yards from the tugboat's anchor. Oohs and aahhs roared in chorus as the swooping jets took their bows. As always, Jonathan felt a sense of pride when the pilots' gold helmets zoomed close enough to reflect the sun. He always marveled how the collection of jets could hold such perfect formations.

The show's grande finale came when one of the jets flew through the Golden Gate Bridge, just feet above commuter traffic busily weaving below. As heads panned 180 degrees to follow the flight of the Navy hotshot, Jonathan's eyes swept across Jacki's face. She was not looking at the jet's final maneuver either; she was looking at him with a smile that brought a shiver.

As the day was drawing to an end, Jonathan couldn't remember when he had last felt so happy and content.

"Jacki, I can't recall having a more enjoyable day in the past few years. Thank you so much for inviting me to join you and your brother on this incredible tugboat. What a wonderful experience!" As he spoke, Jonathan found himself unable to take his eyes from hers.

"I'm so happy you're having a good time. And, I'm really glad the Bay is so calm today." Jacki continued, "I have to tell you, I was dreading the possibility of rough water which would have put a completely different complexion on the afternoon – one with a sick green tint! A dozen men and women heaving over the side of a tugboat is not a pretty sight."

She giggled nervously. A date with her handsome CEO was not an everyday occasion for her. She tried to direct the conversation to a bit of local lore.

"You know, there have been many stories of prisoners attempting to swim to freedom from the island prison of Alcatraz, only to meet a watery grave in these turbulent waters."

As casual as she was trying to be, Jacki was aware of the impact she was having on Mr. Jonathan Grayhall. She knew because she was feeling the same way. Dozens of men had hit on her over the years, but none caught her attention, except this one. There was something about Jonathan's manner she found captivating.

She also realized they both had to tread carefully if this relationship was to grow. Being a subordinate report in the T.V. Neurologicals business setting, a nest of complications could develop that would be as volatile as a case of nitroglycerine.

It had been a perfect day in San Francisco. Uncharacteristically calm seas seared by the Blue Angels' sky high acrobatics painted a glorious picture against the San Francisco skyline and the island of Alcatraz.

Nothing had been planned after the tugboat cruise, so Jacki suggested a visit to Chinatown where she knew an authentic Chinese restaurant patronized exclusively by locals.

It was an innocuous hole-in-the-wall place called Hunan Homes with a preponderance of Asian clientele. Newspapers served as coverings over well worn Formica tables. Both were very good signs that the patrons were culinary knowledgeable and of Chinese heritage.

The pair enjoyed an exquisite, spicy dinner for the princely sum of $65. As the evening wore on, something special was developing in the new relationship. Close to midnight, Jonathan drove Jacki to her brother's apartment on Nob Hill. He didn't want the night to end. As they walked up the stairs to the front door, the heavens opened and raindrops sprinkled over them. Jonathan took off his raincoat and draped it over Jacki's shoulders.

Jacki's brother seemed like a decent guy and the two hit it off famously. In the course of their conversations he had mentioned after the Bay cruise he was taking the tugboat down the coast to Monterey so Jacki would have the Nob Hill apartment to herself. At the time Jonathan wondered if Ravi was trying to tell him something. He had to remind himself Jacki was his employee and he needed to keep his behavior gentlemanly. As they reached the top of the stairs he realized he really hated the thought of leaving her.

"Jacki, you must know I had a wonderful time with you today. You're a very special lady and I enjoyed every minute we spent together. I don't want to do or say anything to spoil such a magical day, so I better just thank you for a wonderful time and say good-night."

"That's it?" she squeaked. "Seriously, Jonathan, you're the best thing to happen to T.V. Neurologicals and I'm so glad you came into my life. But, wow, you really don't know the first thing about women!"

Before he knew what was happening she planted her soft, moist lips on his with incredible sensuality. She sweetly smiled and said, "Good night" and then closed the door.

Inside Jacki stood with her back pressed against the door. A goofy smile plastered her face as she considered how fantastic this man was who had wandered into her life in such a serendipitous way. When they reached that top step, it was all she could do to stop herself from grabbing him by the shirt, pulling him into the apartment, and taking straight to the bedroom. She secretly hoped the day might end with her feeling this way. She wondered if Jonathan might be playing with her, but blew that idea away fast.

Jonathan staggered down the steps and almost tripped because his legs felt like mounds of Jell-O. What just happened? He was experiencing a flood of emotions ranging from excitement and attraction to sheer panic when he realized Jacki was only visiting San Francisco. He absolutely could not lose her, but how could he keep her here?

He would have to think of ways to make this relationship work. It was only a brief kiss, but what an experience! He hoped he was reading Jacki correctly and her feelings really echoed his. If they didn't and she was only being friendly, or worse felt pressured to be with him because he was her CEO… well, crap, that would be awful!

As he reached his car, Jonathan realized Jacki hadn't taken off his raincoat and it was now in the apartment. His wallet and keys were in the front pocket and he could go nowhere without them.

Damn! He had no choice but to go back and get the coat. Up the steps once again. He knocked on the door and there she was. They looked awkwardly at each other before Jonathan started to speak. The gorgeous redhead stopped him dead in his tracks.

"Oh, shut up, Jonathan!" She threw her arms around him and kissed him deeply as she pulled him inside and silently led him upstairs. If he had taken the time to look, he would have found his raincoat already hanging in the hall closet. Jacki had no intention of returning it that evening. Their relationship was moving at lightning speed, faster than either could have imagined.

Jacki led him to the bedroom where she had a fragrant candle burning and soft music playing. With great tenderness they undressed each other and slid under the covers. Their lovemaking was incredibly passionate and urgent. Jonathan's head was spinning at this remarkable turn of events. It had been a long time since Tina had died and he felt certain his first lady love would have approved of this new woman in his life.

Jacki moaned softly as her lover entered her. She wrapped her legs tightly around him, never wanting him to leave her embrace. She was so feminine, so loving, and moved her hips in ways he'd never experienced with sensations that drove him crazy.

Then suddenly she started to cry. Alarmed that he had done something wrong or hurt her, she was quick to reassure him. "These are tears of happiness. I was beginning to think there would never be anyone in my life to curl my toes the way you do." Jonathan smiled and pulled her to him.

"I guess we're a perfect match because you're my first in the years since I lost my wife. Until today I simply could not comprehend being with another woman."

Words were lost as the pair coupled frantically until a harmonious crescendo was reached by both.

The next morning they showered together, playing and laughing under the pulsating streams of water. Laughter gave away to passion as they playfully made love once more before toweling off and getting dressed. They kissed at the door, eyes searching for confirmation of what they were feeling.

Jonathan retrieved his raincoat from the hall closet and was about to ask how she could have hung it up without noticing the noisy keys clanking in the pocket. Of course she'd heard them rattle; she had every intention of keeping him for the night. The keys were a convenient catalyst to make things happen.

"I don't want to leave, but we both know I have to go. It was a wonderful evening and you are absolutely incredible." Jonathan kissed Jacki softly and skipped down the steps to his car.

As he approached the Audi, he spotted a parking ticket under the left windshield wiper. Usually the only ticket that could infuriate him more than a speeding violation was a parking ticket, but this morning he could only smile as he pocketed the flimsy pink paper and drove off.

CHAPTER SEVENTEEN

Mildred

S everal months passed since the initiation of the SRD 6969 clinical trial. Life continued to be better than grand for Mildred
and Harry. Mildred joined the longer-term trial designed to mea-
sure the indication of sexual enhancement in women. It was more
exciting than the first study which only targeted restless legs. That
problem had long flown out the window. Mildred and Harry were
still thrilled with the honeymoon urgent sex that was rekindled
after Mildred started taking the daily drug.

Truth be told, intimate activity had slowed somewhat compared
to the initial rush Mildred had experienced after first taking SRD
6969. The happy couple was definitely more sexually active than
before the start of the trial, but just like their first honeymoon,
urgency ebbed as time passed.

Dr. Rivers wasn't involved with the new trial as T.V. Neurologicals
had abandoned the restless legs indication for SRD 6969 and
was now building a cadre of physician specialties including doctors treating women's issues, including enhancing female sexual

responsiveness. This was not exactly the typical patient seen in a neurologist's office.

Mildred did see Rivers for the wrap-up of the initial restless legs trial when he studiously asked her if she had experienced noticeable side effects. Mildred recalled occasional bouts of somnolence, but couldn't be sure if they were drug-related. Nevertheless, somnolence went into the report as a drug-related side effect forever to be stored in the data banks.

After examining Mildred and listening to her account of drowsiness, notably experienced on an empty stomach, Dr. Rivers decided the simplest remedy would be to take the pill with food. This process when repeated with patients across all trial sites is what formed much of the side-effect profile seen on drug package inserts.

When he finished his formal patient review, Dr. Rivers switched gears to a non-medically related topic and posed a question. "Mildred, do you remember I told you at the beginning of the year that I had never participated in trials for blockbuster drugs? Well, I'm going to amend that statement because from what I've observed, the T.V. Neurologicals drug is as close to being a blockbuster as I have ever seen. What makes this exciting for me is soon after the trial got under way, I purchased several thousand shares of T.V. Neurologicals at $13 and today the stock is trading at more than twice that, a hefty $28 a share!"

Mildred's response took him by surprise.

"Well, isn't that a coincidence, Dr. Rivers! After starting the trial Harry and I had a big disagreement, the first big fight since we've been married. I wanted to take a third of our savings and invest in T.V. Neurologicals stock but he wanted to leave it in interest-bearing notes at a whopping three percent. I stood my ground and as the result we ended up netting about $200,000 when we recently sold the stock for a handsome gain." Mildred's quick and assertive response caught Rivers off guard.

He made a mental note that his once shy patient had seemingly developed a higher level of self-confidence that he found quite refreshing. He also noted the drug might have an effect on brain chemistry, which had been completely unexpected.

"Mildred, forgive me for saying so, but I can't help but notice a level of confidence that's a few notches higher than was evident in our discussions just last year."

Without hesitation Mildred responded with a smile. "Dr. Rivers, Harry tells me I'm a different woman, and it's for the better. I found I could finally believe in myself and the result of that mind change has been very positive, especially concerning our financial portfolio. I told you about my investment in T.V. Neurologicals stock, well. I'm also looking at ways to leverage my experience as a clinical trial participant. You'll be hearing more about my ideas when I finalize discussions with a local venture capitalist firm willing to back my proposal."

"Well, I'll be! This news is certainly quite impressive and I'm pleased SRD 6969 had an unexpected effect on you. This drug just might have the potential to drastically alter the behavior of men and women in our society."

Rivers' thoughts went even further as he considered the wealth of possibilities the breakthrough could bring, even wondering if the drug could have an effect on altering brain chemistry in Alzheimer's patients. He made another mental note to raise the issue at the next T.V. Neurologicals advisory board meeting. Hell, it could mean his fantasy Porsche 911S would be a reality and parked in his garage sooner than expected!

Rivers and his happy patient said goodbye as Mildred thanked the good doctor for the wonderful changes and opportunities he'd brought into her life. They were both confident the simple drug trial demonstrated a unique ability to enhance Mildred's sexual activity, possibly leading to other clinical benefits.

Sally-Anne

There is no drug that can truly claim 100 percent efficacy and 100 percent absence of undesirable side effects caused by taking it. The Zuckermans were initially pleased with the results of SRD 6969; it seemed to boost their sexual activity which was top priority for both.

However, in their zealousness to boost sexual explorations and exploits, the couple failed to notice that over time Sally-Anne had developed a serious problem. Before the trial began, Sally-Anne already enjoyed a healthy sexual appetite. Although not convinced she really had a problem with restless legs, decided to enter the trial, claiming no harm no foul.

After several months on the medication Sally-Anne found her sexual appetite had grown exponentially and was creating major issues for her and her husband. Sally-Anne developed a bizarre craving for sex that was similar to a narcotic junkie searching for the next fix. She found herself needing larger doses of fucking at higher frequency to meet her sexual needs. She was starting to spin out of control as she clamored to feed and satisfy her carnal hunger.

Early on it was easy to find satisfaction with the South American tennis pros at the club who were quite willing to help her out by performing a tandem act. Sally-Anne was convinced the tennis players' eager participation was enhanced by the opportunity for bisexual relations without admitting as such. Along with her increased sexual proclivity, the young woman had developed a devil-may-care brashness that gave her husband Dennis pause for concern as her sexual partners became more reckless, bawdy, and demanding.

It was fortuitous when Dennis caught her in the moment with the tennis jocks, later surprising her with the suggestion that they start an underground "couples' club" in the Villages. This idea provided new outlets for satisfaction and Dennis could choose to participate or hungrily watch, whichever suited his mood.

The Zuckerman's were flabbergasted when their fledgling sex club took off like wildfire. Who would have thought an elderly, white, conservative segment of the population living in Central Florida would rush to join a swingers' club? So great was the intrigue of wanton coupling that it set off a spike in demand for antibiotics to treat a tidal wave of venereal disease, a story that made it to the national news. It didn't take long before things really got out of hand as the swingers became more outrageous. When Villages Security was called to bust a Crisco party of naked seventy-something's performing every sexual act known or imagined in backyard pools, the Zuckerman's were declared persona non grata by the Baptist dominated Property Owners' Association and were asked to leave the community, immediately.

Trial patient data recorded for Sally-Anne was deemed inconclusive regarding the effectiveness of the drug for stimulating sexual demand. Sally-Anne did not complete the study as the preliminary data indicated she already had a voracious appetite for sex far exceeding the norm. This skewed the study as Sally-Anne came with a bias in behavior. The tech who followed Sally-Anne in the study noted in his comments, "No nymphos need apply!"

Old Dennis Zuckerman was smart enough to realize Sally-Anne's sexual activity after ingesting SRD 6969 had far exceeded normal bounds and she had developed a serious problem and needed professional help. It was quite possible there could be a lawsuit in their favor if he could find the right ambulance chaser to prove his wife's aberrant behavior was T.V. Neurologicals drug-related. But, this could be difficult to prove. Secretly, Sally-Anne was convinced the drug did nothing to stimulate her sexual behavior. She knew she was just a hottie.

The couple debated reporting the behavioral side effects to the clinical team, but was hesitant to expose the sordid details of their relationship so they blamed occasional bouts of nausea as the reason Sally-Anne exited the study and so this was entered into the drug file.

After experiencing much harassment, condemnation, and labeled as satanic sinners by local church groups, Dennis and

Sally-Anne decided to move to Las Vegas where they felt their life-style might be more amenable in the faster pace of Glitter City.

Alice

Of all the participants in the clinical trials, the early favorite for the most successful patient outcome would undoubtedly have been Alice.

There had been an incredible transformation in the woman's appearance, self-confidence, and, according to her husband, a substantially increased libido. The development of these attributes led to positive changes in Alice's workplace and helped her land a promotion to an enviable spot on network TV. Only those very close to Alice had noticed changes in her behavior that were not for the better. Casual acquaintances had no idea she had undergone such a tremendous behavioral change.

In recent weeks Alice had become obsessed with her appearance, almost to the level of narcissism. This was manifest by frequent consultations with a battalion of cosmetic surgeons to discuss an abundance of nips and tucks. For an attractive twenty-something woman to be so fixated on cosmetic surgery was plainly ridiculous.

Things had spun so far out of control that her loving but confused husband finally reached his breaking point and moved out of their apartment and was living with a friend. The last time the couple made love Tim caught his wife looking into a hand mirror during the act. He would have appreciated the gesture if watching their passionate performance was a turn-on, but Alice seemed fixated on her face and appeared to be practicing her smile. Along with cosmetic issues, Alice had become an outrageous flirt and exhibitionist and Tim began to suspect she was having an occasional affair.

Both Tim and Jacki agreed SRD 6969 gave a boost to Alice's self-confidence, but the drug also carried baggage loaded with side effects which elicited unusual, almost bizarre, behavior.

The uninvited and unexpected open-mouth kiss that Alice had planted on Jacki in full view of a crowded restaurant was a classic example. The clinical reports were blind so it was not possible to identify data associated with individual trial participants. In her pharmaceutical role, Jacki had access to the overall data bank, but it was not labeled to identify individual participating patients. In her review of the general data contained in routine clinical follow-ups, the abnormal and undesirable behaviors in Alice that had been causing Jacki concern were not yet observed by clinical trial monitors. Jacki felt certain it would only be a matter of time before these behaviors would emerge in the larger trial population and would be recorded in the side-effect profile of the drug.

Once reported, it was very likely sales projections for SRD 6969 would drop accordingly, thereby putting the future of T.V. Neurologicals at risk. Jacki knew how Jonathan lived and breathed T.V. Neurologicals and how much he was counting on SRD 6969 to be his blockbuster drug. If there were serious behavioral issues identified with the drug, there was no telling what that tailspin could do to the company, not to mention the effect it would have on her "future husband." Jacki debated alerting Jonathan to her concerns, fearing how such news might affect him.

CHAPTER EIGHTEEN

Jennifer Wright was saddled in her office reviewing the audit report she had commissioned from a leading consultant in corporate compliance. A whole new industry sector handling compliance related issues had erupted as a result of pharmaceutical companies facing sizable financial risk for questionable corporate practices. Public opinion put wind behind the sails of State Attorney Generals throughout the country, fueling the perception that drug companies had deep pockets and were undoubtedly gouging the public with excessively high prices for prescriptions.

SAG political aspirations were enhanced by taking issue with the reported negative behavior of said money grabbing drug companies. Seldom did federal attorneys lose a case brought by the government in which a whistleblower, usually a one-time employee of the company, offered the SAG office a bundle of sensitive internal information. Whistleblowers faced no consequences if the case fell apart, but stood to reap huge financial returns should the case be won, or even merely settled, by the government. Government stood only to lose time and effort should they lose, but massive fines added to the till should they win. In many cases it was an all around win-win situation to prosecute.

On the whole, T.V. Neurologicals performed its business operations in a responsible fashion. Inevitably there were a few outlier behaviors that hovered outside the acceptable norm, but not many. The consultant's report identified functional areas that needed systems strengthened, but this was not surprising and was, in fact, expected.

Jennifer put the 50-page document face down on her desk and leaned back in her chair. For the most part, the report suggested none of the infractions appeared deliberate or heinous; this was a good sign.

The consultancy engagement designed for T.V. Neurologicals cost in excess of $150,000 for the initial audit report. External consultants serve a useful function because they are expected to be objective and bring a fresh pair of eyes to the exercise. More often than not, a study would uncover problems in areas requiring an extension of service, thus further expanding the fee outlay. The downside to hiring consultants was the heavy expense required to hire expertise from reputable firms. Past experience taught Jennifer that a top consultancy like McKinsey or BCG could demand a fee of well over a million dollars, a figure that would not be acceptable to a company the size of T.V. Neurologicals. She knew she had to develop a creative alternative for handling the most critical issues T.V. Neurologicals faced, but the rest would have to be addressed over time.

Of particular concern to Jennifer was the sheer number of violations that required follow-up, particularly in the field sales and medical departments. She recognized early that the work burden laid out by the report was simply too much for a fully staffed department to handle let alone one person. Jennifer also recognized she didn't have a cache of developed relationships to penetrate those working outside the home office. Field personnel differed in degrees of freedom because they didn't enjoy the face-to-face influence of supervisors on a daily basis. The compliance report indicated a strong need for change in certain potentially dangerous activities promoted by the sales force and medical affairs teams.

Jennifer was drowning in paperwork and putting in an unacceptable number of hours, but it was imperative she stretch the T.V. Neurologicals compliance reach far outside the home office walls.

She had a scheduled appointment with Jonathan later that morning to discuss the developing situation. Approvals for headcount additions that didn't directly increase sales were as rare as braces on hens' teeth, but Jennifer felt she had little choice but to make her request for help known. Jonathan had a reputation for being stingy with department additions so Jennifer knew she had her work cut out for her.

CHAPTER NINETEEN

In the T.V. Neurologicals executive suite Jonathan was crumpled behind his desk, door closed, head in his hands, and taking no calls. If his employees only knew the mood that pervaded their CEO's office they would have been floored. The strong, decisive CEO was visibly distressed and indecisive. Mr. Cool and Controlled in the most stressful business negotiations was a mess. There was only one possible explanation how a man of Jonathan's composure could be reduced to a quivering mass. A woman was at the center of his soul!

It had been two long days since he left Jacki at her brother's apartment in San Francisco. The pain and desire he felt for her were feelings he hadn't experienced in many years. In their short time together, she had become special to him and he was terrified of the possibility she might slip away.

What made the situation more explosive was her status as a T.V. Neurologicals employee – a ticking HR time bomb for sure. Jonathan knew his random concerns were impinging on his ability to function, and with high corporate stakes now on the table, he had to be at his CEO best.

For hours Jonathan had furiously run through all the scenarios, best and worst case, he could imagine, but it was not until he walked to Pete Ames's office and data-dumped the challenge on his irreverent friend that a reasonable solution began to take shape.

"As I see it, the solution is quite simple," Ames announced with a haughty grin. "Shoot yourself, just shoot yourself! Get it over with. *Ha! Ha! Ha!*"

"You dolt! Get serious for once. I really need your help. This woman is someone who's becoming important to me, the first in a long, long time. I find her wonderfully attractive in every way. She's gorgeous, a pure knockout. I'm as sure as I can be, the feeling goes both ways. She's a rare combination of beauty and brains.

"When we chatted about issues faced at T.V. Neurologicals, she had insightful thoughts and I could tell we share similar visions and values. She's the one!"

Jonathan spun around and crashed into the low leather sofa in a corner of Pete's office. He looked more like one of the lost boys than a corporate executive. "Let me cut the crap, I've really fallen for this woman and I don't want her to leave."

"Well, hell, that's it," declared Ames victoriously.

"That's what? What are you talking about?" Jonathan was hopeful that his Boy Genius had conjured up one of his brainstorms.

"I've spent quite a bit of time with your compliance officer recently and it's clear to me the woman desperately needs an assistant to work with the field employees. You know how the outside the office staff generally holds contempt for the home based crowd."

Jonathan smiled; he had forgotten it was Jacki's friend Jennifer who'd made it possible for her to attend the conference. Of course! He could carve out a bulletproof case for Jacki to join the compliance effort. This idea had real potential and he couldn't come up with one reason why it wouldn't work. Jonathan suddenly became like a man who'd discovered a buried bottle of water after being lost in the desert for a week.

"Thanks, bud. I definitely owe you one!" Whoosh, Jonathan was out the door and rushing back to his office leaving Pete leaning back in his chair, both feet up on the messiest desk in the Valley. Pete smiled and was happy for his friend who had finally found someone to heal the hole he had been carrying in his heart for several years.

"Susie, absolutely no visitors and ask Jennifer to come by in one hour."

Not sure how his compliance officer might react to the suggested addition of her friend to her office, Jonathan developed a plan to approach Jennifer. This was a decision that could not be forced; ideally Jennifer would independently come to the conclusion that she needed help. Decision made, Jonathan felt his head clear and his legs return to pillars of bone instead of mountains of mush. He had to resist the urge to beat his chest and bellow . . . "I'm baaaaack!"

The hour passed as Jonathan put his game plan together. He was ready to meet with Jennifer, armed with a stack of reasons the compliance department should expand. Not realizing he would be preaching to the converted, Jonathan wondered how his compliance expert might react.

Finally the knock came. Show time!

"Hi boss, it's Jennifer. I was going to ask you to meet with an old friend of mine who works for T.V. Neurologicals as an MSL, but I think you beat me to the punch."

During the short time the two worked together it was clear Jennifer had developed an excellent rapport with her boss. She felt she could speak openly on any topic without fear of reprisal, but was still unsure what his reaction would be to a headcount addition.

"If it's about your friend Jacki, you're way too late! You are here-by sentenced to thirty lashes for not arranging a more appropriate introduction for such a special lady. Jokes aside, I'm sure you've spoken with her and know we spent a delightful time together in San Francisco over the weekend. I was quite impressed by her un-derstanding of the issues you and I face on the compliance front, and was taken by the corporate integrity that radiates from her."

Radiates from her? Jennifer got the distinct impression Jacki hadn't shared everything there was to know about the weekend. Sensing this might be a good time to hit him up with her request for additional resources, Jennifer launched into her prepared spiel.

"Jonathan, I have plans for the department I would like to review with you. We're accomplishing a great deal at T.V. Neurologicals and are well on our way to meeting your vision of leading the field in positive corporate behavior. I've given it a lot of thought and decided for our goals to be fully met, it will require an additional resource to spend time on field-based issues."

Jennifer began the review of reasons supporting her request for an additional person in the office, but Jonathan interrupted her before a minute passed. With such a quick response, she wor-ried he was going to nix the whole idea before she could present it.

"Before you go any further, let me run something past you, but please know the decision of yea or nay is yours to make. There's no pressure on you at all."

He wondered if Jennifer had any inkling of what he was about to suggest.

Spewing a volcano of words, Jonathan spoke quickly. "What would you think about bringing your friend Jacki into your depart-ment to fill the need you've identified?"

He paused to see if he could read a reaction from Jennifer. "From what I've seen, your friend looks like a pretty good candi-date to give you a helping hand."

Jennifer couldn't believe it! This was not exactly the play she apparently had in mind, but now that it was put on the table she was happily receptive. Jennifer turned her head upward as if she was searching for something high above.

"Well, why not? What a great idea! Jacki would be a tremendous asset and she's certainly well qualified." Jonathan felt a wave of re-lief, his plan had worked!

"It's settled then. Go ahead and work with Rachel to prepare an employment offer and present it to Jacki no later than tomorrow. If you need any help with the offer package or selling the job, let me know and I'll help anyway I can." I love it when a plan comes together, he thought.

Later back in her office, Jennifer pulled her personal iPhone from her purse and dialed a number. The person on the other end picked up and Jennifer smugly said, "Well, it worked like a charm, Jacki! I love it when a plan comes together."

CHAPTER TWENTY

Pharmaceutical entrepreneurs often begin their journeys with visions of building a company which fits the image they hold in their imaginations. If a company manages to carry a product through the FDA process and can successfully commercialize it by building strong sales and marketing teams, there's a good chance the company's stock will appreciate dramatically. Over time significant wealth could accumulate for those holding ownership. In most cases, this is the expected satisfactory financial outcome.

But, there's another route to financial wealth that takes the previously described scenario and puts it on steroids. This situation occurs when wealthy mature companies demonstrate a significant need for new products to add to their portfolios and are willing to pay a significant premium for the product alone, but often will outright buy the entire company.

For a purchase offer to be attractive, a premium over and above current sales must be offered. It is based on the increment believed can be attained in the future if sales and marketing strategies are developed under new guidance. The cost for acquiring companies is never modest and corporate boards often believe they can do better promoting the purchased drug than the company currently owning the rights can do.

Sometimes a company founder doesn't want to release his vision which he often refers to as "my baby." Or perhaps the company owner is genuinely concerned for the well being of the tightly knit staff he's lived with for many years and had proved to be loyal and instrumental in helping achieve the company's success. Despite early reluctance to sell a company, in almost all cases a tipping point is reached at which the owner will cave and become convinced that selling is the best and sometimes only option. Relentless pressure may come from board members "to take the money and run."

When Jonathan first came to T.V. Neurologicals, it was not in his vocabulary to put the company on the block for selling. His goal was to continue the successful growth of Czuretrin, develop attractive drugs to add to the pipeline, and license-in products from other companies. He knew SRD 6969 was potentially a big win for the company, but had not expected the overwhelming attention expressed by several of the larger pharmaceutical companies that seemed to be interested in the outright purchase of T.V. Neurologicals.

Ten days had passed since Jonathan presented at the January conference and already three companies were camped on their Mountain View site conducting due diligence on T.V. Neurologicals. They were all considering what could be offered as the price to acquire.

Each visiting company dispatched a team of corporate investigators who stationed themselves in conference rooms, known as War Rooms. Jonathan had the responsibility to provide all suitors with whatever documents or information requested. This only happened after a team of T.V. Neurologicals lawyers created iron-clad confidentiality documents.

Hosting the visitors was a draining experience spent answering an inordinate number of questions all day, followed by long evenings spent charming corporate suitors over lavish offerings of food and wine. The whole process had the elements of a romantic courtship; the trick was to remain "unscrewed" until rings were exchanged. Carrying endless piles of documents to a War Room was like laying a dowry of treasures at the foot of the groom to determine if the bride was attractive or worthy enough to seal the nuptial ceremony.

Running a business under such intense conditions could be extremely taxing so Jonathan decided on a relaxing location to review any pending situations with his two trusted lieutenants.   The three were sitting around a wrought iron table on the patio of the Sharon Heights Golf Club after playing an enjoyable 18 holes. The day was especially happy for Jonathan – he was the one who pocketed the princely sum of $20 equally offered between Ames and Hopper. Those two were now grousing about being duped by unfair handicapping. They were also joshing and complaining about insufficient stroke counts.

Ames whined as he held out his hand to show a small puncture in his palm received after a wild drive when he lost his balance, sending his feet flying before he landed hand-first onto the sharp tip of his tee. This happened in full view of a foursome waiting to play behind them and only added to Pete's embarrassment as guffaws echoed over the course.

Hopper had additional sums to pay because an errant 5-iron found its way through the rear-window of a big black Cadillac in the parking lot. Only Jonathan had been on his game and suffered nothing en route to a solid round of 80.

"Guys, I'm really glad you had such a miserable time basking in the California sunshine on one of the nicest golf courses in the state. But, hey, I didn't bring you out here just to have fun. I thought the change in environment might stimulate good thinking."

Ames and Hopper got the message and quit horsing around; it was time to talk business.

"You know, selling the company was not on my agenda when I recruited you to join me. My goal was for organic growth from existing and new products aided by additional drugs through research and development. But, as you know, attractive possibilities have surfaced."

It was Hopper who first jumped into the conversation, clearly excited about what he had to say. "Jonathan, since you spoke at the conference, our stock has shot up to $28 as the word on the street is to expect an acquisition by one of the deep-pocket drug biggies." He stopped speaking when the waitress arrived to see how they were doing in the drink department.

"Three more Dos Equis por favor, young lady," issued the order from Ames. Jonathan raised his eyebrows. They had already downed three rounds, and he sensed they were on their way to limo rides home.

"Hell, yes, the stock is up and rightly so. The market lusts for a female version of Viagra®, but don't we all!" The beers came and each took swigs of the refreshing icy brew. "Miss, could you also bring an order of hamburger sliders? Just add it to Mr. Grayhall's tab, he's good for it."

Jonathan shook his head in mock dismay. "How is it that I won the money, but still sense I'm the loser?"

The three friends laughed and swigged another round. "You know, there are several board members who are ecstatic at the prospect of cashing out their investment. In fact, I had a call from one of the original venture capitalists yesterday who told me not to let this opportunity evaporate."

Unfazed by the importance of the VC's request, Ames blurted, "Aw! Fuck'em! If the guy can't take a joke or an occasional poke to his pocket, he's an ass. On the other hand, there is the challenge we could face if we go it alone with the launch of SRD 6969.

"Jonathan, you recall the question that baby-face analyst asked in San Francisco? He wondered how a small company like T.V. Neurologicals would have the promotional reach needed to impact the extensive primary care and OB/Gyn audiences for our female product. The kid also asked about our marketing expertise for this particular segment, especially regarding direct to consumer advertising."

Jonathan responded easily. "That snotty-nosed kid asked some very penetrating questions, that's for sure." Some of the same concerns were ones Jonathan had posed to his staff about SRD 0011 and the cardiologist targeted audience when he first joined the company.

With only one product to sell, a new sales force would not be very efficient. Jonathan knew T.V. Neurologicals would likely get involved in co-promotion with another company, often the halfway road to acquisition.

Breaking the conversation, the three were momentarily diverted to the 18th green where a golfer was lining up a birdie putt.

"Two bucks he misses the putt!" whispered Ames.

"You're on," Jonathan accepted.

Hopper shifted in his seat displaying discomfort for what he was about to say. "You marketing types will bet on anything, but let me clue you into reality. Very few drugs in development actually make it to market, roughly one in 10,000. What I find attractive about selling the company is it takes the risk out of our hands. From everything I've read and Jonathan has indicated, one of these days we're going to be paid a visit by the State Attorney General who will most likely bring action against T.V. Neurologicals which could result in a substantial fine. By substantial I mean it would put us in a weak position to launch a new product and we might have to go back on the market, or at least be forced to sell part of the company to raise cash."

After Hopper's pronouncement the silence was deafening, broken only by the soft click when the golfer finally putted. He missed!

"Well, Hopper, you certainly are a bundle of fun and cheer, but I hasten to add you are 100 percent correct to point out these considerations.

"Gents, it's getting late and I believe my limo is waiting and yours will be here shortly. I took the liberty of ordering car service because I knew we would be knocking back a few brews while we discussed the strategic future of our company. I believe we are unanimous in saying the decision to sell is a good one, assuming we get the right price. Once we head down that road, we don't want to veer off track as we all know the market punishes as swiftly as it rewards.

"Good night, guys, see you back at the farm."

"Before we leave, a minute of your attention, please." Hopper clearly had something important he wanted to say.

"That matter of the over-budget research funds. Within a short period of time I feel confident I will have the matter fully analyzed as to where it was spent. My guess is you'll be quite unhappy with how it was spent, but pleased with the leverage it gives you."

Jonathan acknowledged his friend's information with a wry smile.

CHAPTER TWENTY-ONE

The next day Jonathan was back in his role of hosting potential T.V. Neurologicals suitors. After making appropriate welcoming remarks to a delegation from a large French global pharmaceutical company, he set off down the hall to join the staff meeting held in Raynard's office where a group of company scientists were discussing the status of clinical trials underway. Raynard had sent him a note earlier indicating it was essential that Jonathan attend the meeting.

The CEO had already planned to be there since he wanted to be updated on the company's clinical studies. Jonathan didn't want egg on his face when negotiating with CEOs interested in acquiring T.V. Neurologicals to boost their lagging pipelines.

Before joining Raynard, Jonathan stopped by his office to see a VIP who'd been patiently waiting. When he walked through the door, *boing!* It was as if he was a teenage guy again. This was the first time he'd seen Jacki since the morning he left her at her brother's house. She was stunning in a deep purple suit accented with silver buttons and he felt himself flush with excitement just seeing her.

Jacki didn't hesitate when she welcomed her lover. She rushed into his arms, kissing him fully and deeply.

"It's only been three days, but I've missed you terribly!"

Jonathan seized a moment of sanity and slammed his door shut so curious hall wanderers wouldn't see their CEO locked in the arms of this gorgeous woman, an employee at that.

"Me too! Me too!" Was all he could murmur as their bodies passionately responded to the moment.

"Now lady, we have a lot of ground to cover so let's sit down and get to it. I've been waiting for you to come into my life for many years so there's absolutely no way you're going to jump on a plane and fly away. I know everything is happening quickly, but I need you here by my side. That's my story and I'm sticking to it!"

Jacki smiled and tilted her head to one side.

"I don't suppose you had anything to do with a meeting I just had with my friend Jennifer. It seems she feels the need to hire somebody to help her build compliance function in the field and she offered me the position. Isn't that surprising?"

Jonathan feigned shock.

"Well, I'll be damned, amazing how serendipity can strike when needed. So tell me, what do you think? Is this something you'd be willing to take on? I have to tell you, this is not an artificial assignment I conjured up to get you to stay. We have a real an urgent need to buck up our compliance department within the company. Well, what do you think?"

Jacki threw her arms around his neck as her answer.

"Of course, I said yes, you silly man. Sorry, now you're stuck with me!"

For the next fifteen minutes the two excitedly discussed the personal and business agenda that lay ahead. As much as he hated to end his time with Jacki, Jonathan had to head to his next commitment. They agreed to meet after work at his place to go over work plans, fueled by a steak on the grill and a few glasses of wine. Who knows what might follow. Yeah, right.

A text ping alerted Jonathan that Raynard was waiting until he arrived before explaining the status of the most critical studies underway. Jonathan soon joined the clinical update meeting already in progress. Walking into the room, he immediately sensed a strange level of tension, something was definitely off balance.

Oh, crap! What the hell could Dr. Dread be up to now?

Raynard had a funny, weird expression on his face. He almost, but not quite, looked happy. Jonathan had never seen this side of him before. The scientist motioned to Jonathan to take a seat.

"Jonathan, there are developments you should know that bear great relevance to the ongoing discussions you're having with interested T.V. Neurologicals suitors. I suggest we clear the room except for the two of us and Doctors Viviane Anderson and Ross Charming."

Anderson was the physician in charge of SRD 6969 and Charming was responsible for the development of the orphan drug. This was unusual behavior on Raynard's part and probably was the most sensible suggestion to come out of his mouth since Day One.

Jonathan nodded his approval. The tightness in his gut intensified as if it were an omen for bad stuff waiting to happen. As the rest of the research staff shuffled out the door, Raynard carefully reminded the doctors of the need for strictest confidentiality regarding all discussions. He almost threatened them with prosecution if secrets were leaked. That sent Jonathan's stomach into spasms as he tried to imagine what on earth was going on in the R&D department.

"Wait, Raynard, I want to check to see if Ames, Hopper, and Hammer are in the building. I want them to be in on this discussion." Raynard nodded his agreement and dialed his secretary to round up the others immediately at the request of their boss.

Within minutes the three executives filed into the room. Getting the signal from Jonathan, Raynard turned to Viviane and asked her to begin her briefing. Viviane was one of the best researchers in the company, which was why she'd been assigned to the lead product. Her credibility and reputation within the organization and with the general scientific community was excellent and Jonathan placed high value on her opinion. He was definitely interested in what this woman had to say.

"Jonathan, SRD 6969 has been a fascinating project to work on and it has certainly captured the attention of the research community, to say nothing of the investment analysts who know big money is out there for anything affecting female sexual response in any way, shape, or form. We have a number of safeguards in place to keep information confidential, but in light of recent observations made by the clinical team, we thought as CEO you should have a heads-up on the speculation teeming within our group of physician experts.

"Let me cut to the chase and say this. When we finally break the code on the trial, we could find that what we initially thought was sexual arousal impacting the genitourinary system, might in fact be related to actual behavioral changes in the brain."

The blood drained from Jonathan's face as he tried to decode the implications of Viviane's words. Sensing Jonathan's obvious discomfort, Raynard interjected quickly.

"Remember, the information we have at this point is not definitive. It's enough to give us reason to question, but still exceptionally speculative given the stage of our clinical trial process. Having said that, I hasten to add there might be very bright rainbows coming over the mountain."

"Go on, Viviane."

"What Raynard is referring to is the excitement the expert group feels about SRD 6969 exhibiting a mode of action that has never been seen before and could have vitally important implications in psycho-pharmacy, particularly in the treatment of depression.

"As you know, depression is one of the largest pharmaceutical markets where there still remains a significant unmet need."

Jonathan started to regain color in his face as he processed what was being said. Raynard, ass that he was, was clearly enjoying himself as he watched his tormentor suffer.

Ames did not look happy with the trade-off in potential indications. In his mind the sexual arousal indication was dynamite and he would have to look into this behavioral concept further before he saw any good news.

Hopper was banging the keys of the financial model on his laptop in an attempt to quantify the news and its impact on stock price. Hammer was concentrating intently and exploring ways to spin information to investors via the various media relation outlets.

Jonathan stood abruptly and started pacing the room.

"So, let me get this straight. The good news is we may have a drug with a unique mode of action for the treatment of psychological disorders, for which you believe there is a substantial market.

"But the bad news is that after all the excitement generated about SRD 6969 impacting sexual arousal, you are now telling me at this eleventh hour that the activity in this indication may not be as we had hoped? Would someone just shoot me, now!"

Raynard smiled like Alice in Wonderland's Cheshire cat and impatiently gestured for Jonathan to retake his seat.

"Jonathan, please remember, this is still very speculative information and we're simply bringing it to your attention so you won't be blindsided with a question from a young Turk doing diligence for his company if he happens to come across information that supports what we are discussing.

"On a positive note, there is the potential for the drug to move into a highly attractive and active field rather than be discarded. I believe you actually discussed this phenomenon at the San Francisco conference using a horse racing metaphor."

"No! It was a carousel metaphor," shot the terse correction from Jonathan.

"Well, I knew it had something to do with horses," Raynard muttered. He was clearly enjoying seeing his CEO sweat.

"Wait! There's more news to add and it's a blockbuster. It may even help turn lemons into lemonade, as the saying goes. Ross, why don't you tell Mr. Grayhall about the exciting developments with the drug you've been shepherding?"

"Delighted to do so, Raynard. Jonathan, I think you'll be very pleased to hear what I have to say as it has the potential to be bigger than anything else we've seen so far."

Ames, Hooper, and Hammer perked up with this promising introduction.

"The often forgotten third research drug in our pipeline was being developed for a rare disease afflicting a relatively small number of patients, hence the orphan designation.

"Working with a drug like this is morally rewarding, but also akin to working with the ugly stepsister as its financial returns are not usually considered to be attractive. But the worm may have turned.

"About a year ago, we were approached by investigators at M.D. Anderson in Houston and the Cleveland Clinic, two of the nation's leading cancer treatment institutions, as you know. Their researchers had preliminary reports about our orphan and they picked up on the mode of action of the drug that they felt might have implications treating advanced forms of prostate cancer. They have been highly encouraged by what they have seen so far in their self-funded patient mini-trials and now the National Cancer Institute wants to run a full-blown clinical trial as soon as the usual logistics are completed.

"The NCI feels so strongly about this compound that they are lobbying the FDA to give the drug and its implication their highest priority. The NCI experts are convinced we might be sitting on the most important oncology breakthrough of the decade."

Ross concluded with a self-satisfied smile. Jonathan felt a wave of relief sweep through his body. What had initially sounded like a flaming disaster had once again become extremely encouraging. Multiple excited conversations flew around the room. After a few minutes Jonathan called all to attention.

"Viviane, Ross, thank you for the excellent updates and for all your hard work. But, please, never put me on that roller coaster ride again. I don't think my stomach could survive another round! Now if you don't mind, I'd like to have a few words with Raynard and the members of the executive committee."

As the two physicians filed out the door, thoughts ran to the implications of what had been discussed and how radically the playing field had changed in a relatively short time. What they were experiencing with the T.V. Neurologicals drug pipeline was not terribly unusual for small biopharma companies that typically lived and died on one or two molecules.

To revert to Jonathan's carousel analogy, horses were being swapped in and out, new directions taken, but all using the same assets. Much had already been invested in the T.V. Neurologicals molecules and the reality was that creative resuscitation was a skill vital to the continuation of the small company.

"So, Raynard, there's not been a lot we've agreed on regarding the company's research strategy in the past, but perhaps circumstances have finally forced us to common ground." As much as he hated to agree with his nemesis, Raynard nodded.

Ames spoke up. "For T.V. Neurologicals to continue to survive we have no choice but to gradually transition SRD 6969 from the 'hot bod' market to that of psychiatry and behavioral change, even though it's not as sexy. Furthermore, it may well be our orphan drug proves to be the biggest surprise of all if it's found successful for treating advanced prostate cancer."

Raynard was more than pleased that Jonathan's backing of 6969 had taken a sharp left turn.

"As the physician and medical expert, I should point out a few highly relevant points to be considered."

No question Raynard was in his element and basking in the attention. "Clinical trials are still ongoing so we don't have statistical information to back what our staff experts are surmising, granted their informed opinion has merit.

"In the world of pharmaceuticals I've never known a situation in which a trial was discontinued because judgments were made through observation, not based on data. This is a treacherous path to follow and the wiser route might be to wrap up the trials and let the data speak."

"Peter, you've been unusually quiet, what's going on in the place you call a brain?"

Ames smiled and shot back, "Did you say space or place? What Raynard said is correct. Pharmaceutical companies never make decisions like this without substantial data in their pocket. The problem is, Hopper and I have been looking at our company's financial model and we simply do not have the funds to complete the SRD 6969 trials, only to put the product on the shelf and then show poor performance. We would be in a tenuous, weak position to start behavioral studies, and would be susceptible to a lowball takeover of the company at an unacceptable price, especially with news about the orphan drug getting out."

Hopper stood and banged the table with his fist, surprising everybody.

"I can't believe I'm saying this, but I think we should roll the dice. Cut our losses on female arousal, and go full bore on behavioral and prostate cancer. If our decisions follow classical guidelines, we are likely to fail. Nobody will sing our praises for choosing the correct decision-making process yet ending up with the wrong answer."

All eyes looked to Jonathan for his take. Their leader was facing the biggest bet of his career and they knew it. He held his head in his hands for almost half a minute, and then stood. He had made his decision.

"Things are not what they seem. Now, where have I heard *that* before? If we're going to risk all our marbles, I first want to hear from our experts to ensure there is or is not sufficient backing for SRD 6969 in sexual and psychological indications.

"This has to be completed yesterday because the next move will be to call an emergency board meeting to explain why our stock is likely to plummet before it eventually returns to the higher atmosphere. Surviving that board meeting will be nothing short of a miracle as some investors think we're already in the money. They're not crazy about change.

"Hammer, please come up with the best damned media relations plan to keep the stock from falling off the cliff until the positive spin gains traction."

Jonathan sensed there must be a solid path through this complex maze. Once found, it would require great skill to maneuver and conquer; it wouldn't be easy and the potential for failure was strong. The T.V. Neurologicals army would need to be well armed.

Never one to beat around the bush, Ames turned to the only woman in the room and implored, "Rachel, you're our media relations guru. Who would you recommend we enlist for this critical role?"

His timing was perfect. Jonathan was concerned Rachel might not be ready to jump into the sandbox with the big boys. The fact she did not hesitate a nanosecond before giving her response assured him she had the moxie to take on the biggest challenge of her career.

"There's a hot PR company based in Santa Clara that goes by the name Media Rx; it's led by the Valley's latest whiz-kid, Roscoe Neer. I feel we need Neer and his organization to pull this off. That team would be like having the Russian Cossack army backing

T.V. Neurologicals. Neer and his boys recently won a large contract with Apple and the word is they're setting a new standard in the industry."

Hopper chimed in. "I strongly support Rachel's choice. The financial community has been talking about the talent stacked in this fast paced organization. Particularly strong is the firm's ability and willingness to turn on a dime, or in this case on our market cap, which is worth quite a few dimes.

"We need to keep it that way or our crown jewels will tumble at a very cheap price. One of the big pharmas will cash in on our pipeline and call it theirs."

It was now after six in the evening. They collectively decided Rachel should reach out to the Media Rx CEO immediately to test his willingness to pull his key staff together for a series of all-nighters.

All-nighters weren't unusual in the Silicon Valley corporate community; everyone knew the New York Stock Exchange would open the next morning three hours earlier when the West Coast was just waking up. Any company expecting big things had better be ready to answer early questions that would blast fast and furious.

"No time to prepare" simply was not an acceptable defensive response. Investors made decisions with or without full corporate interpretation, although some of the more conservative waited to hear it before taking action.

Jonathan was getting antsy and ended the meeting with a challenge. "People, you know what has to be done, let's get to it!"

Pulling off this coup would take more effort and luck than the 1980 USA Olympic hockey team needed to claim their "Miracle on Ice." Jonathan wondered if his team could really make it happen.

CHAPTER TWENTY-TWO

Rachel Hammer left the meeting of the inner circle with a clear understanding of the magnitude of the task set before the key T.V. Neurologicals team members. She was particularly aware of the faith their boss had put in each of them. She appreciated the show of confidence Jonathan had given his top female executive, an attitude Rachel hadn't experienced with previous bosses. Rachel was confident she could deliver a media relations program second to none, and knew the exact company that would be instrumental in reaching that goal. Only the corporate best would do if they were going to pull off their daring and creative ploy. Fees wouldn't be a concern, hiring the most competent, innovative media relations firm was imperative; the survival of T.V. Neurologicals depended on it.

Sitting patiently outside her office Rachel found a nondescript gentleman dressed in a brown suit and dark green tie, which camouflaged him well against the wall. With a nod of recognition she acknowledged him, and turned to her secretary.

"I am not to be disturbed for the next thirty minutes. Now, would you please set up a meeting with Media Rx at their Santa Clara office with the stipulation it is essential CEO Roscoe Neer be in attendance."

Rachel stepped into her office and gestured for the man in the brown suit to follow and take a chair. She settled into the seat behind her desk and studied her visitor for a few moments before speaking.

"So, after two years of investigative probing and pocketing my regular payments into your bank account, I gather you finally have information that may be of value to me?"

Brown Suit remained expressionless, but when he spoke his demeanor and words seemed patronizing. Rachel wondered if this was typical of all private investigators.

"Ms. Hammer, when you first approached me three years ago, I indicated you had very little to go on to locate the perpetrator who assaulted your sister. It's only through outstanding detective work on my part that I've gathered information that may be of value to you."

This was the first time Brown Suit had come to her with anything new about the case and Rachel found herself leaning forward in her chair to catch every word.

"Go on, tell me what you've discovered," she encouraged.

"Well, I've not been able to lock onto the name of the person you're looking for, but I have managed to gather sufficient information so I think it's only a matter of weeks before I have that missing piece of the puzzle. I spent much time and legwork visiting a number of hotels that are popular venues for training conferences. From my expense report you'll see I had to slip healthy tips to the bartenders at these hotels. After talking with several, I was able to identify a possible suspect who was often noted leaving with women who were inebriated. According to the barkeeps, he seemed to be directing them with purpose."

By this time, Rachel was almost tipping out of her chair as she desperately tried to absorb every detail. The search for the domineering beast that caused her sister's death had consumed all Rachel's non-working hours after making the promise to her sister's memory that justice would be done.

"Who is this vile individual? Where can he be found?" Brown Suit raised both hands to deflect Rachel's questions.

"As I said at the start of my briefing, I don't have a name yet, but it's only a matter of time. The suspect was described as a Caucasian of median height and girth, light brown hair, and an accent that was identified as the Yat dialect originating in the suburbs of New Orleans."

A thundering shudder assaulted Rachel as horrific thoughts pounded her memory.

Oh God, it couldn't be! All this time?

She recalled a sales dinner conversation when Ron Daniels described his early years in the 9th Ward of the Big Easy and how he and his friends would greet each other. "Where y'at?" was their welcome from which the supposed Yat dialect originated.

As if it was only yesterday Rachel recalled her first meeting with Daniels; it was his T.V. Neurologicals job interview. She remembered he appeared surprised when he first saw her. It was as if he had met her before and was trying to remember where. Rachel was positive the two were meeting for the first time. She never considered the possibility she might be mistaken for her twin sister.

Brown Suit sighed. Before becoming a PI, he put in twenty-five years as a city cop and had thousands of interviews under his belt. He was troubled by the look he saw in his client's eyes. It carried the realization of bad news, signaling a pile of shit was about to unload. Oh well, he could only do so much before the case was out of his hands.

Brown Suit finished his report in a few minutes. Rachel thanked him, scribbled her signature on a check, and accepted the summary folder offered. She asked to be kept informed if any information of note surfaced. After the man in the brown suit left her office, Rachel grabbed a heavy couch cushion, buried her face in it, and screamed as loud as she could. Could Daniels possibly be the person she was looking for? The very man who worked beside her every single day? She had to play this suspicion out with great care and planning.

"Knock, knock!" Rachel's secretary peeked from behind the door. "Your employee function is about to start and they'd like you to say a few words to the assembled corps of volunteers."

Rachel let out a deep sigh. The function was a visit from the Red Cross mobile blood van. Her initial inclination was to delegate her canned welcome to an associate, but an idea came to mind and injected a shot of energy. The blood drive just might be the very opportunity needed to confirm if Daniels was indeed the bastard she had been looking for all this time.

CHAPTER TWENTY-THREE

It was nearing the end of the workday. For Daniels, his well-honed sense of survival told him his long T.V. Neurologicals career was going to come to an abrupt end soon. He planned to offer his resignation within the next couple weeks. The walls were closing in fast on many fronts.

The sales manager sat alone in his office and for the first time wondered if he'd pushed the envelope one time too many, and perhaps too far. The perennial Mister Suave was experiencing underarm perspiration stains for the first time in memory and the runaway liquid definitely ruined the appearance of the expensive long thread Egyptian cotton shirt he wore. He casually wondered if his fluid fear would seep through the fine Italian wool of his sports coat.

Daniels knew Bernstein was avoiding him. This sent the obvious signal he had been marked as toxic. On the other hand, Susie Quattro was becoming clingy and possessive. Inevitably there would be the piper to pay when he kissed off his sexual playmate.

Daniels noticed something hush-hush was going on in the R&D group. Staff was perpetually meeting behind closed doors and his usual information sources were ignoring him like the Invisible Man.

That very afternoon he'd watched several board members park their pricey German chariots in the lot, most likely arriving for an audience with Grayhall. Something was definitely going on and he wasn't part of it.

Daniels cursed when he saw T.V. Neurologicals stock take a dive. He was counting on his stock options to keep him comfortable, at least in the immediate future. Daniels was confident that in today's environment any employer would negotiate an exit package that included retaining options rather than face the hassle of litigation with the possibility of an adverse outcome if a judge or jury happened to dislike greedy pharmaceutical companies.

On the other hand, it was a whole different ball game if he faced criminal charges. That thought kept Daniels walking the floor at night, concerned he may have been overzealous developing sales promotions that bordered on being downright bizarre and definitely illegal.

To divert focus from his misdeeds, Daniels formulated a plan that hung his colleague Bernstein out to dry. Bernstein would appear to be the likely culprit in this diabolical scheme and Daniels chuckled when he thought how confused the researcher would be. He still had a few ends to tie together, but since time was running short, he knew things had to start happening fast.

A leopard doesn't change spots, even during a crisis. Daniels couldn't resist the temptation to seduce the newest ambitious female recruit training in the home office.

When he'd addressed her training class, the young woman from Indianapolis caught him during a session break to express concerns. She had performed poorly on several of the pop quizzes given by the teaching staff and was on the verge of being sent home. The woman explained how she had busted her butt to get the job at T.V. Neurologicals and felt missing a couple questions on a stupid quiz shouldn't lead to her dismissal.

The pretty young thing had heard rumors about favors being granted by the top sales executive so she asked Daniels if he might coach her one day. Both knew exactly what activity private coaching involved. Without giving his intentions away, Daniels said he'd have to get back with her later.

Daniels looked up from his desk and was surprised to see the petite brunette standing at his door. He hadn't realized the Hoosier honey was so aggressive.

"Hi, Ronnie, I'm here for my coaching session," she exclaimed, shooting him her most seductive smile.

"Come this way, quickly!" Daniels wasn't about to let this serendipitous opportunity pass him by.

He led her to the back elevator before her presence in his office attracted attention. Without speaking, they rode down to the depths of the T.V. Neurologicals basement. Daniels led his conquest through a series of doors and corridors to a little known storage room that had been originally remodeled as a sleep room for the night custodian. Daniels had taken over the long forgotten room by slipping the Hispanic janitor a couple Ben Franklins and threatened to report him to Immigration if he dared open his mouth.

Daniels replaced the janitor's cot with a queen-size bed. A small refrigerator meant to hold libations guarded one corner. Daniels found chilled chardonnay was most popular with the ladies he enjoyed screwing during his rousing romps. If the carnal sessions become hot and heavy, as was his intent this particular afternoon, a shower stall lavished with exquisite European soaps for sensual sudsing offered both a cleansing and erotic experience. Originally designed as a room for storing air-conditioning equipment before the janitor claimed his cot, Daniels was proud of the sensual boudoir he had secretly designed.

"What do you think of my private office, little lady? Why don't you make yourself comfortable while I find us a drink before we begin our coaching session?"

The tiny brunette quickly figured out what the big boss had in mind and was more than willing to comply. She'd do anything; even have sex with an older man, to stay on the T.V. Neurologicals payroll. Within minutes she carelessly piled her clothes on a small red velvet chair and climbed between the sheets. It didn't take Daniels much longer to join her in bed and soon the filly from Indy was moaning passionately, one eye open to make sure her partner was buying her feigned ecstasy.

"Here, take a sniff of this, baby." Daniels broke a vial of amyl nitrate, which gave both an immediate rush and momentarily sent his plaything into a foggy daze. In a flash the predator flipped his conquest on her knees and began entering her from behind.

"Ronnie! You're hurting me, please don't do it that way!" Her pleading excited him as he thrust deeper and deeper causing her to scream in pain.

"Shut up, bitch!" Daniels ordered, crashing his hand hard across her tight little ass. The resulting large red welt was a souvenir she would wear for quite some time. Twenty minutes later, Daniels took the teary eyed trainee upstairs and ushered her out a side door into a cab, assuring her she had no worries about her morning exam.

"Ronnie, I'm really glad you're sticking to your promise after that humiliating experience." As she entered the taxi, he slapped her behind hard, remembering how much he had enjoyed their frolic in the hay.

"Sweetheart, it's in the bag. Now get to your hotel room and pretend to study. I don't have to tell you that you can't say a word about our coaching session to anyone." Of course he had no intention of intervening in the testing process. He would be long gone by tomorrow and knew the woman didn't have a clue that the important Vice President of T.V. Neurologicals Sales was not a man of his word.

Daniels started to return to his office but changed direction when he realized he'd forgotten something. He headed back to the elevator and rode it to the basement. He walked directly to his passion parlor and headed to the refrigerator, searching inside for a blue plastic cooler.

He opened the locked container and there was the deadly ooze he'd stolen from Bernstein's office. This was the first and only chance he'd had to remove it from the building, and the sooner he was able to dispose of its contents, the better he'd feel. The ooze appeared to have diminished in size; perhaps he should just let it evaporate on its own. He quickly thought better of that idea and decided to stick with his original plan.

Now all he had to do was to get the cooler to his car without running into an employee. If he could make it that far, he would be home free.

Daniels made arrangements to stay at a hotel in Half Moon Bay by the ocean, what better place to dispose of the damn thing than in salt water? He debated searching out Susie Quattro for a quickie, but decided that would be a badass idea.

The stupid cow actually thought he was going to file for divorce and marry her! She didn't take it well when he set her straight. After she got over crying and beating her fist on his chest, things turned really nasty. Susie threatened to expose him to Jonathan.

A hard slap across her face with a warning to play it smart unless she wanted to experience the full brunt of her old lover's anger quieted her.

It was at this point Daniels realized the gig was up and he needed to exit the T.V. Neurologicals scene fast.

What the hell, it had been a good run and he was able to cash in most stock options, thanks to the run-up from heavy interest in acquiring the company.

Daniels reviewed the resignation letter he had written citing "seeking other opportunities" as his reason for leaving and decided to drop it on the CEO's desk within the hour when he left the building for the last time.

Heading away from his basement hideaway, Daniels thought he heard something rustle. He stopped, turned, and stared down the dark corridor. He could see nothing out of the ordinary.

That's funny. He could have sworn someone was watching him. Satisfied his active imagination was working overtime, the sales executive made his way back to the elevator.

CHAPTER TWENTY-FOUR

The hours flew by too fast. Jonathan's team was eagerly ensconced with the brightest and best spin masters in the Valley to develop a credible storyline designed to sway key investors who had the power to make or break the company if negative adjustments were made to their portfolios. These days, so much of a company's valuation seemed to rest in the ability to effectively market their story.

Change was roaring at the team like a thundering avalanche rushing down a mountain. Fortunately all recognized adjustments were desperately needed or T.V. Neurologicals would be buried under a ton of misinformation and innuendo. The T.V. Neurologicals team held their own against the top guns from Media Rx led by their new age, off-beat guru.

Roscoe Neer was clearly a genius in the communication field. Time and again he had guided his clients away from using ambiguous messages that seemed harmless to the unknowing, but held the potential for ultimate disaster. Neer had a reputation in the Valley for picking winners as clients. He was self-made, certainly didn't need to make another dime, and seemed to be in the game for the opportunity to engage in battle. Rachel had done well to recruit this Valley icon who ironically was a high school dropout from rural Mississippi.

So much information had to be digested and communicated in a clear and concise way so investors would continue to hold the company's stock. Ideally, the spin would be so pervasive that they would consider loading their portfolios with additional shares. The challenge was to calm frantic naysayers while leading the company from its murky and tenuous position to the dawn of an innovative success story. The catch was the plan and program had to be formulated, polished, and ready to roll in roughly thirty-six hours.

As if Jonathan didn't have enough piled on his plate, earlier that morning he'd spoken with Rachel who shared that Susie Quattro had dropped by her office and was visibly upset. Rachel insisted Jonathan speak with Susie that day; she had a sense something very bad had happened. Jonathan sighed and decided that conversation would have to be shuffled to the end of the day as he was running from back to back meetings.

Great, more baby-sitting, just how I need to be spending my time!

As he hustled down the hall he happened to notice Jacki on the phone in one of the unoccupied offices. He knocked on the door and she wheeled around hurriedly. Jacki gestured madly for him to sit down. He could see she really wanted to speak with him, and now.

Guessing Jacki was probably experiencing the usual sticker shock after checking out the local real estate offerings, Jonathan was ready to reassure her he would make her relocation package substantial enough to adequately bridge any differences in the cost of living so he took a seat in front of her desk.

Jacki tactfully ended her phone call and before she could say a word, Jonathan began his spiel.

"Jacki, I know what you are going through finding affordable real estate in this town, but I want to assure you I'll structure a package that is fair and will keep you happy to be living in one of the most beautiful places in the world. Besides, even though our relationship is just beginning, you must know I'm in it for the long run."

She looked at him quizzically, smiled, and shook her head.

"What are you talking about? Thank you for offering, Jonathan, but I'm quite comfortable with the package you and Rachel put together for me; I think it's very fair and I can certainly make it work. With the generous moving allowance, I can comfortably find a place to live while our relationship grows."

Jonathan relaxed and settled back into the chair. Geez, he was definitely feeling the pressure of his office today.

"So, then what's on your mind, Jacki?" He smiled and jokingly added, "Have you and Jennifer already uncovered a new issue with compliance?" No sooner did the words slip out of his mouth that he wanted to retract them. Jacki's expression told him she was clearly having great difficulty with whatever was on her mind.

"Actually Jonathan, I think you'll be pleased with the plan Jennifer and I came up with to ensure we can communicate the importance of total compliance and how we'll deal with infractions. But that isn't why I wanted to talk with you. I'm a little nervous because I'm used to speaking to you as your lover and this discussion is more like employee to CEO."

"Well, believe it or not, both those personas bring great respect for whatever you have to say, so please take a deep breath and speak what's on your mind." Jacki smiled, Jonathan's words helped ease the tightness cramping her shoulders..

"Jonathan, the topic is quite personal, involves confidentialities and nobody knows better than I do how important SRD 6969 is to you and T.V. Neurologicals. I'm deeply concerned you will think me incapable of keeping a confidence."

"You have my full attention, go on." Jacki related her history with Alice and how it had been Jacki's initiative that encouraged her friend to enroll in the patient trial for SRD 6969. As a consequence, she felt personally responsible for Alice and had to protect her friend's privacy. Jacki explained how a wonderful success story was now looking like it could develop into a serious, if not devastating, problem if the suspicions held by the clinical team became reality.

Jacki had called a few of her former Medical Science Liaison colleagues to ask what they had heard or observed regarding trial enrollees to determine if unusual personality patterns could be defined. Without breaking the code, nothing certain could be uncovered, but there seemed to be increased reporting of behavioral changes, especially noticeable were reports of initial intense sexual responses, which were now diminishing at a rapid rate. Knowing the high profile surrounding SRD 6969 and its importance to the future of T.V. Neurologicals, Jacki wasn't sure she should discuss her "off the reservation" concerns and findings. After a sleepless night weighing the many pros and cons, she felt she had to tell Jonathan what she was hearing from some of her former colleagues in the MSL team. Her conclusion was that she felt this information was owed to her CEO and lover out of loyalty, if nothing else.

Jonathan took a deep breath and took her hand in his.

"Jacki, I take what you've said in good faith and I thank you for trusting me enough to come forward. Of course you recognize your personal involvement with this patient clouds the issue. Furthermore, we are talking about a sample of one, so we cannot regard your friend's case as conclusive. Nevertheless, I know you are fully aware of the importance of SRD 6969 and ultimately my role as CEO so I do appreciate you bringing related issues to my attention."

"Jonathan there's more..." Suddenly, there was a change in her tone and her voice quivered. In the months before I met you I was approached by some unpleasant members of the sales force who wanted me to engage in promotional activities which I knew to be against our code of ethics. I refused, but then received threatening emails which I took to my supervisor only to discover she was involved in the scheme."

Jonathan released Jacki's hand and leaned back in the chair with his hands folded behind his head. He wondered where this conversation was leading as his internal concern barometer began to escalate.

"I am embarrassed to tell you that as a result of my boss's behavior I went to a lawyer to learn more about whistle blowing, possibly bringing a case against T.V. Neurologicals. Fortunately the attorney was a wise man and advised me to think long and hard about such a decision. This led to my trip to San Francisco to hear you speak. Once I met you, I knew whistle blowing was not the path for me and the company I loved. I knew I would eventually find the right way to handle the situation and considered the matter closed."

Feeling a bit annoyed he was hearing this confession at the late critical hour, Jonathan stood up and walked around the desk.

"Is there anything else I need to know?" Jacki's look gave him the answer.

"I hate being a snitch, but I think you should know that when I spoke to my old MSL friends I discovered that word of 6969's side effect profile is spreading and the bad seeds I mentioned were bragging about the money they were going to make through trading on the stock." Jonathan felt like he had been struck by a lightning bolt. He did not need an investigation by the Security Exchange at this time in his negotiations.

"Jacki, whatever reservations you had let them fly out the window because by speaking up you may have saved the company from untold number of problems. Those idiots are playing the markets with confidential information and that's playing with dynamite. Let's get Jennifer in here and determine our plan of action."

It turned out Jennifer had dealt with a very similar situation in her past and knew exactly which government officials to contact and which law firm needed to be brought into the picture. The plan of action she proposed left Jonathan feeling confident that the matter was under control and would never hit the wires. As his compliance officer walked out of the office, he told her that hiring her for this difficult position was one of his smartest business moves ever, which brought a wide smile to her face.

"Jacki, would you please stay behind for a moment, I would like to speak with you." Not sure if she had caused irreparable damage to their relationship by not sharing information earlier, Jacki could not look into his eyes.

"Hon, I know you struggled with this issue, let me just say how grateful I am that you told me about the improper activities within our ranks. Because of you, we have the opportunity to implement Jennifer's plan, take the bull by the horns and begin remedial action on our own accord, not at the direction of a government agency. I can't tell you how important this factor plays at this time when we are negotiating the sale of our company. Millions of dollars are at stake." For the first time in hours, Jacki smiled.

"So, you still love me?" she whispered in his ear, an audible embrace he found extremely sexy.

"Yes, I still love you, but I must insist this conversation stay strictly between us. Not a word to another person. I'll have to move quickly with the board as this incident has shown me that Murphy can strike from out of the blue."

With that Jonathan forced a smile, resisted the urge to wrap his arms around his compliance associate and kiss her silly.

"I hate to leave, but I really have to arrange for the most challenging board meeting I've ever had to face." He winked and

turning abruptly, took off down the corridor to face his next problem. As he made his way he texted Jacki, *C U 2night.*

For his next move, Jonathan called Tim Varter's personal assistant and without going into details, described the need for an
emergency board meeting, giving no apologies for the short notice.
The assistant was not pleased and insisted this would be an impos-
sibility given the tight schedules of board members, but Jonathan
was adamant and would not take no for the answer.

The meeting was eventually scheduled for one o'clock in the afternoon two days later and Jonathan insisted it could not be post-
poned for any reason. He concluded the conversation and hung
up on one very furious woman who worried the messenger, namely
her, would surely be shot. Many board members would have their
egos dented by Jonathan's abrupt summons, that was a given.

CHAPTER TWENTY-FIVE

It was the day before the hastily scheduled board meeting. Hopper was complaining to Pete Ames that he'd been burning LEDs at both ends. Ames wondered what on earth Hopper was talking about.

"Hopper, light emitting diodes are known to give off cold light, there is no burning to speak of." To which Hopper retorted, "Pete, you need to get with the Silicon Valley jargon. To say I have been burning the candle at both ends would be so passé!"

Everyone groaned at Hopper's feeble attempt at humor. It did serve to show the fatigue that had washed over the team after spending hours perfecting the board presentations.

Ames made his familiar whining sound, recognized by all who knew him that he was about to say something that might be a bit sticky.

"Boss, we've kicked around the deliverables for tomorrow's meeting and the team is fully informed since we've kept them current on all events. Now the three of us should have a quick walk-through of the key points, just to make sure nothing is missing from the roster. After that, we want you to go home and get some rest. It's not in our best interest to have our esteemed CEO waltzing around like a zombie in front of the board tomorrow. It's been a helluva day, so go catch a few snores and join us around eight tomorrow morning, all bright eyed and bushy tailed. We'll hold a briefing then and give you the final prep for the meeting."

Jonathan groaned. As much as he didn't want to leave mission control, he knew his friends were right.

"Okay, okay. Let's plow through a quick review so I can be sure you knuckleheads haven't missed anything." Ames and Hopper feigned hurt feelings but the charade lasted only for a minute before the tribunal was back at it with the business at hand.

As he headed home for much needed rest, Jonathan again felt fortunate his two musketeers had his back and now Jacki made it the proverbial three. They were not only his key business partners, but all three had bonded and become close friends. He was fond of all of them, particularly the one with blazing red hair.

It seemed Jonathan's head barely touched the pillow when he heard the alarm ring. Surely it had gone off too early! When he looked at the face, 5:00 a.m. shined back at him. He'd been sleeping like the dead for the past five hours, plenty long enough to recharge his internal batteries. After a quick shower and shave, Jonathan was on his way back to the office, his first stop the mandatory Starbuck's window pick-up.

After leaving his car in the lonely parking lot and entering the almost vacant building, Jonathan passed his secretary's empty desk and wondered if Susie would show up that day. He vaguely recalled he was supposed to talk with her, but that agenda item had slipped his mind. Susie had recently taken several sick days without calling in to extend her days out. His radar signaled something was off, but this was not the time to get into that. Questions to ask the woman swirled in his mind.

Blinking lights on his desk phones indicated multiple voicemails had collected over the past few hours. Jonathan quickly reviewed all who were trying to reach him and triaged their importance. He was not in the least surprised to see a flock of stock analysts had called to juice rumors about SRD 6969. What did surprise him was the number of CEOs from leading oncology pharmaceuticals who wanted to meet. Jonathan counted three serious contenders.

Secrets were incredibly hard to keep in an industry where so much opportunistic wealth was at stake for those connected with the best sources of information. The recent loss of interest resulting from changing gears surrounding implications of SRD 6969 could be more than offset by large wealthy oncology companies desperate to buy the next breakthrough for treating prostate cancer.

The clock showed Jonathan had less than ninety minutes before his board meeting was called to order. Two of the three cancer drug company franchises were headquartered on the east coast. If he was lucky, he might pick up valuable information to help him through what was surely going to be one heck of a day. Jonathan wondered if most thought he was crazy for thinking of switching priorities within the T.V. Neurologicals research portfolio without the backing and support of strong clinical data.

He turned to his keyboard to check the price of T.V. Neurologicals stock. In after-hours trading the share cost had dropped to $16. That significant fall suggested at least one investor had been involved in a significant "Sell" transaction, but how could information leak so quickly and at this point, who would take the risk of blatant trading using insider information? What little annoyance he held that Jacki had not told him sooner about her near whistle blowing action was forgotten and forgiven. Yesterday Jacki clearly put Jonathan's interests as her top priority and in the process may have saved him from putting out yet another fire at this critical juncture in negotiations.

Substantial and deserved scrutiny were paid to maintaining careful watch over the release of clinical trial information, but as always, somewhere in the chain somebody might be willing to take a chance with the SEC by trading on privileged information. No matter what the case, Jonathan knew his board would call for his head if he couldn't present a solid solution to the T.V. Neurologicals dilemma. Before making his way to the most important board meeting of his career, it was imperative Jonathan return those phone calls from serious company suitors.

But, first things first. The young CEO desperately needed to sink a few baskets to center his frame of mind.

As he was ready to grab his squishy Nerf ball and take aim at the small basket, Susie poked her head into his office. Just as he was about to tell her he didn't want to be bothered, she primly announced, "There is a lady who wants to have a word. I tried to tell her you were busy, but she is insistent upon seeing you." Before Susie could continue, Jacki edged her way past the door.

"Susie, it's okay, I asked Jacki to stop by to give me information for my upcoming meeting." Looking disturbed at her boss's casual dismissal, Susie reluctantly shut the door.

"I'm feeling mighty frisky this morning, Mr. CEO!" Jacki's words made him smile and buoyed him for the upcoming grueling session. Jacki walked behind Jonathan's desk, twirled his chair around and plopped unceremoniously on his lap. She snuggled close and kissed him hungrily.

"I just dropped in to wish you all the best, although there's no doubt you'll ace the gig."

"Can't think of a better way to start the morning than to have my lady ravish my body and wish me well."

"Betcha I can score two points before you can!"

In college Jacki had been a basketball point guard, a tidbit of information she hadn't bothered to mention before. She made an enthusiastic athletic fake right, moved left, and then cut right and reached for the Nerf ball sitting on the corner of the desk intending to steal it and sink a two-pointer.

What happened next seemed to take place in slow motion. In retrospect, it was one of the worst moments in Jonathan's life.

He saw Jacki's winning smile and her move to the left and the fake right. He reached to capture the ball but she beat him to it. Jacki palmed the sphere, but suddenly looked both surprised and puzzled.

Her features morphed from coquettishness to shock, and then formed into a distorted grimace of anguish and pain. The transformation was horrific. Her screams echoed far down the hallway. Jonathan tried to process what was happening, but only confusion and disbelief filled his senses. Waves of nausea erupted from his gut as he helplessly watched his lover writhe on the floor, white spittle escaping haphazardly from her open mouth.

Jacki dropped the Nerf ball as if it was hot lava. Within seconds her hands became a mass of ugly red welts as large blisters formed filled with dark fluid. The pain she was experiencing was clearly intense as the march of welts crept up her arm. As blisters grew too large to contain the build-up, they exploded into fountains of purple with a horrible odor defying description. Jacki convulsed, projectile vomited, and then mercifully passed out with open eyes that appeared unseeing.

Jonathan desperately tried to keep from lunging into a state of panic. Bizarre fragmented recollections of long ago Boy Scout instruction and gym class training shot through his consciousness. Tearing off his shirt, he swathed it around his lover's arms so whatever was filling the blisters wouldn't transfer to his hands or other parts of Jacki's body. Arms wrapped around the unconscious victim, he cradled her head in his arms as tears welled in his eyes. He plaintively screamed, "Susie, get in here now!"

What seemed like hours were mere seconds before a shocked secretary opened the door to discover the horrendous scene. Voice wavering, Jonathan begged, "Call 911 and get an ambulance here stat! Hurry!"

Tears now flowed freely and the always-confident CEO felt as helpless as a kitten as he tried to decipher what had happened. Obviously a trap had been set for him, but Jacki had intercepted its consequences. Speed to treatment was a critical element to survival and Jacki was fortunate that an empty ambulance happened to be passing by less than a minute from the T.V. Neurologicals building. The efficiency of the paramedic team in delivering her to the ER and Jonathan's insistence that the medical staff consider box jellyfish toxin as the offending agent probably saved Jacki from a more severe outcome or even possibly death.

Two hours later Jonathan was stationed outside Jacki's hospital room at Stanford Hospital, desperately looking for answers from the ER physician in charge of her care.

Discovering the attending physician was one of the best on staff, Jonathan felt his pulse rate gradually recede from its previous astronomically high levels. The physician completed a thorough examination before updating Jonathan on Jacki's prognosis.

"We have our patient on high dose steroids and multiple pain medications. She is mildly sedated to get her through this rough period. From the appearance of the lesions, they seem to be subsiding and I hazard a guess that your lady friend will be released in a few days, good as new. I think we were lucky that the exposure was to her hand and not a more sensitive part of the body. To be perfectly frank, I've never treated a contact wound like this and had it not been for your insistence, we would not have considered a jellyfish capable of this much tissue damage. Do you have any idea of the origin of the offending agent?"

Jonathan certainly carried thoughts about who and what might be responsible for this travesty but could not comprehend why his prime suspect would be so carelessly obvious. Within minutes after sending Jacki off in an ambulance, Jonathan had carefully packed the Nerf ball and rushed it to a local laboratory for analysis. He was already convinced results would show the ball had been coated with box jellyfish toxin straight from Bernstein's lab. He would have much preferred to be in the ambulance with Jacki, but felt he had a responsibility to make sure nobody else was injured. Secondly, he knew how much importance rested with the results of the outside lab.

This was obviously an attempt to sabotage Jonathan's critical board presentation that day. He knew the poison was meant for him. If the initial plan had worked, Bernstein would substitute for Jonathan at the board meeting and who knows what that insecure man so desperate for peer recognition would present as the official T.V. Neurologicals research pipeline strategy.

Yet Jonathan couldn't believe Bernstein would be so foolish to orchestrate the event knowing circumstantial evidence would point directly to him. Bernstein had his faults, but Jonathan had never seen a cruel streak in the man's personality and the researcher was certainly not stupid. He wondered how the hell he managed to sneak the substitute ball into his locked office anyway. The evidence definitively pointed to the head of R&D as the culprit, but a nagging suspicion told Jonathan that accepting the obvious might not be the correct conclusion.

Sitting in the fold-up chair someone had placed by the door leading to Jacki's bed, Jonathan's brain kept playing the day's events over and over. His iPhone chirped and the small screen informed him of an incoming call from the lead analyst at the lab whose name was Andy Scores. He had asked to speak to Andy to make sure the analytical procedures were well understood.

"Andy, this may sound absurd, but I suggest you investigate the sample for toxin inflicted by box jellyfish. Please let me know what you find and call me later at this cell phone number." He slipped the cell phone back into his pocket and faced an agonizing decision.

Jonathan didn't want to leave Jacki's bedside, especially since she was still unconscious. But, he had to go. He walked over to the ER doctor who was making calls at the nurses' station, and said, "You've assured me Jacki will be back to normal within 24 hours, but if anything should change, I want you to call me at this number at any time."

He handed the doctor his business card and set out for the delayed board meeting. Jonathan was shaken, but rather than submit to defeat and confusion, he resolved to give the finest presentation to his questioning and now cynical board. He knew Jacki would expect no less from him. Later he would deal with the person responsible for her condition, forcing the asshole to face wrath like he had never seen before.

CHAPTER TWENTY-SIX

Tim Varter enjoyed his board position as Chairman Emeritus for T.V. Neurologicals. He was paid a cool $50,000 to attend no more than three meetings each year at which he might be asked for his opinion, but bore no real accountability for the outcomes. He was familiar with the people sitting around the table as several had been by his side since the beginning of his venture.

Eight members created the board, including Varter and Jonathan Grayhall. Four were venture capitalists with offices bearing prestigious addresses on Sand Hill Road in Menlo Park. All four drove expensive European automobiles that expressed the success of their respective enterprise. Today two showed up in golf attire, their links plans interrupted at either the Los Altos Country Club or the more proximate Sharon Heights Golf Club. One junior member of the VC contingent wore a relatively inexpensive coat and tie likely purchased at Nordstrom rather than fitted by a personal tailor. He was still in the process of building his company's portfolio and spent his waking hours looking for the breakthrough deal that would cement his reputation and establish his standing in the Valley. Occupying seat seven was the lone token physician, a neurologist representing a Manhattan-based hedge fund.

An extremely successful former big pharma CEO occupied the final board seat. A Ph.D. by training, Julius Dario was highly regarded for his deal-making expertise and his uncanny ability to pick winners. Julius was in it strictly for sport, being a millionaire several times over. Julius helped recruit Jonathan and had been a strong supporter since Day One.

Remembering the raucous meetings during the early days of his tenure, Varter was looking forward to seeing how the new kid on the block would handle his first major crisis. This certainly was not the first time T.V. Neurologicals had faced a potential disaster, nor would it be the last. The risk quotient at smaller pharmaceutical companies was certainly higher than in big pharma and life or death decisions far more frequent. Varter reflected comparing the two environments as playing roulette versus chess.

Observing Jonathan's demeanor as he sauntered into the meeting room, it was difficult to imagine this man was facing one of the most difficult meetings of his career, especially coming on the heels of a terrible personal experience just hours before. News of the morning's horror had not made it to the members of the board and nothing in Jonathan's expression or carriage suggested what he had been through.

The CEO made his way around the table greeting each member with a smile as he shook hands. Some on the board returned the smile, but most didn't. Emergency meetings called at the eleventh hour never went over well. One member avoided looking at Jonathan as they clasped hands, a clear signal of disappointment and disgust at the newly established negative status of T.V. Neurologicals. Rachel followed her boss around the room using every bit of her skill and charm to soften the situation.

It was time to begin. As the clock pointed south to 1:30, the T.V. Neurologicals CEO started his PowerPoint presentation at the front of the room. Jonathan had practiced every page with his in-house executive team and the hired gun communication specialists countless times and was ready for most anything the board could throw at him.

"Gentlemen and lady, good afternoon and thank you for making time in your tight schedules to attend this impromptu emergency meeting. Since we last met, there have been monumental developments coming down our research pipeline and as board members; I must bring you up to date. I regret the short notice, but the information I will be sharing will affect T.V. Neurologicals stock price in the near term. These developments led to important changes regarding ongoing talks with potential suitors for our company."

Although he was barely into his presentation, Arthur Blake, the Varys VC who had earlier avoided looking at Jonathan, could not hold back his annoyance any longer. With anger filling his voice he stated, "After years of hovering in the low teens, our stock finally broke into the 20s with substantial upward potential if an acquisition was announced. I can't believe you couldn't move fast enough to seal the deal! Now we're moving in the opposite direction with the last quote I saw being 16 and falling."

A rumble erupted in the room as individuals expressed a round of opinions. When the din became unbearable, Julius abruptly stood up and thumped his fist on the table.

"Gentlemen! Let Jonathan speak!" he implored. "We must hear about the factors that have driven the stock price down and what our options might be in the new game. After we have the facts, we can debate the correct path to take." The rumblings and mumblings quieted and Jonathan resumed his talk.

"Just before I walked in, I checked the price of our stock and found it had dropped to 12 before the SEC put a hold on further trading." A collective groan swept the room.

"But, I'm going out on a limb to tell you I expect a full recovery and much more." Jonathan paused for effect. "All I ask is you hold off expressing your opinions until you hear everything I have to say."

Jonathan's words captured the attention of the table although the mood seemed mixed. Was Jonathan blowing smoke to save his ass or did he truly have a plan that would bring a whole new vision to the future of the company?

Sensing all ears were his, Jonathan launched into the first of his PowerPoint slides. He skillfully brought the board up to speed on the recent developments observed in the SRD 6969 trials, explaining the expectation that the drug was not going to succeed for its targeted indication of relieving sexual dysfunction. He carefully pointed out that none of the interpretations described had been backed by empirical data. That they were discussing strategic decisions based on purely observational instances violated all principles of clinical trial management. That was clear to all.

Despite red flags, Jonathan crafted his case that T.V. Neurologicals would be financially crippled if they didn't take immediate action, assuming the clinical trial outcomes proved to be as predicted. He argued that bold, confident action would demonstrate a clear strategy and decisively showcase the ability of T.V. Neurologicals management to adapt to a dynamic set of changing circumstances. The CEO spoke, and the board finally listened.

"I am confident our management team has developed a bullet-proof communication that puts a credible, positive spin on the change in indication developed for SRD 6969. Yes, sexual dysfunction is a substantial and expanding market, but so is clinical depression. The key will be the novel mode of action that psychiatrists have never holstered in their armamentariums."

Julius Dario was the first with a question.

"Jonathan, what makes you so confident that 6969 has such strong potential for treating depression?" Jonathan had counted on this question being asked and was well prepared.

"Julius, before accepting this conclusion, I personally met and spoke with over a dozen leading clinicians in the field of psychiatry. Thanks to an excellent data sharing system, all are well acquainted with our molecule. In fact, all have been using it in their locally initiated trials with promising results.

"Our pipeline progress has been detained by a T.V. Neurologicals research department that has been looking inwardly and totally fixated on developing the unsuccessful molecule called SRD 0011. We should have been listening and communicating with physicians all along. If we'd done that, we would be well into a clinical development program by now."

Silence filled the room as the board digested the missed opportunity that had occurred under their watch. Jonathan's stage was now set to present the board with his tipping point.

"I am now going to bridge to the second chapter in the T.V. Neurologicals repositioning strategy. In the interest of time, I'm going to get straight to the heart of the matter to give you encouraging news."

Arthur Blake was definitely having trouble buying into what Jonathan was saying.

"I admire your courage, but do you really believe we have a life preserver to throw into the raging waters so the company will be saved?"

Jonathan positioned himself in front of Arthur Blake, looked him directly in the eye, and announced, "What a brilliant metaphor you've provided, Arthur! The answer is an unqualified yes! You all know of our orphan drug program and the pressure brought upon me to discontinue studies because such a limited population would actually benefit from the drug.

"Once again our research department did not keep abreast of external interest and the possible use of the molecule in another profitable market. The bottom line is there is much support for the drug in prostate cancer treatment from the M.D. Anderson facility and the Cleveland Clinic, which in turn resulted in the National Cancer Institute instigating fast-track discussions with the FDA. I can tell you the projected combined value of T.V. Neurologicals molecules in treating depression and prostate cancer far outpaces the lost potential in treating sexual dysfunction."

When Jonathan finished his spiel, the tension in the room seemed to dissipate. Even Arthur Blake had no further concerns to express. Finally the hedge fund neurologist spoke.

"As a physician and a scientist, I must say what you are proposing is very persuasive, but goes against my years of training and experience. It's my job to protect the investment of my partners back in New York when I cast my vote."

Julius Dario interjected at this point.

"It is precisely at a time like this when we earn our pay as board members. Jonathan has clearly shown we cannot afford the luxury of waiting for results as that would spell financial doom if they confirm our best, educated guess as managers. Look at it this way, if the data somehow shows trial success in enhancing female sexual response, we'll have the benefit of two indications for SRD 6969. Granted, we would have a little back pedaling to do, but nobody objects when there are more goodies to fill a basket, only when the basket comes up empty."

Another board member added a voice. "There would be no 'Attaboys' given if we chose to run with the conventional decision making process but end with an unfavorable outcome." Heads nodded like a mass of bobble heads in a stadium souvenir stand. Jonathan sensed it was time to go for the close.

"There's an additional tidbit I would like to add for your consideration. While we may have lost partnering interest from a few companies for SRD 6969, other companies are lining up. Just before I came to this meeting, I spoke to the CEOs of three oncology oriented companies who expressed high interest in what we have to offer. They are aware of our molecule and are interested in starting discussions immediately. Let me assure you of one thing, these are deep-pocket companies."

With that comment, Tim Varter called for a vote. It was unanimous that Jonathan should move forward with his team's plan.

The meeting was adjourned as each board member approached Jonathan and expressed their appreciation and confidence that the company was in good hands. Especially warm congratulations came from Varter. Julius added his stamp of approval with a hearty slap on the back.

The meeting was over, but there was still much to be done. Jonathan bolted down the corridor to the small room where his team was anxiously waiting. He walked in the door and gave a thumbs-up, resulting in a raucous cheer.

"Great job, team, great presentation! It went like a hot knife slicing through butter, but now that the concept is sold, it's up to us to implement our communication strategy. You all know we have an enormous job ahead so let's get the damn spin masters spinning! To the team from Media Rx goes a special word of thanks; you really earn kudos for your assistance developing our strategy. We now need you to set your foot soldiers free to contact key targets to implement what we have on paper."

The crew was high-fiving each other as Jonathan pulled Rachel aside to congratulate her for her role convincing the board to go along with the plan. She was even able to convince Media Rx to accept T.V. Neurologicals stock as part payment of fees. This was Jonathan's idea and the thinking behind it was that Roscoe Neer was more likely to be motivated by having skin in the game than by cash, something he had more than he knew what to do with anyway.

"Congratulations to you, boss. It's a real feather in your cap to convince that hardcore bunch that we really have a plan that's going to make them a ton of money.

"I checked the appointments on your calendar for the rest of the day and you have three VIP calls from CEOs of oncology companies who insist they must speak with you today. Before you get to that though, and I'm really sorry to keep bugging you about this, you really need to take twenty minutes to speak with Susie Quattro. She just handed in her resignation and is waiting outside your office."

"Rachel, this was a team effort and the team should take the credit, not any one individual. I will deal with Susie, but I noticed you're not yourself these days. You seem subdued. Is something bothering you?"

Rachel calmly replied, "Nothing I can't deal with, Jonathan, and it has nothing to do with work. It's a personal issue that I've been trying to right for several years."

He looked into her eyes and again found deep darkness, something he could not understand.

"Well, if there's anything I can do to help, just give a shout. Now wish me luck on the next part of the plan!"

Rachel surprised him with a kiss on the cheek and added, "I know you're going to be successful, very successful." He sensed she wanted to tell him something but could not bring herself to do it.

As he made his way to his office, Jonathan knew speed was of the essence in dealing with the CEOs who were interested in the T.V. Neurologicals product molecule or better yet, the company itself. But first he had to meet with Susie to see if she would confirm his suspicions regarding the incident that had hospitalized Jacki.

Susie was slouched uncomfortably in a chair next to her desk and he could see by her swollen, red eyes that she had been crying.

"Hello, Susie, please come into my office." Jonathan beckoned her to sit in a comfortable leather chair and found his place across from her. He reached to the coffee table between them and poured two drinks from a silver flask, offering one to her. Susie couldn't bring herself to look at her boss and instead stared at the ground as her body racked with sobs.

"Well, Susie, I understand you've resigned but wanted to speak with me about matters that I suspect are causing you a great deal of sadness. You have my full attention for the next fifteen minutes but then I must get to a scheduled meeting, so why don't you get started?"

Susie struggled to regain composure and had trouble getting her thoughts out at first, but once she started talking, words rushed like a raging waterfall.

"I guess I should start at the beginning. A few years ago Ron Daniels and I began an intimate relationship. My feelings ran deep and I thought he felt the same about me, but about the time you arrived at T.V. Neurologicals I noticed a change in him."

She paused to read Jonathan's expression, but he showed nothing.

"About three months ago, Ron started acted suspiciously. First I saw him taking my office keys from my purse and returning them a few hours later. UPS delivered a package one day and he tried to hide it from me, but I saw the delivery slip. The box contained a Nerf basketball game identical to the one you have hanging in your office."

Jonathan shook his head as things became clear. "Did you discuss any of this with a colleague?" he asked.

"No, I didn't. I had fallen in love with Ron and thought my feelings were reciprocated. This morning I told him I knew about the keys and the Nerf game and that I had packed a suitcase and was ready to leave with him that very morning."

"How did Daniels react when you asked him to run away with you?" Jonathan asked, now feeling his blood start to boil. Any hope he might forgive Susie went down the toilet when she mentioned the Nerf ball. The image of Jacki suffering flashed through his mind. Susie's reveal confirmed what he had suspected. The conniving Ron Daniels had set up Raynard as his fall guy. Controlling his emotions, Jonathan asked Susie to explain further.

"He laughed at me and said there was no way he was going to divorce his wife and screamed I was a stupid cow. After a barrage of tears I realized how wrong I'd acted and now I desperately hope you can forgive me."

Susie was wishing Jonathan would show sympathy and somehow keep her at T.V. Neurologicals. She was seriously wrong in her assumption.

"Susie, I've heard enough! I want you to pack your personal belongings and be out of here by the end of the workday. There is no room on my team for someone as untrustworthy and disloyal as you have shown yourself to be!"

Susie tried to protest but Jonathan wasn't interested in her excuses.

"But I've told you all you wanted to know! I have nowhere to go and nobody to go to." Jonathan repeated his instructions and firmly told her not to bother requesting a recommendation because none would be forthcoming. He picked up the phone and called HR giving instructions that Susie was to be accompanied by security until she had finished packing her personal belongings and left the building. With that he abruptly left the sobbing secretary alone in his office.

It's all because of that bastard Ron Daniels, Susie thought as she angrily threw years of collections in cardboard boxes before heading to her car in the parking lot. Her Honda had a hatchback allowing her to quickly jam several boxes haphazardly in the rear.

That bastard ruined my life, but he's not going to get away with it! I'll make him regret what he has done to me.

Leaving the spacious tree lined parking lot for the last time, Susie Quattro traded her tears for a sense of purpose and revenge like she'd never experienced before. Her new life was just beginning.

CHAPTER TWENTY-SEVEN

I t was now after seven, and what a day it had been! First the atrocity committed with the crazy Nerf ball, then the stressful presentation at the board meeting, and finally the angry confrontation with Susie. All early indicators conveniently pointed at Bernstein as the poisonous villain, but Jonathan now knew Daniels was the culprit. Still, he needed to find out if Bernstein had a secondary role in the assault on Jacki.

Jonathan was almost certain the toxin extracted from the box jellyfish would be identified as the offending poison. When he put the Nerf ball into the shoebox that he personally carried to the lab, he noticed the color of the ball was off, it was slightly more orange. How could he have missed that? Jonathan blamed his carelessness for what had happened.

As he walked to the company parking lot, he saw Bernstein's office light was still on. Good! He wanted to confront the man and get at the truth. Jonathan turned quickly and within minutes entered Bernstein's office. Without saying a word he purposely walked to the aquarium. Looking at the ghostly inhabitants with his back to Bernstein, Jonathan slowly made his observation.

"It's been quite a day for a multitude of reasons. Are you up to speed on what's been happening around here?" Jonathan fully expected an arrogant response from the researcher, but this time a subdued and a nervous voice answered him. Now, that was interesting!

"Well, I heard your meeting with the board went extremely well and our company is the talk of the town as a result of the media relations program. Congratulations!"

"Anything else?" Jonathan asked suspiciously.

"Do you mean your unwarranted criticism of my department not keeping informed of work being done by key centers treating depression and cancer?" Bernstein went bright red when he spoke the words that seemed to burn in his throat.

Jonathan pursued his course. "And what else?"

"Of course I heard about the terrible accident involving Ms. Striker, but I know very few details. It was quite a shock to have something like that happen to an employee."

Bernstein's voice was quavering; he was obviously stressed and nervous. Jonathan was still staring at the aquarium as if hypnotized by the floating creatures. Finally he casually remarked, "That's funny, the last time I was here, I could swear there were more of these bastards floating in your scummy pond. I only see a few now. Where is the missing piece of shit?"

Jonathan deliberately name called Bernstein's pets as a last ditch effort to get the man to slip, but surprisingly there was no reaction. For the first time Jonathan considered the possibility that Bernstein may not have been involved in the plot at all.

"You are correct. One of my jellyfish is not accounted for and I've asked maintenance as well as the aquarium serviceman repeatedly if they have any idea what happened to it."

Jonathan sensed Bernstein might actually be telling the truth. The day was catching up with him and he was beginning to feel ripples of exhaustion. He didn't think any further progress was going to be made that night so he walked to the door.

Jonathan stopped in the doorframe, turned slowly, and issued a warning. "There's something not right in this building and I'm going to get to the bottom of it. When I find whoever is responsible for the attack today, rest assured that person will not only lose their job, but will be marched to the police station to face criminal charges. Wait, let me rephrase that. What's left of that person will be escorted to the cop shop.

"I suggest if there's anything you think I should know, you'd be doing yourself a big favor by coming forward with that information."

With that the troubled CEO left Bernstein a quivering, questioning human mass of confusion.

CHAPTER TWENTY-EIGHT

Although he was exhausted, Jacki's condition haunted Jonathan. Before trying to sleep, he telephoned the hospital to ask how she was doing. Learning Jacki had regained consciousness and visitors were permitted for another hour, he immediately drove back up Bayshore to Palo Alto and headed straight to her hospital room.

When he walked into the sparse room decorated only with tubes and wires and saw this beautiful woman lying in the bed pale as a ghost, he felt terrible knowing he was the intended target of the attack. Jacki was lucid and happy to see him, but he could tell her injured, heavily bandaged hand was still causing substantial pain.

"It's so great to see you, hon! Tell me how your presentation went."

Jonathan walked to the cumbersome bed, leaned over and gave the patient a tender kiss.

"I'm so very sorry. Jacki. You were the victim of something meant to put *me* out of commission. This was never intended to harm you. I promise I'll find out who did this and make them pay. I promise!" For the thousandth time he wished he could take the pain on himself.

"Oh, please don't worry. I won't deny it hurts like a son of bitch but the painkillers are doing a good job and the docs say I'll be fine in a couple days." Jackie smiled and squeezed Jonathan's hand.

"Just tell me your presentation was successful so I can rest knowing I took one for the Gipper."

They both laughed, easing the tension. Relying on his best cheerful manner, Jonathan updated Jacki on the positive outcome of the meeting. Twenty minutes later, just as he was wrapping up the drama, the nurse came in to announce visiting hours were over. He hated leaving Jacki alone, but knew her body needed time and sleep to recover. He sighed, got up, and started for the door.

Jacki called after him. "Before you leave, I need to tell you about a strange visit I had from Rachel. To tell the truth, I'm not sure it really happened. Maybe I was dreaming or the drugs were making me crazy." She appeared confused.

"Interesting you should mention Rachel," Jonathan noted. "She did a helluva job for us on the media relations component of the plan. Following the team debrief I had time with her alone and found her to be somewhat restrained and vague, despite her great accomplishment. I sensed something wasn't right; something was eating away at her but she wouldn't let on what it was." Jonathan walked back to Jacki's bedside to hear what she had to say about Rachel's visit.

"When Rachel came in I was heavily sedated and drifting in and out of consciousness. I seem to recall the first thing she did was go to the supply cupboard and take out a pair of rubber gloves, which she put in her purse. She came over to my bed, sat right where you are, and didn't say a word, but cried quietly for a long time. Then she spoke to me even though my eyes were closed. I must have looked like I was deep in sleep. Here comes the weird part, and I can't tell if I really heard this or if I dreamt the whole thing."

For the life of him, Jonathan couldn't figure out where this was headed. "Go on, this is really starting to get interesting."

Jacki continued.

"Rachel kept apologizing to me for what had happened and said if only she had picked up on the clues earlier, she could have dealt with the problem and none of this would have happened. After all the apologizing she assured me she had a plan in place to take care of everything. I was not to worry and said all would soon be fine again. The next time I opened my eyes she was gone and like I said, I couldn't tell if she was ever really there."

Jonathan sat back in his chair and took a deep breath.

"Well, I don't know what that's all about, but I do know I'm on the verge of providing the police with what they need to arrest the person responsible for your assault. At first I thought Bernstein was a co-conspirator, but I'm now convinced this was the heinous work of one man acting alone, Ron Daniels.

"Prison seems to be too soft a sentence for such an asshole. As far as Rachel and her conversation with you goes, I have no idea what that could be about."

CHAPTER TWENTY-NINE

I t was late and most of the T.V. Neurologicals staff had left the building hours before, but Ron Daniels was still roaming the hallways. With nobody to watch him, he made his way to the CEO's office to drop off his carefully worded letter of resignation. Mission accomplished, he left the building for the final time and walked to his car. Daniels glanced around to see if a straggler might be in the parking lot, but it was empty as a tomb.

In his right hand he carried the blue cooler containing Bernstein's missing jellyfish, which he'd had in his possession since stealing it days before.

Now he had to dispose of the slimy creature so there would never be a link back to him. Daniels first thought was to flush it down the toilet. But he visualized the unusual mass clogging the pipes, which would then require the services of a plumber. He didn't need questions about a strange creature swimming in the toilet bowl.

He decided the easiest solution was to take the cooler and its contents to the beach at Half Moon Bay where he could toss the translucent bitch-creature into the ocean so recovery would be impossible. Once in the water, it would most certainly never be seen again. Satisfied all was copasetic in the parking lot, he placed the cooler on the seat next to him, cracked open the lid and peeked inside to confirm the contents were safely in place.

The gelatinous mass with the hideous beak was snuggled in a corner and if he didn't know better, the thing looked ready to pounce on unsuspecting prey. As he looked at the little beast he thought it seemed smaller and wondered how that could be. He convinced himself the creature had become dehydrated since leaving its aquarium home. Satisfied all was as it should be, Daniels closed the cooler lid and pulled out of his parking spot. As Daniels turned onto the main road he took pains to drive slowly and follow all the rules of the road so a Mountain View police cruiser would have no reason to stop him. He chuckled at how paranoid he had suddenly become.

Daniels paused to look at the night sky through the moon roof in his car. Rain had started to fall and given the drought that had plagued the area for the past year, streets were likely to be treacherous.

Hilly terrain lay ahead requiring concentration to negotiate the forty-five minute drive to the coast. An accident and subsequent police involvement would not be a good thing, especially with the unusual cargo he was carrying. Office mementoes and supplies were packed in boxes and stacked in the back seat of the car. Daniels had a good run at T.V. Neurologicals, but now the time had come to move on. For days Daniels had sensed Grayhall breathing down his neck, not to mention the regulatory authorities who would be arriving soon, thanks to the bitch in compliance. Daniels wasn't worried. He had accumulated a nice emergency fund and intended to enjoy a well-deserved treat later that evening to welcome his new life.

He would soon be checking into the Ritz Carlton at Half Moon Bay and if all went to plan, that little Cuban trainee he met at last night's training dinner would be spending a few days of R&R with him in a beachfront boudoir.

As Daniels turned on Shoreline Boulevard, he was so absorbed in thoughts of debaucheries that he didn't notice the compact car turning on headlights and falling in line a hundred yards behind him. He made his way down Shoreline and heard music blasting from the county amphitheater where he had attended some of the best rock concerts ever. Recollections of The Eagles and Crosby, Stills, Nash and Young came to mind. Those cool California evenings were scented by the familiar sweet odor of burning grass. He would miss living in this part of the country and all it offered.

Daniels slowly made his way to Highway 85 and turned north onto Highway 280 toward San Francisco. The rain was now coming heavy, which was a bit unusual for California. He wondered if he would have to pull to the side of the road until the downpour ended. He quickly dismissed that idea; he had things to do and a lady to screw.

Daniels enjoyed driving on Highway 280, one of the most beautiful stretches of road in the country with spectacular views of the coastal mountain range. The town of Half Moon Bay was on the other side of the range that stretched south of San Francisco. To reach the coast, motorists were forced to negotiate twisty Highway 92 running East/West before joining the 280 connecting to the Pacific Coast Highway.

Motorists reached the summit of 92 and started the downhill run; the series of swooping curves were not often given the respect they deserved. As Daniels made his way, this section of road was further handicapped by dense fog and the light rain served to lift the surface oil that had been deposited by traffic. All served to increase the potential for accidents and fortunately, the weather dissuaded most drivers from venturing out this night. Daniels pretty much had the road to himself.

He headed down the switchback section of Highway 92 at a comfortable 50 mph; he felt safe at that speed even in the rainy conditions. Daniels smiled as he thought of the Cuban chick waiting below in a beautiful beachfront room decorated with a spread of champagne and caviar. The man felt great, the best he had felt in a long, long time.

Without warning, his body was jolted. The Buick had been hit hard from behind causing him to temporarily lose control.

"What the fuck!" Daniels cursed at the stupid ass that had rammed into him. Fortunately he was an experienced driver and quickly regained control of his vehicle when *thunk!* He was hit again! This time the car was smashed into more forcefully and went into a four-wheel skid sliding toward the guardrail.

"What the hell! Who the hell?" For a moment he thought he would be able to maneuver through the skid and once again regain control. Hope evaporated when there was a loud *crunch!* And the third swipe into his fender flipped his car over the guardrail and sent it hurtling down the side of the mountain. As his car rolled, the headlights of the offending car no longer blinded him and for a split second he caught a glance of the crazed driver in his rearview mirror. He couldn't believe the eyes he saw staring back at him.

"Omigod, it's you! How? When did you know?" His questions were lost to the sounds of crunching steel as his car was pounded by rocks on the steep, unforgiving mountainside. Daniels and his green Buick performed multiple somersaults bouncing high in the air before meeting the earth again. The tumbling came to a jarring stop when the mangled car struck a large boulder.

Above, the road was deserted except for the Honda that had given Daniels the hefty nudge down the hill. The driver monitored the action from the top, a satisfied grin covering her face.

A bystander witnessing the accident wouldn't take bets on anyone surviving the maelstrom. Odds would be slim to none.

The Buick settled at the bottom of the hill but didn't catch fire. By a quirk of fate, Daniels' screams indicated he was very much alive.

"How disappointing."

This was a disturbing outcome for the assailant who quickly made her way back to her car and started driving down Highway 92 toward the mangled wreck. On the passenger seat she found the mask she'd purchased earlier at a costume store and covered her face, presenting a truly bizarre appearance at this time of night on this dark section of road. She slipped on a pair of thick rubber gloves knowing she needed to protect herself for what she was about to do next. The figure with the ghostly mask reached down to the floor and lifted a small cooler to fit on the seat beside her. She knew what she had to do if her victim was able to exit his car.

With the Buick looking like an upended turtle, Daniels was strapped upside-down in his seat unable to move. His collarbone was smashed and his body was held tight by a jammed seat belt. Blood dripped from his head into his eyes, finally pooling on the gearshift below him. His head was throbbing and his vision blurred, but he was alive and reasoned emergency teams would soon be on the scene to rescue him. All he could do was sit back and wait. Be patient, he told himself over and over. Out of the corner of his battered eye he saw something that caused a wave of horror and nausea to envelop him.

Through a ridiculous sequence of events, the blue cooler had bounced around the car's cabin and jammed between the brake pedal and accelerator and was now positioned directly above his crotch. Daniel's horror quotient jumped when he realized the lid was slowly opening and the gelatinous mass was seeping through the crack.

From his bat-like perch, Daniels tried to reach above to grab the box or jiggle it so it was no longer positioned as a lethal weapon.

His futile lunges were hampered by the broken collarbone and confining seat belt. The ooze continued its relentless march of death toward him. Within seconds Daniels saw the single-fanged beak appear under the lid. In a last ditch effort, Daniels screamed as he dislocated his shoulder allowing him to slip off the seat belt to escape from the car and the offending predator. After a long roll in the dirt, he struggled to his feet.

"Shit, shit, shit! That was too fucking close for comfort!" Checking his bearings he saw he was near the bottom of the hill and only a few yards from the side of a road.

Hell, I'm going to be okay, but I must get to the road so EMTs can find me.

Bleeding profusely and his shoulder and arm worthless, the crippled man made his way to the roadside where he hoped a passing motorist would come to his rescue. Headlights came around the corner, a car was approaching! *Thank God!*

Using his good arm, Daniels frantically waved at the approaching car and begged in a feeble scream, "I need help, please!"

Daniels was relieved when the small Honda approached and the driver rolled down the passenger side window. As the car came to a stop, Daniels stuck his head in the window to appeal for assistance. At that moment, he knew he was doomed. The driver he thought would be his savior appeared to be a monster from his worst nightmare.

Sitting behind the steering wheel was a person wearing a mask he knew only too well, a rubber Scream mask. Scream was an appropriate descriptor because of what happened next. In a flash, the driver dipped a gloved hand into a small cooler and scooped up a gelatinous mass. Before Daniels could react the driver threw the mass at the open passenger window directly in Daniels' face. The burning pain the toss brought was excruciating and like nothing he had ever known.

A large chunk of a box jellyfish covered half of Daniel's face like the mask worn by the phantom of the opera as the first of a hundred cnidocysts shot poisonous darts directly into his eye causing immense pain. When he thought he could take no more, dart after dart penetrated his face until he passed out. Direct exposure on such a sensitive surface was far more toxic than what Jacki had experienced. Daniels fell to the side of the road, folding into a crumbled mass as seizure after seizure assaulted him.

The driver of the Honda calmly rolled up the car window after making sure all remaining jellyfish residue had dissipated before removing her rubber gloves and depositing them into the cooler.

She took a quick look around to make sure she was alone and then calmly drove off leaving Daniels writhing at the curb. Several cars drove by but didn't bother to stop figuring the body by the side of the road was just another drunk sleeping it off. Daniels lay unconscious for twenty minutes before a motorist finally stopped to help him.

The incident was reported in the local news as an accident attributed to excessive speed on the slippery road and the injuries were the result of multiple traumas received from the hillside roll.

Daniels' savior was a migrant farm worker who loaded him in the back of his pick-up and drove to the nearest emergency room. The doctors were unable to explain the long streaks of apparent burning on the victim's face given the lack of flames as the car careened down the hill. The doctors remarked the burns were some of the worse ever seen in that ER and had severely disfigured the driver's face. It would be some time before it could be determined if the driver would make a full recovery. It was doubtful.

CHAPTER THIRTY

News of Daniels' accident quickly spread around T.V. Neurologicals and met with a cool employee reception. This was testament to the negative feelings the company population held for the former VP of Sales. The usual goodwill gesture of sending a bountiful fruit basket to a fallen employee's hospital room on behalf of the company never happened. Few, if any, visited him.

Half Moon Bay police officers frequently tended to visitors from the "other side of the mountain" who were unable to navigate the treacherous road leading to the seaside town. The police declared the Daniels' incident to be a driver-related, one car accident. There was little for them to examine at the scene because the car and its contents eventually caught fire after the driver managed to escape.

Jonathan and his executive team had no reason to think anything different than what the police report offered and wrote the incident off as an accident in which Daniels got his just desserts, basically taking one problem off the table. Feeling no guilt, Jonathan was relieved he wasn't going to be the one to bring bodily harm to Daniels. If that would have happened, he probably would find himself in trouble with the law. He was crazed by Daniels' assault on Jacki and had no doubt he would have worn blood on his hands if he'd met the ass in a dark alley.

For the next four weeks it was full spin ahead on the research carousel as the T.V. Neurologicals executive team and Media Rx formulated and reformulated the company story. Repositioning the drug pipeline and romancing the market potential for T.V. Neurologicals stock took extensive planning and work. All indications showed the company's new image was being well accepted so the stock halted its decline and was now back on a strong upward track. Buzz about potential acquisitions fueled the financial community; the company was rockin' and rollin' to heady levels of success.

The "come to Jesus" moment for T.V. Neurologicals involved breaking the code connected with the SD 6969 sexual arousal studies. As had been predicted by management, without statistical data, the results were mixed and non-definitive. A heavy sigh of relief from the executive team echoed through the halls as there would have been hell to pay if the company's repositioning data supported continuing on the Lady Viagra® path. Purists would have criticized the folly of making such important decisions without substantial supporting data. Jonathan knew they had been damn lucky to sidestep disaster. If presented with a hundred similar decisions to call, Jonathan would have waited for conclusive data before calling the shot. For whatever reason, his hunch this time resulted in a winning play.

Information obtained from the study couldn't have been better when it came to supporting the strategic decisions made. There was strong evidence of behavioral changes in the defined patient population, supporting the decision to fashion studies with a psychiatric bent. Dozens of psychiatrists clamored to be part of the clinical study and now were being carefully screened. A leading researcher at John Hopkins developed a rat model supporting the theory that the drug operated on a different pathway with respect to brain chemistry. This novel approach created a great deal of excitement within the discipline of psychiatry. Every indication showed the active model could lead to breakthroughs treating certain psychiatric disorders. Researchers were keen to engage in new clinical trials to evaluate just what had landed in their laps.

For Jonathan and his executive committee, the high-risk gamble to make decisions without the benefit of final data paid off. To bet on clinical outcomes based purely on observation prior to the statistical analysis of trial data was quite atypical in the pharmaceutical industry. In fact, it was considered extremely unscientific and dangerous as all hell. But, if Jonathan and the team had not taken the gamble, they would have been swamped by the public relations tsunami associated with unmet expectations.

Jonathan knew having the right skill set was important to success in any endeavor, but nothing could ever beat the infusion of old-fashioned good luck. Such was the case with the drug previously given the bland name "orphan." More than once, a drug started life in one indication and through serendipity was found to be active in another situation. This was the case with a leading erectile dysfunction drug initially studied as a cardiovascular treatment before creating the enormous erectile dysfunction market. With excitement created by the prestigious National Cancer Institute, Media Rx's job was made easy and Jonathan had no end of suitors interested in sharing T.V. Neurologicals spoils through partnership or acquisition. The market was kind to T.V. Neurologicals knowing the company was poised to play, so much so that the stock jumped to $32 and pundits were claiming the ceiling was yet to be reached.

One morning while sitting at his desk with a Starbuck's coffee in one hand and a Nerf ball in the other, Jonathan did a quick mental calculation of his net worth should the closing price affected by acquisition hit his target of $45. If the target price became reality, he would be worth in the vicinity of $120 million. Not in his wildest dreams did he ever think his trip to the West Coast would bring such riches! No wonder Silicon Valley was Mecca for those seeking fame and fortune. Stories of amassing overnight piles of wealth were daily occurrences.

With the specter of a business collapse behind him and the demise of Daniels, only the nagging question of what to do with the VP of Research remained. Raynard had not directly participated in the incident involving Rachel, but he was a co-conspirator in other ways and Jonathan felt he should not escape without consequence.

Jonathan glanced at his Seiko watch; it was time to catch the meeting called by Hopper. Ames had also been invited to pull up a chair.

Jonathan entered the meeting room and sensed good vibrations. The meeting began with each of his confidants reporting on their respective sphere of influence; all was going exceedingly well on every front. Commercially, Czuretrin was continuing to outperform; the market research Ames had conducted on the orphan drug and the potential of SRD 6969 in the field of psychiatry had been better than expected. The promise of strong sales was comforting after enduring the recent stressful period.

Ames informed his colleagues he had finally lost his mind and had proposed to the longtime girlfriend he dated back in North Carolina. He had moved her to Mountain View where she landed a great job. Congratulatory high-fives circled the room, everybody was happy the bodacious marketing executive had finally captured his soul mate.

"Since Pete is sharing his nuptial announcement, I guess I have to let this motley crew know I'm also taking the plunge."

"So, aren't you going to tell us the lucky lady's name?" Hopper begged, although they all knew perfectly well the bride-to-be was Jacki. The "Two Js" had become an inseparable pair, their pending engagement was the worst kept secret in the Bay area.

Another round of congratulations circled the three before Jonathan announced it was time to cut the chatter and get back to business.

Hopper updated the two on the due diligence progress. Two large East Coast companies with deep pockets were head to head in the final stretch in the race to acquire T.V. Neurologicals products for their pipeline.

"All is going well, but I must warn you, there could be a potential snag. I received a call from the Boston Department of Justice and their key players are flying out next week to have a discussion with us. You all know this might be the beginning of an investigation, but we really won't know until they get here."

Groans traveled around the room, although the three had been expecting the news. Jonathan was happy he had invested heavily in a company compliance program to keep past or future problems at a minimum.

Hopper continued. "It seems the Department of Justice has taken major exception to the activities of our former vice president of sales, and just about the time Daniels recovers from his injuries, his presence will be requested at an inquiry." Ames snickered at the thought.

"During his hospitalization there was considerable chatter about Daniels' sexual playtimes with several of our young recruits. Seems he was promising them the moon for a roll in the hay. Others have come forward with damning information about his approach to off-label use. Unfortunately, T.V. Neurologicals will be dragged into the muck and there will be penalties to pay, but Jennifer has done a bang-up job implementing the compliance programs and I think the fines will sting, but won't maim. In any case, Daniels is going to be far less successful romancing young ladies wearing the deep scars now covering his face."

"Kinda reminds me of the ancient practice of branding offenders," added Hopper.

A wicked grin creased Hopper's face. Jonathan knew something interesting was about to come out of his mouth.

"Okay, Hopper, spit it out!" Their friend was obviously taking great delight while hiding whatever news he was about to reveal.

"There is a God and I never cease to be amazed at the stupidity of some very smart people." Jonathan couldn't figure out where Hopper was going with this.

"Come on, Hopper, don't leave us hanging!" Hopper took his time, shuffled a stack of notes, and got up to grab a cup of coffee. He was about to be hit with the board duster in Ames's hand for taking so long to get to the point.

"I think it's fair to say we would all like to see justice done when it comes to our jerk VP of Research." Heads nodded.

"You know I've been complaining about the difficulty I'm having implementing the Sarbanes and Oxley accounting guidelines. I hardly expected while reviewing our accounting methods I would find unusual indiscretions involving invoices.

"To make a long story short, I did a little forensic accounting and discovered that of the $50,000 expense overage I found many months ago, half went to the Contract Research Organization, or CRO, and half went to unidentified accounts held in the Cayman Islands. I then discovered over the past three years, a half dozen similar invoices ranging from $75,000 all the way to $300,000 had a similar trace. It took a bit of detective work since funds were deposited under a number of pseudonyms, but with the help of a private investigator, I was eventually able to identify the owner of the accounts. It was our very own Raynard Bernstein!

"It seems Bernstein was in cahoots with the owner of the CRO and the two had a busy and lucrative embezzling business on the side. What I found most astounding was Bernstein, the would-be Nobel scientist, was using his share of the stolen funds to supplement what he saw as gaps in research money for his pet project, SRD 0011. What he couldn't secure for his research budget, the fool embezzled and reinvested with outside CROs to make his mark in the scientific community using his pet project. We have him by the short and curly with grounds for dismissal, and best of all, it comes without an exit package required."

Hearing this incredible news, an ecstatic Jonathan jumped out of his chair.

"I'll be damned! Great work, Hopper! You made my day!"

But Hopper wasn't finished; the guy was on a roll.

"But wait, there's more as they say in the infomercials! When the cops came to cart him away, Bernstein complained of chest pains. His final diagnosis was gastric reflux disease. Here we have a cardiovascular physician who could not distinguish GERD from a heart attack!" All three roared at Hopper's crazy update.

"You know, now that we know Bernstein wasn't the architect behind tainting the friggin' Nerf ball, I actually feel sorry for him. He was played the patsy by Daniels too."

Jonathan was remembering how Daniels babbled incoherently about ghosts and jellyfish in the ER after his accident. Police investigators were able to piece together enough information to book him for the assault on Jacki.

"I always thought it was too obvious that every indication pointed to him. Bernstein wasn't the smartest man, but he wasn't a complete fool."

"Nah!" Ames retorted. "He was a blithering idiot and got what he deserved. By the way, I was talking to the officer in charge of the case against Daniels a couple days ago, and have you heard the latest?"

Grayhall and Hopper gave their friend full attention. "It turns out Daniels was involved in a series of rapes of young women at sales conferences and used chemical agents to subdue his victims. The police received an anonymous tip that provided details found on his travel calendar for the past couple years. They were able to link him to crimes involving several women."

Hopper shook his head in disgust; he really hated that man!

"Well, the guy is sure going to have his jets cooled." Their discussion was just about over when Jonathan indicated there was one more item to talk about.

"It's amazing we're going to kick the butts of two negative blots sitting on the executive committee, but regrettably we're going to lose another one and this is a genuine loss.

"After doing a bang-up job in media relations, Rachel Hammer decided it was time for her to move on. She told me she never really settled into the Silicon Valley lifestyle so she's returning to the Midwest where she has a long-standing personal issue she must deal with. When she came to my office to tell me about her decision, she looked happier than I've ever seen her."

Grayhall continued.

"Something about that girl wasn't sitting right, but I could never figure out what it was."

Hooper added, "I know what you mean. Rachel came by to speak with me about options available and I assured her we'd take the necessary steps to build her package so she doesn't walk away from the share she deserves. Rachel wasn't exactly bringing in the big bucks and never received the moving package all of us managed to negotiate when we were hired."

Jonathan signaled it was time to end the meeting.

"Okay, gang, we're doing a great job, now let's take the ball across the goal line."

CHAPTER THIRTY-ONE

Mildred

M ildred Gamble was very happy she had participated in the clinical trial for restless legs. Not because she found relief for her nightly agony and not for the sexual arousal she experienced, although she and Harry were thrilled to welcome a passionate rush into a tired marriage. Mildred was happy because somewhere in the mix of drug trials and human experience she found her self-confidence and ultimately a successful new career.

Throughout her adult years Mildred was always playing second fiddle, even when she should have been the one taking the fade-away shot at the final buzzer. She was smarter than most as demonstrated by near perfect SAT scores and graduating magna cum laude in her class at Radcliffe. For whatever reason, Mildred just didn't have the confidence to step into the limelight.

The change came about largely by observing Dr. Rivers who she considered to be a decent man. Not brilliant, but by no means dumb. She saw how he leveraged his clinical practice into a moneymaking machine with his ability to rapidly enlist candidates for drug trials.

Slowly Mildred convinced herself she could become a broker for clinical trial patients. She was sure she could enlist women using her Web database by convincing them they would get the real scoop from a kindred soul rather than from a physician who thought he was anchored at the right hand of God.

Mildred differentiated her business model from a typical physician's practice because she didn't keep all the profits. A good percentage of her take went to "Mildred's Mob" in the form of benefits. Mildred purchased a fleet of vans to pick up patients from their homes and deliver them to and from the lab site, offering complimentary shopping transportation after medical appointments. Another perk received from joining Mildred's Mob was a restaurant lunch voucher to places most patients couldn't afford. Mildred's common sense, great personality, and strategic thinking made her business proposition successful in more than thirty states. Shy Mildred eventually became a power broker in the world of clinical trials. How much of this aggressive business behavior was influenced by the cognitive properties of SRD 6969, nobody would ever know.

The day her company booked one million dollars in a single month, she drove to Dr. Rivers' office and took him for a lunchtime spin in her new Porsche 911 Carrera S4. After the drive she parked her 911 next to his Boxster, a nice car, but not quite a 911.

Sally-Anne

Life for the Zuckermans had not gone well since they left Florida. The couple moved to a home in a condo community outside Reno that not only looked tired, but was being repossessed by the bank for missed mortgage payments. It seemed Zuckerman's erectile dysfunction was playing havoc with his self-image and the result was a fall deep into quicksand called illegal pornography. He was exposed for his indiscretions and forever after would carry the label of sex offender. No longer able to pay his wife's credit card bills or keep her sexually satisfied, he wasn't surprised when Sally-Anne left the marriage and her husband behind.

With no marketable skills and a sacred vow never to return to dancing at men's clubs, Sally-Anne faced an uncompromising dilemma. How was she going to provide for herself in the manner to which she had become accustomed? More to the point, how was she going to find food and shelter?

She realized the one thing she was best at was an ability to attract men who, under her coaching, became excellent lovers. The two Argentine tennis players were great examples. When she first undressed the men and settled her playthings in her bed, they were a pair of fumbling, clumsy oafs. After three months of working with them, the boys became skilled in the art of love and could bring her to multiple climaxes every time they hit the sheets. The pair quickly became experts in vaginal, oral, and anal adventures, using tricks and techniques most couldn't even imagine.

One afternoon Sally-Anne's girlfriend treated her to a massage. As they lay side by side on the tables, her friend complained about how difficult it was to find male escorts who could give a really good, sexy massage. She grumbled that few men were good looking, good company, and good at giving a relaxing massage. She wanted all three!

Eureka! That was it! Within days Sally-Anne personally recruited and trained a stable of male escorts who were guaranteed to please on all three counts. Word spread faster than wildfire and Sally-Anne's clients reported their dates were sensational and eagerly signed on for additional sessions. With money coming in faster than she ever dreamed possible, Sally-Anne grew her business and soon was known as the leading male escort provider in the West.

Alice

Of the three women participating in the restless legs trials, the greatest success story and yet the greatest failure belonged to Alice. Starting out as an ordinary mousey girl providing gopher services at a local TV station, Alice became a new woman after taking SRD 6969. Overnight Alice transformed into a voluptuous, ravishing beauty who quickly became one of the station's rising stars.

As quickly as she ascended, her star began to fall when she showed signs of addiction to cosmetic surgery. Alice became obsessed with the world of nips and tucks and soon carried her interest and participation to an unpleasant extreme. Alice landed in a place where she was convinced she needed drastic surgery on her cheekbones, nose, lips, and boobs. For her exclamation point she planned a trip to Rio to have a Brazilian butt job performed by a charlatan plastic surgeon carrying no credentials

Fortunately, before she could alter her rear end, Alice suffered a nervous breakdown and spent the next three months in rehab where her body was able to rid itself of the SRD 6969 molecule. Without the drug's punishing effect, she reverted to the Alice of old - a sweet, quiet girl, naturally attractive but poorly groomed.

Through all her travails and transformations, one person stuck by her side, her old friend Jacki Striker. Jacki made sure Alice had the best care possible and helped her return to normality, whatever that might be.

CHAPTER THIRTY-TWO

I t took longer than expected for the sale of T.V. Neurologicals to be completed. Eleven months after diligence began, a new parent company was announced. T.V. Neurologicals now had international tentacles having been acquired by a Swiss pharmaceutical giant. Jonathan's preference would have been to go with a Manhattan based company as the final buyer. His choice was based on the years of experience he had in North Carolina working for a Dutch parent and making all too frequent trips across the pond. There was definitely a toll taken on a body due to air commutes - the six-hour time difference, variations in business and social cultures, but most challenging was the language.

Europeans have a leg up on Americans because in general, citizens are multi-lingual and often speak English as a secondary language. Problems frequently occurred when not all participants in a business discussion had multi-lingual abilities. To the chagrin of colleagues, some with excellent language skills conversed in languages not universally understood. This frequently caused resentment by those missing out on the conversation. There had been gains made due to growth in the Hispanic population, but a long way remained before Americans could match the average Swiss citizen's ability to converse in as many as five different tongues.

Primarily the delay in closing centered on the investigation launched by the Boston State Attorney General. The Massachusetts government team came in with guns blazing. Their intent was to nail the company to a cross as an example of how not to behave.

It soon became obvious to the investigators that any serious infractions committed by the company were not done under the watchful eye of the new, highly capable compliance officer who, under the guidance of the CEO, had established a standard for other companies to emulate. The steps taken by Jonathan to enforce a culture of compliance were exemplary and received praise from the investigators who asked if they could use T.V. Neurologicals as a model for other firms. The cherry on the sundae was the investigators' interview with Jacki who relayed her personal experiences at T.V. Neurologicals telling how she moved from critic to partner/ambassador to the compliance field.

The net of all this was that in an environment when fines typically ran in the hundreds of millions of dollars, and over a billion in some cases, the fine levied against T.V. Neurologicals totaled a mere $30 million. The market had already discounted the stock by a more significant number so when the penalty announcement was made, the stock soared to new heights. T.V. Neurologicals had all the elements of a healthy, attractive acquisition.

Jonathan Grayhall was sitting in a lounge chair by the infinity pool in his newly acquired house high in the Los Altos Hills. He and Jacki shared the 8,000 square foot mansion for which he paid the ungodly sum of $10 million. While unheard of in most parts of the country, this price tag was not an unusual price to pay for one of the finer homes in the hills.

That morning Jonathan officially resigned his post at T.V. Neurologicals and was literally counting the money due him as the result of his change of control agreement that covered senior management at T.V. Neurologicals. Much to the chagrin of the Swiss acquirer, Jonathan elected not to stay on as CEO, wanting to try his hand at new pursuits.

As such, he was now a member of the VC Brotherhood on Sand Hill Road. One of the most prestigious of the venture firms made him an offer he simply could not refuse. The $150 million net he pocketed from the transaction allowed him to pay cash for his new residence and add a bright red Italian stallion to the stable in his garage. Jonathan's fleet occupied three of the four garages, the fourth being designated for Jacki's new car, a wedding present from her adoring husband.

The road Jonathan had traveled was not what he had in mind when he first arrived in the Bay area, but was certainly nothing to complain about. In many ways Jonathan followed the same yellow brick road as his predecessor Tim Varter did and found more success than he ever thought possible. At the beginning of his tenure, Jonathan's vision was to bring new drugs to market for the benefit of mankind and by doing so he would reap benefits and gradually accumulate wealth. He certainly succeeded in the wealth accumulation department, but the path Jonathan followed was really "the business of business." He juggled the carousel's "horses for courses" and although none had grabbed the brass ring, Jonathan had come to be exceptionally successful in many ways. Hell, they never taught this stuff in business school!

Pete Ames was another overnight multi-millionaire but was not ready to bow out. Pete was probably better suited than Jonathan for the business of business and wanted the chance to run his own company. His track record afforded many opportunities and he ended up as CEO of a North Bay start-up genomics company. Always the crazy one in the group, Pete decided he was not going to celebrate by purchasing Italian or German horsepower. To raise a glass to his newfound wealth, Ames purchased a franchise of his favorite eatery – McDonalds. He and Jonathan remained lifelong friends over mounds of fries and gallons of milk shakes.

Hopper was a dyed-in-the-wool finance jock and as such did not know how to celebrate with a big wad of money stuffed in his back pocket. So used to holding expenses to budget limits, Hopper was a conflicted mess having the freedom to spend vast personal sums without constraint.

Finally after much head banging, his friends Ames and Grayhall bought him a ticket to Australia and told him to go walkabout until he learned the secret of spending money without feeling guilt. Hopper took to the city of Perth and bought a beautiful ocean-going sailboat staffed with a full crew. Before long, he found a gorgeous, long-legged Aussie first mate to help him sail the seven seas.

CHAPTER THIRTY-THREE

A blue Honda with multiple scratches on the bumper and a dilapidated headlight was on the road to Phoenix. Susie Quattro's sister owned a condo in the 'burbs and being a good big sister, was willing to let Susie move in for awhile to piece her broken life back together.

Susie decided to make a clean break with Ron and the fast life she'd once enjoyed in California. She eventually found a secretarial job and a husband who owned a tire outlet. Her new husband treated her like a princess, having made a great first impression when he repaired her broken headlight suffered when a deer jumped in front of her car one dark stormy night.

※

Standing outside the showroom of the Mercedes dealership in Indianapolis, Rachel was very happy with her piece of the acquisition pie. After much coaxing by her new husband whom she met at a church social, Rachel finally agreed to trade in the clunker she had driven since her days in business school. While waiting for the salesman to drive up in her new AMG CL 55, the young service attendant asked, "Excuse me, lady, could I bother you for the keys to your trade-in? If you don't mind, would you point it out to me?"

Rachel flashed her classic smile at the young man. "Certainly, here are the keys and the car is the red Honda Civic with the front bumper that collected a few bruises, including a cracked right turn light."

The attendant had no trouble finding the Honda and the lady hadn't exaggerated about the front bumper's poor condition. The bruises she spoke of were actually heavy blotches of green paint, probably the result of contact with another car. He thought he'd better move the eyesore off the Mercedes lot before his boss gave him hell.

The AMG finally pulled up and Rachel slipped into the soft premium leather seat, put the car in gear, and headed for the hills. In the corner of her eye she saw the little red Honda for what she hoped was the last time. Too many liabilities surrounded that car and Rachel couldn't understand why she had such difficulty parting with the old heap. As she entered the freeway, she reflected on the circumstances that led to the nasty incident on California Highway 92 almost one year before.

The puzzle pieces finally came together for Rachel the day T.V. Neurologicals hosted the Red Cross mobile blood bank when all employees were encouraged to turn out to give blood. While being milked, Rachel overheard a technician talk about a donor having a rare blood type, Rh69. Apparently the type was extremely rare, occurring in 1 in 10 million persons in the United States. This piqued her interest. When her twin sister gave birth to the child she put up for adoption many years before, a blood transfusion was needed for the baby to treat a minor problem. At the time there had been difficulty finding a match for the father's blood factor, coincidentally it was Rh69, a designation she would never forget.

Information about blood donations is deemed confidential so Rachel couldn't ask for the name of the T.V. Neurologicals donor. But when the technicians left the caravan for lunch, Rachel slipped into the bloodmobile and searched through the records. Her blood went cold when she located the entry. The donor with blood factor Rh69 was Ron Daniels!

Rachel found herself shivering uncontrollably on that warm California day. Was it possible for so many years she had worked right next to the rapist who had so violently violated her sister's body? Was it too much a stretch to think Daniels was the man who drugged and raped her at that seminar? Since that night so long ago Rachel had terrible nightmares that haunted her sleep. She was suffering for her sister and couldn't escape.

After finding the Red Cross record, Rachel remembered walking back to the building in a fitful daze. Alone in her office, she was at the point of dismissing the absurd possibility that Daniels was the monster she had been looking for when a sobbing Susie Quattro poured herself into a chair and confessed to an incredibly long list of wrongdoings. When Susie mentioned the package Daniels had received containing an almost identical Nerf ball to the one in Jonathan's office that clinched it.

Listening to the woman, Rachel's suspicions exploded into intense rage. She was now convinced Daniels really was the man who had raped her sister, but still wanted absolute proof. Driven by revenge, Rachel set out to nail the bastard. With a great deal of detective work she was able to obtain the list of registered participants at the seminar her sister had attended. She scanned the pages quickly and there he was - Ronald Daniels.

Rachel felt sick and felt she was going to vomit. Sure, it was all circumstantial evidence, nothing concrete, so she decided to confront Daniels directly.

As she approached his office, she saw him leaving with a pretty, young sales rep he'd recently hired. Rachel followed them, making sure to stay out of sight. The two entered a service elevator and apparently descended into the bowels of the building. Rachel wondered if anyone else knew this netherworld even existed. She located a flight of stairs and quickly crept down.

Daniels and the young woman entered a small room and closed the door. Soon after, unmistakable sounds of heavy sex echoed in the hall. After a few minutes vicious slaps joined the moans of pleasure and she heard once passionate utterances erupt into screams of agony. Should she try to stop the lovemaking that had so suddenly accelerated from pleasure to pain? She knew the woman had been turned from lover to victim and was helpless to fight against Daniels' perversions. Rachel decided interfering wasn't the best way to stop Daniels permanently so she stayed hidden and emotionally endured every slap the young woman suffered.

When the sobbing woman and her tormentor finally entered the elevator, Rachel searched Daniels' sex room and found a small blue cooler in the refrigerator. When she opened it and saw the lethal contents, she almost fainted. Immediately her initial fright morphed into fury.

The jellyfish nestled in a corner of the cooler left no doubt that piece of shit named Ron Daniels was the one responsible for Jacki's painful stings that could have proved fatal. The extremely rare blood factor made it likely he was also the person responsible for her sister's rape and ultimate death.

Rachel went on full alert when she heard the elevator lurch. Daniels was returning! She had to get the hell out of there! Before leaving she needed a sample of the jellyfish. She pulled out the pair of rubber gloves she'd lifted from Jacki's hospital room earlier that afternoon on a hunch they might prove useful. She was now very thankful for the protection they offered from the jellyfish toxin. Frantically searching through a drawer, she found a small knife and a plastic butter bowl and lid. She carefully sliced a piece of the animal, including a mass of stinging tentacles.

She hurriedly returned the cooler to the refrigerator exactly as she had found it, then hid deep in the corridor's shadows. She watched Daniels remove the cooler, glance around the room, and leave again with the insulated box secured under his arm. Rachel followed him back to the elevator and froze when he turned and stared into the darkness. Had he sensed her presence? Apparently satisfied he was alone, Daniels continued down the corridor and entered the elevator.

Rachel was certain he was heading to his car. She rushed up the stairs to catch a glimpse of him unlocking the door of his dark green Buick.

Crouching behind a row of cars, Rachel carefully made her way to her red Honda and waited for Daniels to make a move. She wasn't sure what she was going to do, but knew she wanted to destroy the bastard. When Daniels exited the parking lot, she followed at a distance.

He took Highway 85 to the 280 and then headed north, traveling at speeds unsafe for the increasingly slick road conditions. As she weaved behind Daniels to keep pace, her rage accelerated as she recounted the atrocities so many women had suffered at this narcissistic monster's hands. By the time the two cars approached the exit to Highway 92, Rachel knew she'd lost control of her thoughts and actions; revenge only mattered now.

The light rain quickly turned into a deluge and it became difficult to see the highway markings. Rachel realized this created the perfect cover to bump the Buick as it headed down the hill toward the coast. Just enough of a nudge to cause Daniels to ride the guardrail was all she planned. Then horrific runaway thoughts of pure destruction raced through her mind.

As the two cars started down the hill and approached a bend, determined rage drove Rachel. It was now or never.

She accelerated and hit the rear bumper of the Buick. The big green machine swerved hard to recover, but Daniels was no match for nature's torrent. Seeing him lose control gave her an incredible rush. Rachel had no idea it would be so easy to send Daniels spinning out of control and scare the shit out of the bastard. Then something inside her snapped. Nightmare visions of the pain Daniels had caused, the suffering, and the incredible loss filled her head. Hate and anger grew into frenzy and she screamed, "Fuck it!" and rammed the accelerator to the floor. The little Honda was fueled by rage as it hit the Buick's right rear fender again and again causing the front wheels to careen to the left.

Rachel then banged the left bumper of the Buick sending it into a wild uncontrolled spin. Daniels totally lost control and the car smashed through the guardrail and flew over the barrier.

Rachel saw the Buick somersault down the hill and dearly hoped its driver would not survive the fall. If he did, her life would be toast, but hell, there was nothing she could do about it now. She stopped her Honda by the side of the road and looked down at the mangled green Buick lying 100 feet below. Her first inclination was that it would take a lot of luck to survive the somersaults down the hill. Her thoughts were rudely shaken when she heard screams from below signaling her prey was still alive. When she saw a figure pull itself out of the wreck and crawl toward the road, she knew that she had little time to think and had to take action.

Mere seconds later, Rachel was headed down the twisty road taking no heed of the dangers of the slippery road. Knowing the risk she was assuming she took one hand off the steering wheel and frantically pulled on the rubber mask that lay on the passenger seat. Her Honda swerved wildly. Managing to regain control she saw the beat up body of Daniels climbing over the roadside barrier and headed straight for him. She stopped, alongside, quickly put on a pair of gloves also lying on the seat, reached for the small red cooler on the floor and opened it.

Ron Daniels' face framed itself in her car window and an expression that started as one of relief transformed into a visage of sheer and utter horror. Before he could do or say anything, Daniels felt a jelly-like substance hit him flush in the face. The horror he experienced next was indescribable and would haunt him the rest of his miserable life. He screamed like he had never screamed before!

She didn't notice any cars on the road to witness what had happened, so Rachel quickly accelerated to leave the scene before the police arrived.

After a few miles of panicked driving, sweet, gentle Rachel regained her composure and leisurely continued down the coast and headed to Santa Cruz.

What had she become? First worried she was now as bad as Daniels had been, Rachel soon recognized she had eliminated a brutish fiend from the world stage and felt no remorse. For years she'd suffered sleepless nights, but tonight she knew she would sleep well.

EPILOGUE

The big Delta jet's dance was choreographed to gently kiss the San Jose jet way as passengers arriving from Boston eagerly collected their belongings from the overhead bins. The six flight attendants were still buzzing about the tall, dark, and exceptionally handsome executive who was traveling in business class. Particularly noted was the lack of a wedding band on his left hand.

Robert Statham had been headhunted for the CEO position with a West Coast subsidiary of a major Swiss pharmaceutical company. He was interested in the opportunity because he liked the allure of Silicon Valley, the domicile for the company. Robert had never occupied the position of CEO and was looking forward to the opportunity to make his mark in the world of biopharma. There had also been a nasty divorce back in Beantown he wanted to escape after discovering his wife was having an affair with one of his golfing buddies.

There was substantial work to be done to develop his new company's research pipeline. As frequently happens, many of the subsidiary's scientific staff resigned after the acquisition by the Swiss company. With a good share of the wealth from the company sale, key staff members and department heads enjoyed the freedom to be selective about what they wanted to do next. Most went back to working for pharmaceuticals, but some took radically different paths, like opening a restaurant.

Robert was most interested in preparing the company for the launch of a new oncolytic for prostate cancer, which seemingly held great potential. His extensive marketing experience with cancer drugs and his close ties with groundbreaking physician-related research and patient advocacy groups were important reasons he was selected for the job. Good thing too because the company had no experience in marketing cancer drugs and would have to build an energetic and capable marketing and sales organization from scratch.

Robert also wanted to strengthen the company's research portfolio and diligence. After researching his new company, he was nervous about developing a product for behavioral abnormalities in psychiatric patients without a concrete empirical plan in place. He sensed the company was lacking in know-how in this sector of the business.

What intrigued him was a third drug candidate swaying on the sidelines. All he had uncovered suggested the drug might have a future in cardiology, specifically relating to heart failure.

After leaving Baggage Claim, Robert spied a limo driver holding a sign with his name in black block letters. He expected to be met at the airport, but hadn't expected to see the driver wearing a black suit accented with a black tie. He thought everybody in California dressed casually. In minutes he was on his way traveling north on the Bayshore Freeway.

Along the route he noticed a travelling honky-tonk carnival set up in a hotel parking lot adjacent to the freeway. Dozens of colorful whirling rides reflected the California sun, but one stood out as king of the show - a Merry-Go-Round or children's carousel.

Robert rolled down his window and listened to the lively music played as the beautifully painted horses spun round and round, up and down.

Minutes later the long limo approached the entrance of his new company, a rather modest looking building given what was paid for the acquisition. Things apparently didn't move quickly on the West Coast since the name of the original company was still prominently displayed.

Robert made a note to have the T.V. Neurologicals name and logo removed no later than tomorrow so work could begin on the company's new identity and culture he planned to introduce under his vision and leadership.

Made in the USA
Charleston, SC
11 April 2016